GIL HOGG

THE CRUEL PEAK

Matador
9 Priory Business Park
Kibworth Beauchamp
Leicestershire LE8 0RX, UK
Tel: (+44) 116 279 2299
Fax: (+44) 116 279 2277
Email: books@troubador.co.uk
Web: www.troubador.co.uk/matador

ISBN 978 1780883 038

British Library Cataloguing in Publication Data.
A catalogue record for this book is available from the British Library.

Typeset in 12pt Bembo Pro by Troubador Publishing Ltd, Leicester, UK

Matador is an imprint of Troubador Publishing Ltd

Printed and bound in the UK by TJ International, Padstow, Cornwall

1

He had a sense of ownership as he drove into Springvale town in South Canterbury; it was his town, known like a well-read book on his shelf, but a book that he hadn't looked at in years.

The town was still rousing itself in the morning sun; it was 10am. He slowed the rental car in the deserted Seddon Street. The outline of the two- and three-storey shop buildings suggested a past he remembered as a kid; some corrugated iron awnings above the footpaths, with not quite vertical supporting poles; a few shop windows crammed with merchandise, never dusted by a shop assistant or touched by a customer; the faded advertising signs of *The Smart Dry Cleaners* and *The Fresh Fish and Chip Parlour*. But there was change too. More of the windows now confidently displayed a single stylish dress or lounge suite, and there was a newly tiled mall entrance. Light flashed on chrome chairs set outside an empty coffee shop. Springvale, population about three thousand, looked neater, brighter than he remembered it.

The Royal Hotel was a slightly buckled, two-storey wooden building with a red roof, at the end of Seddon Street, or rather where the shops ended and the car and tractor sales yards began; it had stood since the early part of the twentieth century, and now bore a fresh coat of cream paint. He parked the car in front of the hotel and walked up the wooden steps and across the creaking floor of the lobby to the reception.

He coughed and moved about, and a girl came from

behind a curtain with a gummy smile. "I have a reservation, Tom Stavely."

She looked down at a screen. "Oh yes, Mr Stavely. You're early, but the room's ready." She paused, meeting his eyes and opening hers fully. "That's a name around here… Robyn Stavely the actress, and Petra Stavely. I remember Petra at the Primary."

He didn't think the receptionist was being nosey. She was friendly and interested, the way people often are in small towns. He decided to share a harmless piece of information with her. "I'm Petra's father." He was uneasy as he said the words, not because of this girl, but because he was announcing a role he would have to play, one that he was not really used to.

"Oh, right. I see the booking was made from London. You've come from London for the wedding? Gee, I believe it's going to be a really big shindig. Out at Tamaki Downs?"

He nodded. He wondered if the girl was asking herself why the father of the bride was staying here; it must seem un-family in this very family town.

"We're fully booked for the wedding. I suppose every hotel between here and Christchurch is too. Do you - um - know the district?" She stumbled on the mismatch between a London father and a local daughter.

"I was born here. I went to Springvale Primary myself," he quickly assured her.

"Oh, really? I only came back six months ago. It's real peaceful. My boyfriend and I were in London. That's a fun place."

Real peaceful. She might have meant it wasn't fun here. He looked down at her swollen belly. "But you came back."

"Uh-huh." She too looked down, her smile flecked by a grimace.

She gave him a sealed message and a key on a string with a large piece of numbered plywood. He got his case from the car and dragged it up the stairs – there was no lift. The room was at the back and looked over a wild garden, strewn with a rusty boiler, and a tractor without wheels resting on blocks; beyond were rows of cabbages and turnips, and then pastures. The room itself was comfortable enough; an old four-poster iron bed on bare boards, with a few mats, a giant mahogany wardrobe, and a dresser. He visited the bathroom down the hall. On the wall was a Pirelli calendar of 1985 which could probably pass as interesting memorabilia, rather than disregard of the passage of time.

He looked at the rust-stained bath. His mother used to work here as a maid; she had probably cleaned the bath before he was born. He tried to visualise what she might have looked like as she was scrubbing; slender, pale, earnest, her female attraction smothered by lumpy clothes; apprehensive, hoping she might be saved from drudgery by the arrival of a William Stavely or similar.

In his room he opened the message. It was from Petra's mother, Robyn, his former wife; an invitation in her large, assertive handwriting to stay at the Downs, rather than 'that dreadful place, the Royal Hotel'. He expected the invitation, although it was belated; the Downs was to be the centre of the celebrations. Later he would ring Alison, his present wife, in London, and tell her, and she would probably say, 'I knew Robyn would try to drag you up there,' as though Tamaki Downs was a wicked place, and perhaps to Alison it was. He would deny that he cared much where he stayed, but the truth was he wanted to be at the Downs; he expected to be there, and in a way he had a right to be there.

After a quick shower, he changed into casual slacks and a

sweater and decided to go to Tamaki Downs now, leaving his luggage at the Royal for the moment.

He drove west at a brisk pace, passing the outlying farms, always climbing, with the Southern Alps sprawling in the sun before him. The farms looked, as ever, comfortable and withdrawn, hiding their prosperity.

He knew some of the farmers around here; he had been to school and grown up with them. George Hedley was one. George had stayed with him in London a few years ago and announced proudly, 'I'm a multimillionaire now, Tom, do you realise that?' If Tom had replied candidly, he would have said, 'I wouldn't have been prepared to serve a twenty-year term of imprisonment on fifteen hundred acres for the money,' but George wouldn't have seen it that way. He had come as a youth to work the farm, married the farmer's only child, served well and been compensated for his term of incarceration. He was a happy man. Unfortunately, he never lived to sell the farm, but his wife did. Tom reminded himself that he ought to telephone Patricia Hedley while he was in town.

The pastures of late summer were dry and yellow, the sky a vast pale blue bowl, with tumbling white clouds; remoteness was a quality in the air. This was high country, undulating in hills and dales. The road unreeled before him, sometimes new tarmac but the same old curves, and after about two hours, a roadside notice said Tamaki Downs was a mile ahead.

The house came into view only after he had passed through the stone gateway and driven a further half mile; it was built in a wide valley, protected from the south. The two-storey grey limestone central block with two wings occupied the same site as Joe Ashton's cabin in 1870. He knew the history. The high-ceilinged lower storey allowed rooms of grand proportions with tall windows. The roof was blue-grey slate, the window frames white, with a white conservatory and verandah across the front. The building sprawled comfortably amid lawns and walls of varying levels, with beds of wind-burned roses and a surrounding shelter belt of pines and gums. The Tamaki Downs homestead looked much the same as it always had.

A young woman was tending the potted geraniums on the front steps when he drove the car up to the entrance. She had bare feet. She could not have been much more than twenty-five. Her loose black hair hung down to the middle of her back. She wore a black dress. The wind blew the thin material of the dress against her body, which just escaped being thin. Her skin was golden. She greeted him casually and helped with his small gifts of choice liquor, chocolates and perfume.

"I'm Tia. And you're Tom. Where are your bags?"

"At the Royal. I'm staying there."

She looked puzzled. "I thought you were staying here, Tom. Your room is ready. Stuart has a problem with one of the contractors. He's over on the west side."

He stepped into the panelled hall, pleased that he was expected. The smell was familiar, but difficult to identify; dying blooms perhaps. He might even have detected a whiff of decay. A portrait in oils of Celia Ashton, Robyn's mother, long dead, glinted in the gloom. Painted in her thirties, it depicted her as an imperious lady, but he remembered her as a mouse. He placed his jacket on the hall stand by a vase filled with yellow gladioli.

"Come and I'll show you your room, Tom, or maybe you know it. I'm told you're used to being here." Tia picked up his jacket.

"Not in recent years." He followed her to the familiar double bedroom upstairs. The paper on the walls and the bedcover had a faint pattern of green scrolls. "You've redecorated."

"About time. Like it?" She dropped the jacket and the duty-free presents on the bed. "It's a koru design."

She disappeared before he could reply. He could see from the window that the trees in the garden were more profuse. He still had a sight across the downs to the Thums, and Mt Tasman, purple in the distance, with a smudge of snow. For a few seconds, he slipped back in time to himself at ten, twelve, fifteen. Mostly enjoyable times. Then he went downstairs. The house was quiet. He found Tia in the kitchen, occupied at the sink. Her bottom was outlined in the thin dress.

"Let me get you a drink, Tom. If you want a shower, there should be everything in your bathroom. I'll send Ted to collect your stuff."

"No thanks. Nothing to drink and I'm not sure if I'll stay here. I'll talk to Stuart. I don't want to get in the way." He wasn't going to leap at the invitation.

"You're Petra's father. How could you be in the way?"

He countered with, "Where's the new Mrs Ashton?"

She looked over her shoulder with a scratchy laugh. "I don't *work* here, Tom. I'm Mrs Ashton."

Stuart's wife! *How was he to know?* "Well... he told me on the phone that he'd married. We didn't get much further than that. I asked him to tell me about his wife, and he said she was a lovely girl."

What he had actually asked Stuart Ashton, with a tinge of sarcasm, was 'Who *is* she?' expecting to hear a South Canterbury family name that he recognised, or at least a list of her academic accomplishments. Stuart had evaded the question with 'a lovely girl'; on appearances, that much was true. But to him she had looked like a young woman helping in the kitchen. Stuart was in his forties after all.

"We didn't have a big society wedding, like Petra is going to have. We had a hangi at the marae."

"I wasn't invited," he tried to joke.

"You and a lot of other people. We just decided to do it."

He felt foolish and defensive about his mistake. "I haven't heard much from Stuart. Occasional, very occasional emails and phone calls don't really bridge the gap to London, do they? For a writer he's a lousy correspondent."

He would certainly report his gaffe to Alison in a tone of annoyance that he had to conceal now. 'Wouldn't you expect your close friend to tell you about his bride?' he'd say. Alison was bound to reproach him for insensitivity in classifying the girl.

"I don't know about the gap between here and London," Tia said. "I've never been there. Stuart's going to take me some time."

"Do you… go with Stuart when he's on his… projects?" He groped for words, wary of sensitivities.

"Oh, yes. He does a column in the national papers, and occasional nature television shows. We get around the country to film. We go to *Erehwemos,* the house in the Sounds. You know it?" She pronounced the name as though it was a Maori word instead of a snooty jibe at Samuel Butler.

"I've never been there," he had to admit. *Erehwemos* was one of the houses and apartments that the wider Ashton family had scattered in various countries for their pleasure. And investment. What exasperated him about *Erehwemos* was that he had been hearing what an idyllic place it was for years without ever being invited there. Even during his

7

marriage to Robyn, when the opportunity to go arose, Robyn found an excuse not to go, and it wasn't particularly one of those Ashton advantages that he was going to beg for.

"It's beautiful. Stuart likes to write there. He says the vibes are bad here. And another thing we do, whenever we're in Christchurch to record a show or something, we go to see Len. Poor kid. It must cause you a lot of pain. What a waste."

"I stayed over in Christchurch when I arrived and went to see him myself."

"How is he? It's a month since we were down there."

"About the same. He can't improve, I'm told."

"Petra sees him. She loves her brother. And of course Robyn visits regularly. I guess he misses you." She looked at him, her eyes like dark mirrors and hard to read.

He wasn't sure Len missed anything or anyone, but it sounded callous to say it. He struggled to find an appropriate reply, but his long absences from the neurological care home where his son lived were an implicit indictment.

"What's the matter, Tom? Are you surprised your friend's married a Maori?"

This was a startling swipe. "Not at all! I was thinking of Len... And as for Stuart, I'm just surprised he's married!" he said explosively.

She turned toward him, wiping her hands on a cloth. She had a brooding look, seeking offence, he thought, but then he had already offended. "Is your family... from this part of the island?" Again, he was treading carefully.

"We've been around here for hundreds of years," she replied curtly.

This piqued him. "Actually, there weren't *any* Maori families in the Springvale district thirty or forty years ago."

"The only ones you'd remember are the itinerants who came to de-horn or castrate the cattle." She spoke with a slight sneer.

"There weren't many of them either."

"We're not all labourers, you know."

"Are you still fighting the Maori Wars?" he asked, lightly.

She surprisingly returned a wide smile. "You bet. And we're winning. You want to speak to Stuart?" She held up a mobile phone.

"Let's wait until he gets here."

"Why don't you ride out to see him? I can tell you which way. I'll come out to the stable with you. Hack or bike?"

"I haven't been in either saddle… forever. I'll wait until he comes in. He works on the place now?"

"When it's necessary."

"What's stopping him?"

"Don't you know? The war. And he hates working here."

"A feeling we share - about working here. I've done a spot of it myself." He had expected to hear that Stuart was writing another book, or preparing for an adventurous expedition. "I know he served in Afghanistan."

"Bloody Afghanistan!"

"He retired sick?" He had never been able to penetrate the fog around Stuart's retirement from the army.

"He wasn't actually wounded, not physically."

"What happened?"

She tapped her forefinger on her temple. "Headaches and nightmares. He didn't tell you?"

"No. He wouldn't want to admit weakness to me."

"You men… I'm a bit worried about him, Tom. He's depressed. I don't know why. It could be something about Mt Vogel, although that sounds silly."

9

"Vogel is old history. What about it?" The mere mention of the mountain was enough to prick a nerve in him.

"Let him tell you. I'm not sure I understand. Maybe you can cheer him up. Robyn told me you were big mates." The way that Tia crimped her mouth made this a criticism.

"Partying?"

"I think you've done a lot of yarning and boozing together, from what Stuart says."

"Sure, and arguing. Don't assume we're all that compatible."

"If you're not going out to meet Stuart, are you going to look in on the old man then?"

"How is he?"

She frowned. "Without chemo, which he refuses, he has six months or a year. And he has a dicky heart. He says there's no point in a bypass." She was unemotional, her face stiff.

"His health seems to have collapsed, when you think he was once an athlete. You don't get on with him, Tia?"

There was a silence and a sigh. "Right."

"That makes two of us - well, three including Stuart. Are Stuart and Ernest still skirmishing?"

"Sure." She seemed to relax. "Ernest's much vaunted liberal views are bullshit, Tom. The only Maori you'll find at dinner at Tamaki Downs, when he's inviting, apart from me, is one who's a Member of Parliament, or an All Black."

"Surprise me... I've known him all my life. Look, first I think I'll take a walk around the garden. Maybe see the old house." He wanted to get away from her before they had a row and he wasn't interested in rushing to see Ernest Ashton.

"The old house? You mean the ruins? Why go down there?"

"Where I used to live."

"Down there? I didn't know that. I'll come with you."

She had a curious smile and a proprietorial air.

He didn't want her to come, he positively wanted to be alone, but he couldn't resist her courtly motive. She pulled a baseball cap on to shade her face and slipped her feet into a pair of training shoes. They went out of the back door and walked through the lawns, a hundred yards down a cobbled slope to a lane of closed sheds.

"You don't use these for storage any more?"

"No. Working the place has changed in the last few years. We have contractors who shear and take the wool, and others who manage the stock. And we now have deer and alpaca too. There's no killing on the place. Hides and meat and wool are just pieces of paper on Stuart's desk. He coordinates things, sorts out some day to day problems with the contractors. He's not a real manager. I help him."

"Why not get a *real* manager?"

"We might. We need one. I'd like to do it, but I want to go with Stuart on his longer trips. I'm spoiled."

He swept his arm across the horizon. "You know all about this stuff?"

"Sure."

He was confused, but Tia didn't give him time. She had a hint of his incredulity.

"You don't think a young Maori woman could manage this place?"

"Tia, it would be an unusual job for *any* young woman."

"Balls. There are plenty of women managing farms or stations."

He didn't say, 'Not as big as Tamaki Downs,' because she probably had an answer to that. He didn't want an argument. He kept quiet. They had come to the end of the lane where the land fell away, disclosing the rolling downs, yellow in the sunlight, broken by groves of pines, and stretching into a

11

haze which ultimately rose toward the Alps.

He stood for a moment, viewing the landscape of his childhood. He realised then that he could only appreciate it fully if he was alone. Tia was as edgy as he was; in this atmosphere, instead of stimulating his thoughts, the scene was static, a landscape painting.

"Look, Tia, I think I better go back. Ernest will be wondering why I haven't been in to see him. I can visit the old place later. It's only a trip down memory lane."

She dropped the corners of her mouth. They turned back, remote from each other.

His sometime father-in-law Sir Ernest Ashton lay in state upstairs in 'the big bedroom'. Ernest's outline had shrunk, judging by the only visible parts of him above the sheets – his head, shoulders and arms. The skin on his arms was like an old brown jersey several sizes too big. His square jaw and high-domed head with a wisp of brown hair was hollowed and threatening like a Maori carving.

Ernest turned stagnant eyes slowly toward him as he entered, full of reproach. "So you're back. Good journey?"

"Not bad." He didn't offer a hand, and Ernest didn't stir the claw resting on the coverlet.

"You've taken your time about coming in to see me. I saw the car out of the window."

"I wanted to find out about you first. See whether you've been round the stock this morning."

"You've been talking to the housemaid."

"Is that what Tia is?"

The old man avoided the question with a grunt. "You've come for Petra's wedding, eh? Why bother? You've ignored her all her life."

"Maybe, but it is her wedding." He remained standing and Ernest Ashton didn't proffer one of the armchairs by the bed.

"Going to play the fond father, are you? She's marrying a clod. But you wouldn't know."

"She's got to make her own choice."

"How righteous. You want to pose as the father of the bride. You've come out of your hole in London for a moment in the sun." Ernest's rictus represented a smile. "Maybe you were right to bunk off to London; children are leeches and thieves, they suck and take; they don't come to you and say, 'I'd like this,' or 'Can I have that?' They don't make a deal with you; they take over your life; they *live* your life themselves. You become an appendage to them. If parents are always living for their children, whoever is living for himself?"

"You can't get rid of the illusion that your kids have let you down, can you, Ernest? Not even at this late time?"

"I've given them everything. That's no illusion. And what is Stuart? Is he a farmer, a writer, a mountaineer, a soldier? What the hell is he? A bloody dilettante."

"Aren't you a farmer, a writer, a mountaineer, a businessman?"

Ernest let out a throaty growl. "I've had a fair degree of success at all of them. Stuart can't even make a decent profit out of this place. Instead, he's married a child who thinks *she* can. Bugger me, I've never heard the likes of it."

"Maybe Tia can manage this place."

"You don't learn to run a station like Tamaki by getting a university degree in how to bottle-feed lambs."

"Maybe you do. Times have changed. And what's wrong with Robyn as a daughter?" He asked because the old man – he was only in his early sixties – was like a politician; press

13

his button and the story would be repeated.

Ernest's pale lips drew back from the dark teeth. "Theatricals and booze."

He couldn't resist drilling further into the abscess. "You'd like her better as the wife of a national politician, or a judge, with a neat little family?"

"I'd like her better if she reflected some honour on the household."

He didn't have any brief to defend Robyn, but Ernest's pomposity chafed him. "She's a highly regarded theatrical director."

The clouded eyes swivelled toward him. "Used to be. But you had the answer to her career, didn't you? You dumped Petra and Len with Robyn."

He had had these strictures from the old man before in a milder form, and he wasn't particularly surprised that they should take on more stridency as the illness progressed. "Do we have to be like this, Ernest? Robyn insisted on having the children, you know that."

"You scarpered off to Britain with the parson's wife."

This was bile, which Ernest liked to regurgitate whenever they met after a long absence.

"The parson's widow, to be precise. I did."

"You were shagging her long before Hewart died. Robyn told me. And you had a couple of kids from her later, ignoring Petra and Len."

"I wouldn't say ignoring. I've been back here. I do live on the other side of the world, you know."

"Well, what the hell are you doing *there* anyway? At least if you were here you could see that broken boy occasionally."

"Let's continue this pleasant talk when you've had a rest." He turned to leave.

"You didn't want for opportunities here, Tom. I got you

a good post at Gottley's with Clyde Porter." The old man's tone was unaccountably warmer.

"You bought it for me as Gottley's biggest client."

"Well, lucky you! And what did *you* do? Got yourself fired in six months!"

"Clyde Porter, personally, was a shit. I explained it to you at the time."

"He became one of the most respected judges in the country."

"But nevertheless..." Tom said, as he moved toward the door.

"Just a minute. Have you spoken to Stuart yet?"

"No. He's out on the station playing the part of a farmer."

"Well, when you do, don't believe all this crap from him about Mt Vogel."

"What crap?"

Ernest raised a tired hand dismissing him. "Remember what I said."

He left Ernest to go downstairs, the mention of Mt Vogel lost in the cauldron of emotions which his meetings with Ernest always aroused, emotions too about Reginald Clyde Porter.

The Ashton influence had propelled Tom as a young law clerk to Gottley & Son, solicitors in Christchurch, which had no Gottley and no son, but a very large portfolio of Ashton interests, as well as a thriving court practice kept alive by the prominence of Reginald Clyde Porter, who appeared in some of the city's most notable cases.

Although he resisted it at first, he surrendered to the invitation engineered by Ernest Ashton, and told himself that even if he joined another firm of his own choosing, some of the Ashton work would follow inevitably, and he would be looked upon as a golden boy – so what was the difference? And a golden boy he was at Gottley's. Clyde Porter and the other three partners could scarcely contain their pleasure at this almost infinite source of future fees, assuming he served his clerkship and became a partner. Although it was contrary to their feelings, the partners all treated Tom Stavely as a rather important young gentleman amongst the clerks.

Gottleys occupied rooms on the first floor of the Temperance Building on Chancery Lane. The décor was original – what it was when the firm first gained the tenancy forty years before: the furniture a dark, dry brown, the walls the colour of milky tea. Piles of papers and old books littered every available shelf and cabinet. On his first day, while he was waiting to meet one of the partners, he turned idly to a file on the top of a cupboard and saw the title *Enquiry into the sinking of the SS Suva Rose, August 1938.* The firm had moved reluctantly into the late twentieth century with a few word processors, laser printers, copiers and a telephone exchange, but it could not shake off the detritus of an earlier era.

Tom's relationship with the esteemed senior partner started on a note which made him uneasy. His first sight of the great man, then in headlines in the newspapers on a lurid case, was sitting on a chair in the Christchurch Law Library. Clyde Porter crouched, his bespectacled eyes bright and beaky nose up, staring straight at Tom as he came in the door. He had scarcely entered when Clyde Porter launched himself across the floor to grasp his hand. 'I've heard a lot about you, my boy, from Professor Phillips. You're just the person we need! You'll do very well! Exceptionally well, a

lad of your talent. I have to get away now. Justice calls!' He
dropped Tom's hand, which he had wrung unceasingly, and
bolted out of the door. Thus Tom was inducted into the firm
of Gottleys without a question, without being able to ask a
question, without being acknowledged as anything more
than the words on a curriculum vitae, and a certified
harbinger of Ashton munificence.

Tom's job was to devil for Clyde Porter – prepare a legal
basis for his cases. Often, Clyde Porter asked him questions,
the answers to which Clyde Porter already knew very well.
'Thomas, what's the Rule in Babcock's Case?' 'You can't
remember?' Or he would have Tom leaping at the
bookshelves to find law reports. 'Addison v Symons isn't in
the King's Bench Reports, Thomas. All-England. Didn't you
know that?'

He felt rebellious at being humiliated, but said nothing.
Most of Tom's colleagues in the law told him he was lucky
being able to work for such a man.

In the back room of Gottley's, on the light well which
admitted little light, Fred Needham, a qualified solicitor had
worked for seventeen years. He did the prosaic but profitable
work of conveying houses, arranging mortgages, and drafting
leases. He sat at his desk like a doll, his straight black hair
parted in the middle and shining, black eyes as still as two
beads. He could be relied upon to be there from eight
o'clock in the morning (having already collected the mail
from the firm's box), until the staff left at six in the evening.
He was, for Tom, a friendly repository of technical and
procedural information about the law.

Fred was not a partner. When Tom asked one of the
clerks, Roderick Crawford, why, Crawford said callously,
'Not the right material.' The tea-room gossip belittled Fred.
He wasn't married. He drank too much beer. He always

wore the same grey double-breasted suit; it had become baggy, and the lapels had acquired a greasy sheen which was unpleasant to see. Doris Crail, the office matriarch said, "It's no laughing matter. It's a disgrace, and something ought to be done," but Fred appeared to be impervious to hints, and blind to his appearance.

One morning, Fred failed to arrive at the office. Doris's testy call to his landlady elicited that he had the 'flu. A call a few days later found that he had been taken to hospital with what his landlady now described as 'a nervous breakdown'.

After a week, when Doris Crail had to collect and sort the mail, two hostile letters from mortgage companies were discovered demanding their long overdue securities, and a threatening letter from a client requesting his title documents.

When Doris showed the letters to Porter, she reported to the tea-room that he looked nauseated. "Get the files from Needham's desk and I'll have a look at them," he demanded.

Tom was summoned to the back room by Doris. "I can't move this drawer. It's locked or jammed," she said.

"Let me have a try." He shoved the drawer roughly, and accidentally pulled it out of its slide. The contents fell on to floor; pencils, rubbers, note-pads. With the drawer out of its place, he was able to look down into the space below where a profusion of legal documents rested. He plunged his hand down through the top opening and scooped up mortgage documents, transfers, titles, tenancy agreements, wills and letters, all of which appeared to have been thrown in at random.

"My goodness. What is it?" Doris said.

"Looks to me like a lot of work not completed."

When Tom, accompanied by Doris, placed the pile of incomplete securities and files before Porter, he spent a few moments picking them over. He groaned. His calculating eyes knew at once that here was a hoard of documents neglected over months or perhaps longer, obligations unfulfilled. He was contemplating the certainty of claims against the firm for negligence and damages.

"No wonder Fred insisted on collecting the mail," Doris said.

"He's let me down, and he's let the firm down," Porter said, exhaling heavily.

"The firm's let *him* down in a way," Tom said in the silence.

"What do you *mean,* Stavely?" Porter looked at him like a bird of prey, beak poised, ready to strike.

Tom had always been Thomas. He hesitated, because his comment had been almost involuntary. "I mean... in the back room... for seventeen years."

"Mrs Crail, I would be grateful if you would leave us!" Clyde Porter said, bringing both palms down heavily on the desk.

When Doris had gone, Clyde Porter struggled off his chair, stalked across the room, slammed the yet partly open door, and turned fiercely on Tom. "How dare you speak to me in that manner! And in front of Mrs Crail!"

"I spoke quite civilly. It's... what I think, that's all."

"I'm talking, Stavely, about the *substance* of what you said. It was insulting, uncalled for from a clerk in your position, and entirely without foundation. And unless I have a forthright personal apology from you within twenty-four hours, you will find that you don't work here any more. Is that clear?"

A silence.

"Well, Stavely?" Clyde Porter cocked up his beak, waiting.

A few more seconds passed in silence.

"May I go now, sir?"

2

His untimely departure from Gottley & Son was still capable of stirring him today, but he calmed as he entered the 'drawing room' as it was called; it was lofty with an ornate plaster ceiling, the tall windowpanes displaying a wide view of the lawns and gardens. With its chandeliers, drapes, paintings, tapestries and rugs, the room was a Victorian showpiece, rather than a useful living room. Some of the articles here were beautiful, and priceless; there were two oils by Rubens, a Utrillo, a Monet, a baroque cabinet from the Gobelins' workshops, jewelled clocks and marquetry tables. The antique furniture had been carefully polished and the gold brocade curtains aired by housekeepers over the years, but the room had only seen the most sedate receptions. Nobody in the latest generation of Ashtons had ever used and enjoyed this grandiose space.

The pretentious grandeur was like those salons he had seen - as museum pieces now - in Punta Arenas, where the wealthy Chilean colonists, English, Irish and German, preened and paraded themselves in the latest European fashion more than a century ago, at the bottom of the world; Ernest's forbears at Tamaki Downs probably swaggered about in much the same way.

He was attracted to a deep red velvet couch which lay invitingly before him, still occupying virtually the same position as it had over twenty years ago, in a quadrangle of other valuable hand-crafted couches drawn up around a

Persian carpet. The velvet was only a little faded, and the plumpness had gone from the cushions, but it remained an elegant and inviting seat.

He eased himself down and rested, recalling his triumph when he had sex with Robyn Ashton - he didn't seduce her - on the couch, all that time ago. It was an adventure for both of them in getting to know each other better, but that night one of nature's keys was pressed and consequences followed.

He told Alison a version of the event after they became close. 'Robyn and I didn't exactly grow up together as friends,' he said. 'We were children, playing kids' games in the woods and streams, swimming down at the creek, sailing on the river, riding, camping. Stuart was part of it. But we didn't seem to be children for very long. Stuart and I were working on the place in our early teens, and then schooling broke up our trio more effectively. Sure, they were rich and I was poor.'

'And you resented it,' Alison had said.

'The differences between us were the norm, what I'd grown up with,' he had replied to shrug it off, but even to a six year-old, the differences were glaring.

'Robyn went away to Marsden, a private school for girls in Wellington. I saw her only occasionally and momentarily in summer holidays.'

'You'd sort of fallen for her?'

'No, she was just a playmate.' That at least was true. He had never had romantic ideas about Robyn then or since.

'We began to meet again when I left university with my law degree, and came back to Springvale to stay with a friend of my mother's. I don't think the Ashtons would have allowed me through the back door if I'd been a mechanic or a cabinet-maker, even though I'd grown up on the place, but I was a 'clever boy' according to Springvale gossip, with a 'future'.'

21

Of course he never mentioned the couch specifically to Alison, only the effect. 'It seemed to dictate paths. I wasn't free any longer. The exhilaration of being independent, of having a professional skill that I could practice where I chose, the excitement of the future, all began to evaporate,' he said.

A watercolour portrait of Robyn Ashton aged about eighteen was on the wall of the drawing room, not too far from the couch. The artist had captured her determined stare, the only thing that was remarkable about a soft, small-featured face. She had been sexually attractive, and he was drawn to her - in part - for that reason, but he was also, he had to admit, impelled by another motive which he had never mentioned to Alison or anybody else, although he had always acknowledged it to himself.

He was, at one time, 'Bill Stavely's lad', who could be ordered to milk the house cows, clean the stables or help with the lambing or the fencing. Home was a rickety cottage on Tamaki Downs, but that was in the past at the time of the red couch incident. He had no need of the Ashtons in his new stance as a graduate, and there was a special sense of conquest in penetrating Ernest Ashton's socially sought-after daughter, and Stuart Ashton's beloved sister. It felt as though he was driving a wedge into the Ashton clan's comfortable assumptions of superiority. He knew at the time that such an impulse was ignoble, but it was so sweet!

The triumph was short-lived. In this ultimate moment of his success, he seemed to have locked himself in with the Ashtons forever.

He stood in the bay window before the lawns. He was looking back on a finality which couldn't be unravelled; it was pointless to feel regret; directions he *might* have taken were no more than fantasies, and he rejected them as such, but he wanted to understand where and why he had taken one road rather than another; it was like discovering a map which to some extent explained to him the mystery of himself.

He detected a movement through the trees. A half a mile away, Stuart Ashton was riding up the ridge toward the house on a chestnut hack, straight-backed, like the ex-army man he was. How like Stuart to ride a hack when the other workers rode trail-bikes. He felt uncertain. Although he and Stuart had been apart for years at a time, they had been friends for almost all of Tom's forty-seven years, and there were complicated strands of emotion between them.

Stuart entered the drawing room where he was waiting; they embraced stiffly. Stuart was in stockinged feet, and still wearing his jeans and workshirt. They muttered banalities about a safe journey, and declared their good health and spirits.

"I'm surprised to find you riding the range, Stu."

"I do as little as I can, believe me. Why are you in here, this museum?" Stuart's eyes clashed with the ornate furniture.

"Memories."

"We'd be more comfortable in the study."

"You must tell me about Tia."

"We'd been going around for a while and just decided to get hitched."

Stuart spoke in a guileless way, as though it was a small and pleasant happening, but Tom knew Stuart was not a guileless man. He had seemed, to Tom, set to go on womanising without a lasting attachment. He had a tall, athletic figure and a youthfully thick thatch of hair, now greying. Tom thought him deeply narcissistic. A woman might think his lined, square-jawed face showed strength. He certainly had physical strength. Rich, cultured and capable of compelling charm if he wished to use it, Stuart *was* an extremely marriageable bachelor. Tom hadn't been close enough to him in recent years to know whether his longer-term girlfriends of the past had been cast away, or whether one of them might still be watching from the windows of her apartment and warming a king-sized bed.

"Tia tells me you got married on the marae. Didn't Ernest want a big knees-up?"

"That was a big knees-up. Best wedding I ever attended. In any case, I didn't consult the old man. And he stayed away from the marae." Stuart gave a savage leer.

He would say to Alison, although she would be reluctant to accept it, 'Maybe the marriage to Tia is intended to be provocative.'

The kind of reply that she would make would be, 'I don't know Tia, but I do know Stuart, and he's too dynastically minded to use marriage as a stick to beat his father, Tom. Marriage is a serious business to the Ashtons. You should know that from experience.'

After Stuart had showered and changed, they settled in the study with a beer. "All right," Stuart said, dropping his heavy frame into a chair with a thud that made it cry out. They talked casually, but Tom could see that he was preoccupied. Stuart didn't seem to want to let the conversation ramble casually over their friends and the events of the last few years; after a while, he interrupted the flow. "Hey, you know Tom, something's come up about Mt Vogel."

Mt Vogel again. The red light blinked. It wasn't that he found it a sensitive subject, because it was long past. It was about events viewed as a child, which didn't turn out too badly for him. At the time, he only half understood them, and even now they remained an area of mist and uncertainty.

"We should have climbed Mt Vogel years ago, Tom!" Stuart spoke vehemently, and closed his eyes at the thought.

"It's too late now," he responded quietly, startled by the force of Stuart's regret.

They had talked about the climb for years, always agreeing that they would make an attempt together, but they never did. He knew now that the mountain was out of his class, but he had at one time seriously intended to tackle it. It happened that the tracks of their different lives never allowed them to slow down and do the long-term planning and training that were necessary. When he could have been available, Stuart wasn't, and the reverse. Also, as the years passed, he developed what he would admit only to himself was a fear of Mt Vogel. He read the stories of the climbers who failed or died. His availability to make the climb lessened as his fears increased over time, and as his own modest mountaineering capability lessened. Now, he believed that time had excused him. "Well, we didn't have a go... Only Ernest, and what, one other, succeeded?"

"A Swiss, Meisner... I failed too - twice!"

He had heard from Stuart about his failed attempts. He didn't comment on them now. If he said they were creditable - as they were - Stuart would find it patronising. The failures, given excessive publicity because of his father's success, and the difficulty - near impossibility - of the climb, had lacerated Stuart; virtually shamed him. Tom thought it was daft to feel diminished by these events, but that was how Stuart felt.

"*We* could have done it, Tom. You and I together."

"Ha!" he scoffed. Stuart was talking about a fantasy world. "I've never been your partner on the big ones. I couldn't have managed Everest or K2. I was never good enough, Stu. So the idea that you *and* I somehow had the magic ingredient for Vogel when you've already tried twice is just…"

Mt Vogel lured climbers from all over the world. It was known to mountaineers as a supreme challenge, like K2, although just a hundred feet or so short of Mt Cook in height.

"You don't know… about the shame of public failure…" Stuart disappeared behind his hooded eyes for a few moments. Then he brightened. "I'll tell you what we could do. We could climb Mt Vogel now, Tom. The season is right."

It was as though Stuart hadn't heard him, and he laughed. "That's a mad idea."

"Why not?" Stuart protested loudly.

"I've told you, because I'm not skilful enough – or fit enough."

"We could get you fit, Tom. Christ, you haven't forgotten anything. It's like riding a bicycle."

"Don't be stupid, man. Vogel is challenged year by year. The death and injury toll is terrible. Meisner's success must be over ten years ago. It isn't like Everest. Hillary and Tensing broke through a barrier on Everest, like the four minute mile. Once the barrier was broken and the trail blazed, others could follow. Vogel isn't like that. Technical advances in equipment haven't helped either. Ice and the weather make it a virtually unclimable peak. You know these things better than I do. Wasn't it a Swiss team who got into trouble last year? Frostbite. Broken bones. The idea that we could just run up there because we've suddenly decided we want to is barmy."

"I realise it's difficult for you, Tom, because of your father, but –"

"That's not it at all. As I've said to you before, Stu, it was probably a good thing for me and my mother that my father was killed on Mt Vogel. That sounds unfeeling, but you know why. It's a pragmatic judgment that I made years ago. As far as I'm concerned, Vogel means nothing to me. I doubt if I was a good enough climber to do it ten or twenty years ago. And now - forget it."

Stuart wasn't listening. He was focussing on his own thoughts. "We could get a team together…"

"Why are you bringing it up now? What's happened?"

Stuart drained his beer, stood up and started fussing around the cabinet to get a whisky. He kept his back to Tom, not replying, not having to answer. Eventually, he clinked a couple of ice cubes into a big slug of whisky and sat down with a flourish that looked like a determination to speak. "Like one?"

"Not now. What is it, Stu?"

"I got some information from *The Mountaineer* magazine that the Swiss team who had an unsuccessful go recently, came across an old guy on their way down who spends a bit of time on the slopes. He's apparently been finding equipment brought down the mountain by the glaciers and snows for years. The story is that he has some interesting stuff from old expeditions. Wouldn't it be good to see it?"

"Yeah. That's different. A trek around the area would be fine, if that's what you're suggesting." He had a few days to spare, even with the friends he intended to see. He didn't anticipate that he would have a great deal of time with Petra. "You think this man might have something from the Ashton-Stavely climb? It would be interesting to find out, but it's a hell of a long shot, isn't it?"

His lack of real interest in the relics, if there were any relics, was showing. Stuart's agitation couldn't merely be

27

about the prospect of seeing them. There was another pause.

"Come on, Stu."

Stuart winced, and passed his hand over his face, a web of lines. "There *is* something more. About the mountain."

"What do you mean?"

Stuart looked uncomprehending. He fumbled the glass in his hand and slopped some whisky. He opened his mouth but didn't speak. He gulped the whisky. "A rumour... A vile rumour, that there's some doubt about whether Ernest ever made the summit."

"Ernest didn't climb Vogel?" Tom rocked back in his chair, not sure at first that he'd heard correctly. He took a moment to appreciate this. "How can that *possibly* be! More than thirty years ago. It's stupid! We have Ernest's book. There's a photo of him on the summit. And there was a spotter plane in the air, if I remember. You can't do better than that!"

"You have a good memory."

"I must have read *The Fateful Snows* about three times as a teenager."

"Suppose the photo wasn't the old man?"

"You're kidding. *Somebody* made it to the summit. The pilot of the spotter reported it."

"The pilot wouldn't be able to tell who it was, would he?"

"Then it was *my* father, instead? There were only the two of them. Well, lovely, but I can't believe it." He said this easily, unable to take Stuart seriously.

"What are you smirking at? It isn't funny." Stuart's usually suntanned face had paled and crumpled.

"Let's get this straight, Stu. It's rumoured, merely *rumoured,* that thirty-something years ago Ernest Ashton failed to reach the summit of Mt Vogel, but claimed he had.

That means that Bill Stavely, my father, summited Mt Vogel – because one of them did – and was killed coming down, rather than going up as Ernest claimed."

'That's... the lie." Stuart looked stunned. "The lie!"

His response was dismissive. "Ah, Stu! Be real. It would be monstrous and unthinkable if it was true. And how could Ernest possibly set up such a deception? How did this story start? I mean, we – the whole mountaineering community worldwide have been brought up on the fact that –"

"I know, I know. These Swiss guys apparently looked over the stuff that had been found, bags, maps, gloves, you know, the usual dreck, and read some notes amongst them. Maybe they didn't understand them correctly. They said the geezer wouldn't part with anything. They took what they saw seriously. Maybe they were pissed off about their own failure. When they got back home, they reported it to their club, who no doubt passed it on to the Alpine Club here. Charlie Swift, the chairman, informed me with a sort of 'this is nonsense but we thought we ought to tell you' call. Later, a staffer on *The Mountaineer* magazine rang me. Told me. Asked a lot of questions. That's all I know."

"It certainly has the makings of a very dirty story, but Ernest would never claim a peak he hadn't climbed... I mean, there are limits to the perfidy he is capable of."

He had no liking for Ernest Ashton, but the man did have a public reputation for integrity. He was certainly a famous and respected mountaineer but also a major figure on the country's business landscape through the Ashton Group. He was or used to be, the kind of man whose advice was sought by cabinet ministers.

"Are there limits to his perfidy?" Stuart asked with a distant look, his eyes gleaming from dark pits.

"You hate your old man, Stu. We know that. OK. But

this is something else. You're biased. Horribly biased." He grinned again, unable to restrain himself.

"For Christ's sake, this isn't funny, Tom!"

"Forget the whole business, Stu. I'm serious."

"No!" Stuart bulldozed on. "If Ernest did lie about it, stole *your* father's triumph, and that was shown up, I don't know what I'd do...."

To Tom, the thought was grotesque, and somehow fanciful; a product of Stuart's solitary brooding. Stuart leaned over toward him, eyes fixed on his, like an angry schoolteacher with an obtuse child, trying to communicate something very obvious he thought Tom didn't understand.

"You see, Tom, although I loathe the idea in one sense, I have to admit that my name as a climber and journalist is founded on what my father did. The Ashton name echoed around the mountaineering world thirty-three years ago. *The Fateful Snows* followed, and it's still read and remembered everywhere. It's even on the reading list of high schools now, do you realise that? Vogel was a great conquest. I'm known because, all right, I'm a competent mountaineer myself..."

"You're too modest..." Actually, he thought Stuart immodest, but he wanted to soothe his friend.

"And I guess I could have published my mountaineering writings without Ernest, but there's no getting away from the bald fact that people know me, and want to meet me *because* I'm Ernest Ashton's son. It's what makes me special... There's something about celebrity, Tom."

He wanted to ask what there *was* about celebrity, but Stuart was in no mood to debate. "I understand how important your name is, but..."

"It's my *name* that means everything. I've built a career on it."

"Ease up and forget it, man. And let me have another beer."

"Get it yourself. You don't understand, Tom," Stuart said, aggravated, shaking his head, "I have to exorcise this bloody ghastly idea. That's why I want to look at the mountain man's junk collection."

"OK, OK, we can go to the lower levels of Vogel, but I'm not climbing, understand?"

Tom pondered what *he* was supposed to feel in this situation if the rumour was true. Hurt or let down? No, it was too many years ago. Anger or indignation? His father's death was a release. He and his mother were beneficiaries. Anger and indignation didn't come into it. What about the glory of being the son of the man who climbed a peak that nobody had climbed before, and only one person since? Yes, that glimmer of reflected light might have been desirable for a conceited law graduate years ago, but it would hardly penetrate to a lawyer working in London today. Nobody there was interested in how many peaks your father had climbed. Altogether, he recognised quickly that while this *was* a nightmare possibility for Stuart, it was almost a matter of indifference to him. But he was tense at the way the past might be disturbed by the rumour, and the unknown implications.

"What did Ernest say about it, Stuart?"

"He said it was rubbish, lies, and went into a long self-justificatory tirade."

"It was a hell of a thing to put to him. I would have expected him to explode. You believed him, didn't you?"

Stuart looked at the carpet, and then raised his head slowly to Tom. His expression drained. "I don't have confidence in anything he says. You know that. I haven't for years."

"Don't let your feelings about you father get in the way. I imagine the Swiss team were coming down beaten and broken, possibly even angry at their defeat, and in pain with their injuries. They must have met this feller in a hut. You don't stop to discuss past expeditions on the slopes. They're all stamping round in a small, poorly lit space drinking tea and chewing fruit bars and aching. He shows them his booty. They see some papers. They jump to mad conclusions because they're exhausted. How in hell can they work out anything factual from an encounter like that?"

Stuart was a little reassured. "I have to see this man. Do you get that, Tom?"

3

Robyn telephoned the Downs to say she would be arriving that afternoon. After lunch with Stuart and Tia, he waited for her in the library. There was hardly a place of greater ease for him to meet Robyn than at the Downs; it had ceased to be her home in any real sense long before she left it as a bride. Now, with Ernest's incapacity, it was a kind of lodging-house in the management of a housekeeper, Beryl Dilsey, a retainer of the family when he was a child. The earliest sort of refrain he recalled from Beryl was 'Get away from this doorstep Tommy Stavely, you dirty little boy! You're not coming in here!' She was a broomstick, now topped with a tight posy of grey curls. She took instructions from her new mistress, Tia, he noticed, with an insubordinate blankness of expression. Beryl's view of Tom, it seemed, had changed little. She had always been affronted that as Robyn's husband he sat at the dining room table with the master and mistress and she had to wait on him, a task she avoided whenever she could by sending a minion instead. He had taken pleasure at times in giving her instructions she could not avoid fulfilling. 'Beryl, would you mind passing me the vinegar carafe from the buffet…?'

Although Tamaki Downs held much of the past, it was, for him, neutral ground.

When Robyn arrived, he greeted her brightly with an impersonal kiss on each cheek. She threw her jacket casually over a chair and plumped down in an armchair. She was carefully coffeured and made up, perhaps a gesture to him, but the dryness of her tanned skin, her lacklustre hennaed hair, red eyes and the flabbiness around her middle, suggested a drunk who had tidied herself up. She smiled happily.

"There you are, Tom, looking very youthful. And handsome. How are you?"

He couldn't respond honestly with the same generosity, and besides, Robyn's statements were for effect rather than accuracy. The truth was that his hair was thinning and silverish and he had a lot of lines around the eyes, even if he still had his slim figure. He was, however, glad of the superficial crust of politeness which protected them both from deeper antagonisms.

He mentioned the pedestrian facts of his journey and his pleasure at Petra's forthcoming wedding. "Where is Petra?"

"She's in Christchurch, staying with girlfriends and shopping. She'll be here tomorrow. You can meet her and Darren. She's a lovely girl - and you don't know her."

"Letters and visits help, but -"

"All you know is that she's an attractive, well-schooled girl, Tom. It's a pity you've never been able to talk intimately with her, or help her with her problems over the years. You've missed a lot."

"I have written, but…"

"Tom, you can't expect a young girl in the twenty-first century to sit down like Jane Austen and pen letters in reply."

Why the hell not? he thought. "Emails, perhaps?" He held up the palms of his hands plaintively; it was no use trying to defend himself against his default as a parent. Robyn had condemned him long ago without hope of reprieve.

He would be saying to Alison, 'The cow gave me the usual verbal thrashing…' And Alison would reply, with amusement, 'Maybe you deserve it.'

"And how is Alison? Still sharing your uxorious idyll?" Alison still rankled with Robyn.

"She's fine. She's not coming to the wedding."

He and Alison had wrestled with how to deal with her invitation. He wanted her to come. She didn't want to come. She couldn't stand Robyn and didn't see any point in pretence. Her negative reaction came from the confusion, fuelled by alchohol and sex, which had submerged their lives when they met. It was his wish, not hers, to have their relationship more widely understood and accepted by their New Zealand friends, but he gave in.

"Quite right, Tom - Alison not coming." Robyn said haughtily.

"Why?" He shouldn't have asked, but he was needled.

"Because…" Robyn made a quirky movement of her lips, "she destroyed our marriage."

This was Robyn's fantasy. As far as she was concerned, their breakup was simple, and summed up in less than half a dozen words. She was icily positive.

The rows with Robyn in previous years were equivalent to a heavy bombardment on a war frontier; now, with that long in the past, a shell or two did little damage. He resisted the incitement. He had admittedly been a neglectful and adulterous husband, but she couldn't see that she had been a neglectful and adulterous wife. Well, she would *have* to concede adultery if lightly pressed, but neglect, no. She would never admit neglect. Her husband was stolen by a scheming woman in her view. He thought her absurd attitude had made it easier for her wounded pride.

He sidestepped. "Are you doing any stage work, Robyn?"

"I'm doing more directing. I've got *Oh! What a Lovely War* at the Albion in Christchurch, first night on the 6th."

"You've made quite a name for yourself."

She puffed up. She would be soaking up a bottle of sherry backstage during the performance, and probably having it off with the lighting engineer in one of the dressing rooms afterwards. But what amazed him about her, knowing her rather strange reasoning powers, was that out of the conflict and confusion of casting and rehearsals, she could turn a few pages of script into a living, breathing production. She could give the pages a real stage life. The critics said she was a good director and actor and he respected these mysterious skills.

"I think I do a good job, Tom. But I could never get you interested in the footlights, could I? I couldn't even persuade you to audition."

"I never wanted to strut the boards, you know that. I didn't want to assume a different personality, work myself up into false rages."

"You're timid."

She was right. The idea of departing from his self and turning into another self was disquieting. He couldn't understand himself well enough, let alone pretend to be somebody else. Robyn's ability to fragment her personality, while remaining more or less sane, had dazzled and delighted him at first. It was like loving different people at the same time. Which one would it be tonight? Then it began to confuse him. Did he want this person tonight? Then it began to alarm him mildly. Was she entirely sane? He didn't deny her comment.

"What about you, Tom? With an English wife, and two children born in England, will you ever come back?"

"I'd like to, in some ways." He spoke frankly.

"Never mind. It's your problem. You are Petra's father and your presence now is appropriate, but there's one thing I have to tell you. Petra has decided that she wants Stuart to give her away at the church. After all, he's been like a father to her, and he knows her."

He gulped with surprise. "OK, that's fine with me," he said, but it wasn't fine; it was a snub, perhaps a due snub in view of his paternal neglect. No, it was more than a snub. It was a calculated fucking insult! He could feel his cheeks getting hot and a prickle of sweat on his brow. He would rage to Alison on the telephone later that he had come twelve thousand miles to be treated like a visitor! And she would probably reply that it was rather rude, but if that was how Petra felt... 'It's how Robyn feels!' he would shout.

It was difficult now to talk to Robyn in any depth. When they met, each of them dragged a deadweight of shared experience quite differently viewed; two barges on different voyages, each grinding on the other as they passed. All the embarrassing arguments and insults of the past stained the many pleasures they had taken together. Every present word and gesture had to be filtered through this turbulent past and arrived upon the scene either devoid of warmth or slightly rancid.

He couldn't help regarding his attendance at Petra's wedding as of some importance, but perhaps it was only of importance to him. Ernest's jibe that he wanted to play at being a father came back to him. He guessed his presence was probably, if not immaterial, then of small concern to Petra. Money for the wedding and marriage, which may keep a bride close to her father, wasn't an issue here. Robyn was well off, and although he was making a substantial contribution, it had all been arranged very discreetly by Robyn.

He would be saying to Alison, 'Robyn is more concerned about appearances - particularly the need to underline to her friends that Tom Stavely is still family, but on the outer fringe.' 'But that's where you are, aren't you?' Alison would confirm. He wouldn't use any strong words to Alison which would disclose the bile of his emotions.

"Tia told me you aren't staying here, Tom. But you must. There would have been plenty of room for Alison if she had chosen to come. The wedding's here. I'm here. Everything's here. God, everyone can camp here as far as I'm concerned."

"Sure, if that's what you want. I'll get my bags sent up."

When Alison elbowed him about being seduced into staying at Tamaki Downs, he would retort, 'She doesn't give a damn where I stay, provided it doesn't embarrass the family. Robyn doesn't want me to stay at the Royal. You remember it? Definitely downmarket for the father of the bride. Staying anywhere but the Downs when there are guests there would suggest a schism in the family. Divorce is one thing: bad blood is another.'

"Tom, what is this Mt Vogel business about Dad?"

"You've heard the story from Stuart? It sounds to me like nonsense. He's overwrought and he's talked himself into it."

"Good. Yes, and I thought, what does it really matter after all this time? It would certainly be a disgrace for Dad, for the family name, but particularly for Stuart, wouldn't it?"

He didn't comment. She fired up.

"You haven't changed, Tom. Always noncommittal. You're a bloody lawyer alright. I can never get a straight story from you. Stuart's so jumpy."

"I've more or less agreed with him that we'll make a quick trip to the Vogel area and set the rumour to rest. Stuart's got it mixed up with his - what shall we call it? - dislike of Ernest. I understand his feelings... I can remember keeping my head down, digging post holes while Stuart was being thrashed. I can also remember getting a clip or two across the ear myself from Ernest. A multimillionaire getting his kid to dig post holes like a peasant! But that's all beside the point."

Robyn tightened her lips and leaned away at the unpleasant memory. "Dad's nearly dead. Let him go peacefully. But Stuart… I mean, it's inconceivable that Dad lied, surely? Inconceivable. I'm glad you seem so confident it's untrue. A rumour like this could really hurt Stuart when you think about it. You wouldn't realise it, but he's quite a personality in this country with his television programmes and his newspaper work. As soon as there's some kind of smear, influential people in the media start steering clear."

"And he has a name amongst mountaineers internationally."

"Do you care what happens to Stuart? I've always thought you were secretly envious of him." She spoke with a mischief-making grin that was humourless.

"It depends what you mean by envy, Robyn. Stuart is the man with everything. A handsome athlete, born into an old moneyed family, sent to the best school and university, intelligent, with the whole spectrum of possible careers open to him, utterly financially secure from the time he was in his playpen, and with a name that can open any door he chooses – banking, medicine, science, law, business. Seriously, Robyn, is there *anybody* who wouldn't envy this god?"

"I never thought of Stuart like that." She was pleased.

"No, well there's another side. His father has abused him and beaten the confidence out of him, and he's misguidedly erected his career, despite his own talents, on his father's shoulders. Perhaps it's perversely because of the abuse. It's taken him nearly twenty years to find a compatible woman. He's got a battle neurosis…"

"No, no, no! I don't recognise that Stuart! Dad didn't do that. Dad isn't like that. He wouldn't hurt Stuart. Stuart was bad at times like any boy, so…"

"Robyn, you know that's not right. I've *seen* Ernest in action. Ernest, for some unaccountable reason, hates his son. Maybe Ernest hates himself. Anyway, he's crushed Stuart. He's not a nice man."

"Stuart's not been crushed, he's an expansive, confident –"

"He appears to be."

He would probably put this exchange slightly differently to Alison: 'She's always sniping at me! But being envious of bloody Stuart! That's what she accused me of! He's always been a superior sod, but underneath this carapace he's weak. He's propped himself up on Ernest's reputation. He's parlayed his undistinguished skills as a writer, and his genuine competence as a climber, into a kind of celebrity. It's a slick act, covered with the snotty superiority of a wealthy family name!'

'Be fair,' Alison would say, 'Stuart is a very special friend of yours.'

'I care for Stuart, but what I say is true,' he would insist.

Robyn said, "You always have such distorted viewpoints, Tom. Stuart isn't broken and he has a fine career. And Dad isn't what you say. And what about you? Are you so great?"

"I have my own calling. I won't dignify it too much by describing it as a career."

"I know you're very clever at passing exams, Tom, but you've never really… *done anything,* have you, except of course fuck every woman within reach?"

She eked these cruelly delicious words out, but it was mostly the forthcoming conversation with Alison which occupied his mind rather than a riposte: 'This is what Robyn thinks of me. A nerdy nobody. Ernest is somebody. He has his own achievements. I'll concede that. A swine, but somebody. But I won't allow that Stuart is anybody. He's just a wraith, balancing on Ernest's shoulders. In the interests of calm, I never asked the bitch who *she* thought she was. She thinks she's New Zealand's answer to Stanislavsky!' Alison would say that he was being unfair, and that Robyn was a considerable person. To cap this, he would quote Ernest's recent comment: 'Used to be'. But yes, he was being unfair to Robyn. It was her arrogant assumptions that heated him.

Robyn was sitting back in the pause, pleased with the impact of her words; she was actor-director in this encounter.

He didn't care enough to hit back. "No, I haven't *done* anything in the sense you mean."

Robyn was disappointed. She wanted to joust. After a moment, she took her bloodshot eyes off him, and with a sour simper, banged her small bejewelled fist on the arm of the chair.

"What a mistake we made, Tom!"

At lunch the next day, Tia said to him, "Why don't we walk down to the old houses?"

"Yes, you go with Tia, Tom. I've got a bit of work to do in the study," Stuart said.

He tried not to show reluctance at this proposal, because although he had been thinking of going, he wanted to be alone. Yet it was difficult to resist Tia's pleasure in the invitation, and so he agreed.

It was a few minutes' walk. The lane ran down to a gully where the old house had huddled in the lee of a hill, and out of sight of the Downs homestead. The surrounding pines were stunted and twisted by the wind. Nothing much of the house structure was left now; the wooden foundation posts were almost obscured in long grass; a brick chimney with a blackened fireplace stood alone; sheets of rusting iron scattered the ground, and to one side was a holed water tank and a lavatory bowl lying on its side. Beyond were the ruins of more than half a dozen shacks and bunkhouses formerly occupied by other station hands. He had an image of his father, his mother and himself at differing times, squatting over the ceramic bowl.

"It was a rickety old dump when we lived in it." He kicked through the grass. "Peeling paint, warped timber and a leaky roof."

"You lived here with your mother and father?" Tia said, surveying the ruin.

"My old man was the manager here – at least that's what he was called, although I guess Ernest never actually stopped managing any property or person in his power. I was 'Bill Stavely's boy', always available to help out. And my mother lived here after my father died on Mt Vogel, until she died."

"That was nice…"

"An act of kindness by the generous Ashtons, you think? Sometime I'll tell you the story."

"Stuart talks about you as though you are some kind of legal big shot…"

"Well, I'm not. When I leave my job in London, my name will be forgotten in my office in a month, perhaps in a week."

She assented with an uncertain movement of her head. "All these ruins are scheduled to be cleared next year. This little page of history."

"What are you putting in its place?"

"Nothing. We don't need more outbuildings…"

"A very dog-eared page of history… New Zealand was a place where people reinvented themselves, Tia. Maybe Stuart told you about Joe Ashton in the 1870s. Not by any means an uncommon story. Somebody has to win. He came from Glasgow poverty via the goldfields of Australia and the

West Coast and parlayed his stake into this, hundreds of thousands of acres."

"Yes, Stuart told me. Joseph Ashton was a Pakeha land-grabber," she said, contemptuously.

"There's lots of stories around here about him still. A cruel and domineering man by all accounts. Hardly literate, but deadly cunning. Plucked a woman from a bar in Springvale, fathered children and founded a dynasty. The genes must have been accidentally right. Joe would have had little choice of women. Springvale wasn't much more than a saloon, stables and a trading store at the time."

"It's also a story of sweated labour, tricky land deals, bribery and undue political influence, from what Stuart tells me."

"Right. And it will all end in the hands of a Maori princess."

She smiled thoughtfully. "It means nothing to me. I hope you can believe it. I'm not a princess. I'm Ngai Tahu. These great spaces don't belong to individuals, they belong to all of us. But what about *your* father?"

"He didn't have any steel in him like the Ashtons. A make-do man from nowhere. He was of Scots extraction too, I believe, but he had no past or relatives that I ever heard of. Not one. He appeared over the hill, met and married my mother. She was an emigrant from Norfolk – a hotel maid. I don't know anything definite about her past either. She'd never talk about the past. I was fourteen when Bill Stavely died in 1972. Much of what I know about him is hearsay. He was clever at rebuilding internal combustion engines and a bullying foreman. I never knew him as a fatherly figure, only as a morose and violent drunk."

"Hey, that's a way different picture to the one Ernest paints in *The Fateful Snows*."

"Ernest had to dignify his climbing companion because he's a snob. I bless my good luck that my father died, Tia. No old man to push me into hard labour on the land or an apprenticeship. An apprenticeship would have been about the limit of his vision, from what I know of him. Off I went to Timaru College, where they showed me the track to university. It didn't matter a damn that I was Bill Stavely's raggy-arsed kid, and never owned a tennis racket or a bicycle."

"You were brought up with Stu and Robyn. That can't have been bad."

"Borrowing their bicycles and tennis rackets, you mean? After a while you don't ask. You walk away." He could have added, 'How would you know, anyway?' He had already told Alison, 'I've learned from Stu that Tia is absolutely in the Ashton mould. She's a privileged kid. Loving, well-off parents, the best of schooling and university. She's never wanted or had to struggle for anything, and she's gutsy.'

"You'd have made it to university, Tom, surely, even if your father had lived," Tia said.

"Maybe. I doubt it. I pay homage to those who cut the track from farmhouse to university in earlier days. People like Savage and Fraser. A track for anybody, that was the point. Luckily for me. "

"Aren't you too hard on your father?"

"He was a crushing and depressing influence. And he used to beat the shit out of my mother. It's hard to get your head around, Tia - why a strong man should ache so much inside that he has to beat a woman bloody to relieve himself. How it would have ended, I hate to think - if he had lived. It was a little like Ernest with Stuart. Ernest Ashton and Bill Stavely were very different, but a couple of monsters in strangely similar ways. Ernest beat his son and Bill Stavely beat my mother."

44

He had said more than he intended; it was the effect of standing in these ruins and refreshing his realisation of how damn lucky he had been to rise out of them.

She didn't speak again as they returned to the house, but he felt that there was a togetherness in the silence, and that his thoughtlessness of the day before had left little if any mark.

When they were close to the house, she said, "It was good of you to talk to me, Tom. You and Stuart have a lot of shared history and it's helpful to know some of it. And thanks for agreeing to go to Mt Vogel with Stuart. He needs you."

4

He heard Robyn say, "Your dad's in there," and Petra came into the drawing room, laughing, laden with parcels, and preoccupied with the balancing act she had to perform to keep them from falling. She looked back at the tall young man, equally laden, who swayed his wide shoulders from the hips as he followed. It was a moment before they let the parcels down on the couch, the red couch, and she looked at her father.

"Daddy! How lovely to see you." She came close and gave him a quick hug, withdrawing immediately, leaving a fragrance from her hair which had brushed his face.

He tried to add together the time that he had spent with her in her nineteen years; a month or two, perhaps. He could not expect an affectionate reunion, because there had never been a union. 'Daddy' seemed an impossibly intimate word from this young woman.

"It's good to see you so happy, Petra." He was inarticulate in the swirl of youthful sighs around him.

Petra backed away and turned to the tall young man. "Daddy, this is Darren."

"Hi, Mr Stavely," Darren said, proffering a huge fist, without eye contact, instead looking round the princely room, his eyes shining and mouth slightly open, speechless at the fine things that were happening to him.

"Call me Tom. I've been looking forward to meeting you, Darren."

The last person he was looking forward to meeting was not particularly Darren, but his daughter's prospective husband.

'She's too young,' he had said to Robyn, when she called him in London to tell him of the proposed marriage - Petra didn't telephone herself.

'I'm not calling to ask you, Tom,' Robyn had said. 'I'm telling you. You can't play the stern father.'

'I don't want to. I want you to see sense, Robyn. You understand how we messed up our lives. You can give her some motherly advice. Petra needs to take a decade off from childbirth and have fun. She'll be lumbered with twins at twenty, while her Darren is away screwing a rugby groupie.'

'Don't be so cynical and pessimistic.'

It was to no avail; he was to be a spectator at the starting line of an accelerated race for unhappiness.

"How's the great game?" he asked Darren.

He was always respectful about rugby when in New Zealand; it wasn't so much a national passion as a sensitivity. Kiwis were miffed if you didn't show respect and somehow you were a lesser man. Years ago, at lunch with his fellow clerks at Gottleys, they sat around a restaurant table *every* lunch hour and argued about the selection of the team for Saturday. He had been bored by the game - which he had never had the opportunity to play; it was soccer at state schools in his day - and was slightly repelled by the violence, but too mindful of appearances to show his feelings, or refuse to lunch.

"I'm training hard, Mr Stavely - Tom - and I'll get back to it after the honeymoon," Darren said enthusiastically, running his fingers over the close-cut sportsman's bristle on his head.

"Darren's going to be an All Black, aren't you darling?"

"I think I've got a fair chance," Darren said, opening his mouth wide, as though the credibility of this admission was a heavy weight indeed.

"Uncle Stu could have been an All Black," Petra said.

"I know," Tom said. "He was an impressive sportsman at university."

"Were you, Daddy?"

"No. I got lost in my books."

'Hell, Alison,' he'd be saying to her, 'We got on to this sporting thing as though it was the only thing in life worth doing, and Petra was looking at me as if I only had one leg, comparing me to Uncle Stu.'

"What else are you doing, Darren?" he asked earnestly, wanting to show Petra that he was interested in her man.

Darren placed his muscular arm around Petra's shoulders. "Haaa. Chilling out, I guess." He had a yearning, affectionate look, like a golden retriever greeting its mistress.

Petra laughed and wriggled. Their exclusivity shut him out.

"I meant, are you studying or working?"

"Oh yeah…"

These seemed to be tasks Darren had to call to mind.

"Darren's a representative for Wright Stephenson."

"You're interested in stock agency?" Here was a subject he could chat about.

"Naah, but I've got a great car from the company and as much time off as I need to train and play. I'm in a group hoping to join the All Black squad."

"It's a three litre Mercedes coupe, Daddy. Really cool," Petra said.

"Three litres? Very nice."

"Yeah, she really goes," Darren added, his eyes lighting up.

He'd be saying to Alison, 'First it was sport, and then it was bloody cars! Clanking hunks of metal!'

'They're just kids. They don't have to be serious about the manifesto of the Labour Party,' she'd say.

He hadn't the heart to bring a shrug of confusion to Darren's big frame by asking whether he had any interests outside rugby and cars.

Petra was composed; the curves of womanhood now outlined her slight figure. She was more like her mother than him; long mahogany hair and brown, protuberant eyes. Yet she was not too different in appearance from a hundred girls of her age that he might pass in the street. She had all the untried softness of youth.

"What about you, Petra? Are you going to go on working?"

"No, Daddy. I gave them notice. I didn't like the bank much."

"So what comes next?"

She laughed. "I *am* getting married, Daddy. We'll be buying a house, and it'll take me a while to set that up. All the furnishing and decorating and that."

"You're *buying?*"

"Mummy's arranged it… trust funds…"

"Of course…" What the hell did Robyn think she was doing?

"You'll do some decorating?"

"Ha, ha! I'll choose the colours and materials."

"Choose the colours and the materials. Sure," he said, giving up.

Buying a house. It would be a palace. He would say to Alison, 'You'd think Petra would be up a ladder with a paintbrush. Her idea of decorating and furnishing is to go to a store and say 'I'll have this, that, and the other, and please deliver and install it.'

"What about a baby?" he asked carelessly, a throwaway line for an anodyne answer.

The bridal couple looked at each other and sniggered, holding hands now. "That would be *very* nice," Petra said, two dimples showing in her cheeks. She was glowing.

He didn't think his surprise showed. A baby already? And why should he be surprised? He of all people!

'Can you believe it, Alison?' he would say when he spoke to her. This couple have *everything* from day one. A home. No saving, no waiting, no working. And the usual old hurdy-gurdy has started to turn already. Pregnancy! Then we grind on to marriage, children, parties, adultery, and divorce.'

'It doesn't have to be that way, Tom,' Alison was certain to say.

'The guy is just a thick kid,' he would counter.

'You have law books between your ears. How thick is that?' She would be flippant.

'And why didn't Robyn tell me about this?' he'd ask.

Alison would reply, 'Probably to avoid hearing you yelling, 'Children, children, children!''

After dinner, he and Stuart settled in the study with a bottle of whisky. Tia declined to join them, and was pleased to let them talk. Stuart explained that he was seeking a manager for the Downs.

"Tia could do it. She'd like to, but I like to have her with me up at the Sounds, and when I'm travelling. And I think, why should I make any personal sacrifices for this place? Tamaki Downs is like a ton weight on my head."

He mentioned his television work, but Tom found him unfocussed and depressed, wanting to steer the conversation back to Mt Vogel.

"Do you remember that time a few years ago when we went fishing with John in Cook Straight?" Stuart asked.

He remembered. John was John Ashton, Stuart's cousin, an executive at the Ashton Group. "That was a good day."

"I always think about it because we had a row," Stuart said.

"Merely a tiff."

It wasn't an event which rattled their friendship, but he still had in his mind the picture Stuart painted of his – Tom's – future then, and wondered, when he recalled it later, whether year by year he was moving toward it.

He remembered that it was still dark when they climbed into the car at John Ashton's home in Kelburn, Wellington and began the drive to collect the rest of the crew from a variety of street corners. He was squeezed inside the car, shaking hands with people whose names he hardly heard and whose faces he couldn't see clearly. A befuddled crew of six they were at this hour. He and Stuart had come to Wellington, intending to tramp in the Tararuas for four days. They stayed with John and, as a preliminary outing, were invited for a day's fishing in Cook Straight on the Ashton Group's launch, which John skippered.

It was a Wellington day in March; chilly, cloudy and windy, with a weather report promise of sunshine. When they arrived at the boat harbour at Oriental Bay, a few men and women were on the footpath, setting up their easels in the best place to paint the sunrise. Hills fringed the harbour beyond a foreground of moored yachts and launches, a classic tourist view.

The crew were ferried out to board a forty-foot cabin cruiser with their supply of food and drink. John Ashton declared that they had forgotten the milk. Tom volunteered to go back and try to buy some. On returning to the jetty after his errand, the sun had shown its rim above the hills. The artists, their faces screwed up against the glare, were completing their outlines and applying washes to paper.

The milk quest was futile. He couldn't find a shop that was open. Rowing back to the launch in the dinghy, he unintentionally dug one of the copper-capped oars into the ribs of a pristine cruiser, leaving a black scar. He tied the dinghy at the stern of the boat in a cloud of exhaust smoke. John Ashton was warming the twin diesel engines. Tom announced his failure. The rest of the crew agreed that with so many liquids on board, the absence of milk was really a blessing; they could avoid tea and coffee.

As the craft passed through the Wellington Heads, they were having breakfast which Stuart - the only person whom he really knew on the trip apart from John - produced from the galley in a haze of blue frying smoke. They wolfed down bacon, tomatoes, sausages, eggs and fried bread, served on bright-coloured plastic plates with brown sauce.

The jerky chop of the harbour changed to the swell of the Straight where the Tasman and the Pacific met. The cruiser rose high and fell deeply, keeping a taste of salty sausages in the throat. Miles from the shore John Ashton heaved to. They were alone. Cape Palliser was an uncertain charcoal line on the horizon. Here, wedged between sea and sky, he had the same sense that he had when he was alone on snow at times, of being an irritant in the gleaming void of nature.

They baited the lines with squid and threw them out. The boat lurched nauseatingly. He drank a little beer. Nothing happened; there were no bites. The cruiser creaked and threatened to throw the beer cans on the deck. He had a headache and jammed himself into a space by the radio mast on the top of the cabin. He closed his eyes in the sun, letting the line which trailed carelessly across the deck and over the rail, go limp in his hand. Stuart, on the contrary, soldierly neat in his woollen jacket, bent expectantly over the rail. He had told the others that Tom wasn't a fisherman, and not much of a sailor.

After half an hour, the skipper announced that he knew a groper trench and would reposition the boat. The crew began to bait more lines, tying on the nylon traces for the hooks, and selecting different hooks and weights. Tom was half asleep. His head sagged back against a coil of rope, his legs lodged firmly behind the mast. There was a softness in this repose. He rubbed a smelly hand over his face and looked across at Stuart. Stuart's hair had threads of grey; the smooth, almost characterlessly handsome face was being replaced by a more bony structure. The skull was emerging. The skipper shifted the boat without success. The weather calmed.

Stuart too gave up and settled down beside him in the sun. "It was hell up there, Tom," he breathed, without any preliminaries.

They hadn't had an opportunity to talk much about Stuart's recent attempt on Mt Vogel. Tom knew he had several long monologues on the subject to come. But Stuart was, at least, a skilful raconteur.

"You can have another go, Stu." He cleared his head. "Why let Vogel bother you when you're out here in paradise?"

Stuart ignored him. Vogel couldn't be pushed aside that easily. "It's not just failing to complete the climb –"

"I wouldn't use the word failure," Tom interrupted. "The weather on Mt Vogel can be hellish. It must have become mission impossible."

"The old man did it, but I can't do it. *I can't fucking well do it*. This was my second attempt." He spoke strongly but quietly to avoid the others overhearing, with his lips taut.

"You and your team got a lot of nice publicity. You pushed your luck as far as you could."

The climb had been reported briefly in London and described as a gallant attempt, but there was mention of the father-son rivalry.

"Read more carefully. The newspapers over here were full of it. They gloated over it as much as the old man. Son *fails* - they used the word - to beat father's record. I could have thrown up!"

"Why bother trying? You've proved yourself. The Eiger, Mt Blanc, McKinley, Everest, K2."

"You don't get it, do you?" Stuart said, looking at him bitterly.

"I think I do. Everybody trots up Everest now, but only a select two have ever climbed Vogel. Vogel is like K2 - for experts only. And because Ernest did it, above all peaks, you have to do it too. It's a crucial battle in your war with your father."

"OK, you do get it. But you can't *feel* the way I do. You say, 'Have another try', or 'Why bother?' as though it's trifling either way. Every big climb I've made elsewhere in the world has shrunk in importance each time I've failed on Mt Vogel. Every time I fail, Sir Ernest Ashton's reputation swells, and he exalts. 'You can't do it, can you boy?' he says with his death's-head grin. I'd sooner take a good leathering with the belt from him than defeat on Mt Vogel. Then, all I felt was pain and rage. Now I have to suffer ignominy, crushing ignominy from the old man and the newspapers!"

He realised his friend sought endorsement of this passion. Stuart wanted to be stroked and comforted; he wanted a friend who licked his wounds, but Tom couldn't do that, not even for Stuart Ashton. And if he told the truth, and said that Mt Vogel had become a mania with Stuart, it would only make Stuart reject him. He tempered his words, as he had always done.

"Maybe I'm too close to this to really say anything helpful, Stu. But I'll tell you that my inclination is that you should divorce yourself from Ernest and go your own way. Drop Vogel. There's a world of other things to do in mountaineering. You don't need him. He *is* Mt Vogel. You have your journalism..."

"That shows me that you really don't understand the difference between us – I mean you and me. You want me to potter on with a dull little career in journalism, while you have your head down too, quietly lost in your lawyering. We'll both end up, when we retire, according to your view, in our own cottages in the same leafy lane in Springvale or Brighton, growing roses and playing backgammon. That's your view, Tom. Well, you can have it for yourself by all means, but don't foist it on me!"

"Who do you think you are, Stu? I've grown up with the famous Sir Ernest Ashton, and now do I see the great Stuart Ashton emerging? Or perhaps even Sir Stuart?"

Stuart was without any tincture of humour. "You can be as sarcastic as you like, because you don't know what it's like to be publicly recognised for some achievement. I'm recognised internationally for the climbs I've achieved and for my television and writing on mountaineering. Those are... achievements."

"Heady wine... I hope you've made a will leaving your cufflinks to the Canterbury museum."

"Arsehole!" Stuart got up abruptly and went back to his line.

He couldn't doze now. He had a vision of his future; an aged, thin, tanned, white-haired man tending his cottage garden. A man who had lost his taste for television and books and films and galleries after being satiated with them over a lifetime. A man who was impotent, except perhaps sexually, clinging to the softly agreeable edge of human society. Would he have a female companion or would he be alone? Would he have a child (now an elderly adult) who would be interested enough to visit him? A man who bathed in the Sunday newspapers and the 7pm newscast on television, who led a fortnightly walk for pensioners, and took lessons in ballroom dancing at the town hall. A man in passably good health and poor spirits, who was confronted every day when he got out of bed by the cold fact that he had nothing much to do, and was pained and bored by the effort of doing what little he did do. A man who felt every day that his mind was turning to jelly and tried to disguise it... *is this all there is?*

Then he saw an apple box floating past. 'Rist, rist, rissst,' one of the lines sounded as it ran out from the reel. They all crowded to the stern as the fish circled reluctantly to the surface. Stuart pulled up a snapper with a golden back, perhaps five pounds in weight. 'Risssst!' went one of the other lines.

"Look," somebody shouted. A school of porpoises about half a mile away was leaping and diving in pairs and trios; one shot up clear of the waves to stand on its tail for a moment before crashing down like a hooked game-fish.

Now there were bites on all the lines, and they were bringing up gasping blue cod as fast as they could throw in their baited hooks. Cans of beer were passed around. He hauled a fat, foot-long cod up on his line, and poked diffidently inside the gills of the goggling fish until his forefinger met his thumb. He tore the hook from its mouth with his other hand on the line. He threw the pulsing creature into the box where the catch threshed and thumped. They chopped their bait, now in large chunks, and dug the hooks into it carelessly. The lines were alive in their hands. They called to each other with slaughterhouse excitement.

He heard a chugging in the distance and saw two small boats heading toward them. The porpoises still cavorted a few hundred yards away, and suddenly, all around the boat the surface rippled with the 'siseroo, siseroo sisss', of a school of Kawhai breaking the surface. The sea glittered.

"Hell, you could walk on them!" he shouted, as the carpet of feeding fish made the water boil.

5

He was welcomed as an old friend, with a lot of hugs from both Mark and Felicity Curran. They spread themselves out on the white leather couches in the lounge of the Curran home, with *very* large gin and tonics, as befits familiars who have done a lot of drinking together. Mark and his wife, and their two children (presently absent at Christ's College) lived in a spacious house in the wooded, rolling northwest part of Springvale, settled by the leaders of the community and wealthy retired farmers.

After the smiles and sighs, there was a silence. It had been nearly four years. 'Jesus, Alison,' he would say, 'I sat there staring at them, and them grinning at me, and I had a sudden sensation that nothing had happened in four years. There wasn't anything to say. I might as well not have been away.'

Mark was a heavily muscled man, now paunchy, with a reddish-tan complexion and only a dry lock of front hair left on his head. He was much aged from his days at Otago University with Tom. They had shared lodgings; it was a time when they were each eyeing the other's potential and speculating, sometimes in a drunken stupor, about what might become of them. At one point they were planning to go to Sydney to start an investment fund; a dream of tailored suits and fast cars and champagne and women.

After graduation, for Mark, the lofty talk about conquering the world ended, and he simply said, 'I'm going to find a cushy job and play a lot of golf and tennis.' To Tom's surprise, that is what Mark did; it was a life objective Tom had difficulty with at the time; but as the years went by, and his own affairs seesawed, it seemed to have more merit than he first thought.

"How's the Ashton portfolio?" he asked.

"Very good. You'd be surprised how we've diversified." Mark apparently wasn't sure how much he should say about his client, because Tom was an outsider now.

"Stuart tells me that Tamaki Downs is scraping along," he said, to help.

"It's a vast asset, Tom, whatever happens. Money in the bank."

"Stuart isn't interested in running it," Tom said.

"He's OK. Prices haven't been great," Mark said, protectively. "We're looking for a manager."

"What about Tia?"

"Oh, don't talk rubbish, Tom!" Felicity put in heavily. "She's a kid in her twenties."

"She has the qualifications, and she seems a very together person."

"Ridiculous!" Felicity said.

"Yes, well, it's not for us to…" Mark said quietly.

"If you men are going to talk business…" Felicity said.

Mark had buried his history degree, qualified as an accountant and joined a small but prosperous practice in Springvale, which after a time was amalgamated with a practice in Timaru, and one in Christchurch. Eventually, these were all acquired by one of the big international firms. Mark profited financially; his biggest client was the Tamaki Downs Company. He was also a director of some of the Ashtons' other companies, and a trusted adviser of the family.

He had stuck to sport, his practice and his family, and

there seemed to be no irregularities in his life. Years ago, when Tom and Robyn had begun to heat up Springvale, Fairlie and Geraldine with their parties, Felicity virtually withdrew Mark from the scene.

'I don't care if the Ashtons are Mark's clients,' Felicity said to Tom once. 'It doesn't mean that he has to screw your wife!' This was after Felicity had been to bed with him, which was certainly acceptable to her at the time, but she wasn't going to allow Mark the same latitude with Robyn.

At one time, before he and Robyn married, Mark and Robyn had been a couple, and perhaps Felicity knew this and didn't trust Mark. Tom thought Robyn had liked Mark. He had been attractive to women in those days, in a raffish way. She might have married him. The gossip at that time was that she wanted to, but Mark had withdrawn suddenly, and picked up with Felicity. She was an easier girl to cope with.

Tom had pointed out to Mark, at the time, the Aladdin's cave of treasure that lay ahead with Robyn. It wasn't exactly a novel insight, but a nice subject to contemplate over a few drinks. Mark had been too reticent to say much. He was a shy, nervous man under a businesslike veneer. Tom's guess was that Mark was edgy about a cleverness and sociability in Robyn that he couldn't match. And he may have been overawed by her money; he had none himself. Felicity, by contrast, was a very unremarkable girl from a Springvale farm labourer's family. She had incidentally, at that time, acquired the reputation for being an easy lay. She wasn't challenging.

Tom jumped into the awkward space in the stalled conversation. He assured the Currans that Alison and the children were well, and talked a little about them. The Currans said what a lovely couple Petra and Darren were. Tom listened to the achievements of the Curran boys at Christ's College and heard about the renovation of the family apartment in Sydney and their recent vacation in Los Angeles. One or two local names appeared; a politician who was now a Member of Parliament and a haulage contractor who had died. Tom wheedled Mark's golf handicap out of him. "Six is brilliant," he commented, quite impressed. Felicity added that the doctor had forbidden Mark, with his high blood pressure, to play squash, and to concentrate on golf rather than tennis.

Felicity asked when Alison would be arriving for the wedding; both she and Mark knew Alison from 'the old days'. Felicity gave a knowing nod when Tom said that Alison wouldn't be at the wedding. Neither Mark or Felicity asked specifically why, which was either good manners or a tacit acceptance that the Ashton-Stavely excesses of the past still tainted the air. Of course, the Currans would be at the wedding themselves as valued guests.

"Stuart surprised us by marrying Tia," Felicity said, dropping a baited hook into a pause.

"He must have got tired of chasing South Canterbury debs," Tom said, blandly. He wasn't going to admit that not only was he surprised, but irked that his good friend had told him nothing about the bride.

"It was all very sudden. Nobody knew anything," she sniffed.

"Love can be like that," Tom said, flourishing his drink and taking a large gulp.

"Love my arse," Felicity exploded, "more like a jaded roue's desire for sex!"

"He certainly cut a swathe across the province!" Mark guffawed.

Felicity frowned sharply at Mark. "We know all about that." She returned to the subject determinedly, "What do you think of Tia?"

"Seems a nice girl..."

"Too young for Stuart, surely, over twenty years."

"I don't know. Is it so important? And Stuart needs all the help he can get with the Downs. She's a Massey graduate. Knows ten times more about stock and animal husbandry than he's ever learned."

Felicity couldn't decry this because she hadn't finished secondary school.

"She's a big pea down at the marae I hear," Mark said.

"The marae!" Felicity said, huddling into herself on the couch as though there was a chilling breeze in the room.

"Good luck to them," Tom said, avoiding Felicity and Mark's gaze by tossing off the last drop of his 'big one' and squinting at the elaborate plaster cornice on the ceiling through the bottom of the glass.

"Get you another?" Mark asked, always a pressing host to justify his own replenishments.

Felicity chipped in, "The marae around here is just a new thing, you know, in the last ten years or so. There wasn't one before. It's a kind of..." She trailed off, working her mouth without words. "It's like inventing history."

"Tia's from the Banks Peninsula, I believe," Mark said.

"What's the problem?" Tom wanted to lance the boil.

Felicity jerked, but remained huddled. "All this mystical stuff about Maori land!" she said, exhaling strongly, standing up and crossing her arms as though she was cold. She moved toward the door. "Excuse me, Tom, I promised to ring my mother..." She trailed the words over her shoulder.

Mark gritted his teeth when they were alone, and forced a smile at the same time. "You know Felicity, she's a bit..."

"Why?"

Mark paused. He was used to speaking carefully and authoritatively, but the words came out like a groan. "Oh... I dunno!"

62

It was a question Tom hardly had to ask. He didn't think it was entirely her impatience with near-parallel red lines of culture depicted in the Wellington museum. Ever since their mini-affair, on the occasions that he had met Felicity, she was awkward and withdrew from his company as quickly as politeness would allow. He was a very old friend, but also a memory, and an irritant. It was almost as though she had expected more from him in the past than a casual bedding, and that he had disappointed her. He was sure that she was now the irreproachable wife, but he detected her slight contempt for her husband. She could have been saying to Tom, 'You left me with this guy, now clear out and let me get on with it.'

"So how's the job?" he asked Mark.

Mark swelled his chest and thought again. "Oh, good, great, fine. I spend a lot of my time in Timaru or Christchurch. We're busy."

"Uh-huh. Remember when we were going to chuck things in and go to Oz? Ever think of that now?"

"No, hell, Oz is where I go on holiday. I wouldn't want to live there. Not now. And there's the kid's schooling here."

"Sydney would be a big buzz, and there are plenty of schools there."

Mark sat up defensively. He had small, feminine hands which he waved to express himself better. "Look Tom, I have everything I want. A good wife, kids, a job and money. We have a yacht. We live well."

He didn't reply immediately. Mark didn't look as though he had convinced himself. "It's a bit like living in a village on the Ashton's manor, isn't it? Small town, same people," Tom said.

"There's some wonderful people here!"

"Who are they?"

"Don't be funny."

"So no regrets?"

"Whaddya mean regrets, Tom? I told you, I'm a happy man."

He probed Mark gently, accepting another drink. The 'big ones' were distancing him from the Curran lounge. "Don't you feel kind of restricted in Springvale? I mean, it's a beautiful place, not many people here, in beautiful countryside. It's sort of quiet, and well, beautiful, but… nothing ever happens."

He could have added, 'Nothing except adultery and boozing, and maybe the odd line of cocaine,' but he wouldn't say that, because although the Currans might be heavies on the dinner party circuit, that is about all they were.

Mark was looking at Tom curiously now, his brow corrugated. "Whaddya mean, nothing happens?" Then his expression smoothed into a grin. "Isn't the wedding of Petra Stavely *something*?"

"Sure…" Tom said warmly. "I'll explain, Mark. My plane touched down in Auckland before coming on here. I picked up a copy of *The Auckland Herald* from the steward when we took off. It headlined a taxation niggle, a company fraud, and a Maori claim to fishing rights. I had a sense of déjà vu. I thought it must be the same paper I picked up on my flight four years ago. I checked the date. It was current."

"Yeah, well…"

Mark had set up a defensive wall, and Tom didn't want to appear to be trying to break it down, at least not any more on this occasion. The hazy look in Mark's eyes, and the way he wiped the palm of his hand uncertainly across his mouth, suggested to Tom a reflection on goals set, and not pursued.

He walked across the lawns at Tamaki Downs. The gardeners had fought the wind and the sun successfully and produced a lush carpet. From the pine belt, he could see clear across the golden uplands to the slate gray line of the Southern Alps. At this moment, the snow-topped peaks appeared to be floating above the island like a long cloud. The sight made him want to hoist a pack on his shoulders and start walking; walk out of this thicket of prickly relationships to an icy calm. Then he went inside to a ground floor bathroom with a marble bath and gold-plated taps. On the windowsill in front of him as he used the lavatory was a pink clam shell, and beside it a pile of five smooth, grey river stones, artfully leaning on each other.

He fondled the stones; they were from a stream at Mt Ruapehu, a trophy which Robyn had gathered. She had relegated them from her bedroom, but they had been faithfully retained by the housekeeper in this inferior position. Just as the red velvet couch had attracted him for reasons which were only partly to do with affection, a short time later his fortunes were diverted at Mt Ruapehu.

He returned to sit in the sun on a sheltered chair on the lawn and dozed.

It was about two months after the red couch incident when he swung high above the mountainside at Mt Ruapehu. He could see a puff of steam from the crater of Mt Ngaurahoe. A slight breeze brought a sudden chill. The chairlift passed up a face of rock, a waterfall in summer, now a pillar of ice. The rocks on the face were brown-black, stacked like bricks but crushed into irregularity by the weight of ice above. At the top of the cliff, on gentle slopes, human figures slid down like bright twig insects. Closer, a few teenagers were agilely swerving through a self-made slalom course, throwing up silver veils of snow. After he had been dropped by the chairlift at the crest of the slope, he skied to the end of the slalom course. The children raced past him at speed and stopped daringly near the edge of the cliff in sudden turns; they panted healthy enjoyment.

Then he skied, and by one in the afternoon he was exhausted; his legs were too tired to control the skis; his face burned, a tomato under his woollen hat. He had a sensation of being crushed between the white earth and the blue sky. He snapped off his skis and planted them upright in the forest of skis and poles outside the cafeteria. He pushed slowly through the crowd. He found Stuart sitting on a rail at the top of the cafeteria steps. Stuart pointed to the drink and the pizza he had ordered for Tom.

"Where's Robyn?" Stuart asked.

"I haven't seen her since I left the lodge."

"You two are OK, are you?"

Perhaps he sensed that something was wrong. Tom had an urge to confide in him, but although he knew Stuart better than anybody else, he didn't know how Stuart would react. Stuart had liberal views, but where the Ashton clan was concerned, Tom thought he cherished a spotless escutcheon.

"Of course we're OK. You know she likes to ski blue."

Stuart munched his pizza enthusiastically. He had a way of picking up articles in his large hands, or tasting a morsel of food, which showed the pleasure these things evoked in him. His gusto in doing simple things was infectious. Alone, Tom might have gulped the pizza down without remarking its taste, but today he lingered over every mouthful, so hungry that he couldn't pause to talk, but so anxious to taste every morsel that he couldn't hurry. The lemon drink, half filled with crushed ice, pierced his sticky throat.

He had hardly talked to Robyn of their plight since she told him. His silence was caused by shock; hers – it seemed – by an acceptance of the fact. Even when they arrived at the lodge at Ruapehu, having travelled in separate vehicles, they didn't talk. She glanced at him occasionally from a distance. When he was unpacking his clothes on his bunk, she was a few yards away, chatting to a girl in their party. When he went in to lunch with Stuart that day, she came in later and chose another table, but her powerful, emotional, big-eyed stare rested upon him from time to time. He didn't have the resolve to single her out and embrace her. He supposed he was reluctant because that would be like embracing the situation they were in; it would be a tacit acknowledgment of invisible bonds which threatened to tie him to her.

For the first few days after Robyn's phone call to him in Christchurch, he had nursed the bad news like indigestion, without thinking further than the fact. The implications which came to him increasingly were confused. He was looking for a practice - anywhere in the country, North or South Island - where he could make a good living; this prospect, so bright, was cast into shadow.

The weather changed suddenly. On Sunday, mist closed over Ruapehu and snow began to fall. After breakfast, he moved Stuart's car down to the Chateau park and walked back. In front of the lodge, a crowd of skiiers was hesitant about venturing on to the slopes in such poor visibility. The chairlift had stopped operating. Three people from the lodge, dressed in blue, had walked out a hundred yards across the snow. Their footprints had been obliterated; they were talking face to face, surrounded by depthless white. Their figures might have been cut from a coloured picture and pasted on a plain white sheet of paper.

"You're keeping out of the way," Robyn said to him, in front of the others.

Hastily, he suggested they go for a walk together. "It's no use standing around here."

They headed away silently from their friends, Robyn a few yards in front. She set a course between a line of red poles at the side of the lodge which marked the hidden track. They peeped out from the hoods of their anoraks; large flakes settled on their shoulders like epaulettes, each of them in a silent cell.

As they passed into a clump of trees, he caught Robyn up, pulled her back toward him, and tried to kiss her. His boots slipped. He bore over on her. She thrust her arms back to save herself, dirtying her gloves on an earthen bank. She looked at him disdainfully and then at her gloves. She wiped them across the breast of her anorak leaving a smear.

"There!" she said, tossing her head, and walking a few steps to lean against a tree trunk. "Is it so terrible, having your life messed up with mine? You look so grim."

"There are... problems."

"You have problems? Poor you! Do you have any idea how I'm suffering?"

"Yes, of course..."

"What a damn misery you are, Tom!"

She stamped her foot. She shook a branch and showered them with tiny crystals. The white-laden trees swayed around them like a sugar forest.

He felt another stab of desire. If she was to have his child, he couldn't help assuming a right to possess her. He grasped her shoulders. She evaded him and sat down on a stone.

Their knowledge of each other wasn't exclusively pleasant; they argued a lot. Occasionally, he disliked her, but certain parts of the past had been irrevocably made over to her, and if he parted from her, the memories would lose colour and value. What were they? Their physical intimacies, shared secrets about their lives, shared views about other people close to them, their adventures together, trekking and skiing, and going to parties. It was a hedonistic past, recalled in the belief that it could somehow be woven into a future.

And there was an element of possession too. Robyn was known amongst their friends to be 'his'; predatory males were implicitly warned off. He couldn't help liking this. The knowledge that Robyn could have a future in which he did not appear except as a memory disturbed him. He had little idea that these thoughts might be a feverish confusion brought on by a young's man's desire for intimate sex, but he was sure that they did not add up to love. He couldn't have defined what love was, but he believed his feeling for Robyn couldn't qualify.

At that moment, with her sitting disconsolate at his feet, whatever he felt, he ought to have said – as he understood in retrospect – 'I love you,' but he couldn't bring himself to it. It wasn't that he was averse to lying about his feelings. He didn't have the will to use the words; they simply wouldn't come, and he wasn't aware what a fulcrum for future action they could be in the mind of somebody like Robyn.

"You know how I feel," was all he was able to say.

She shook her head. "No I don't. I don't know at all. I love *you*. That must be obvious. I can't give any more than I've given."

He then protested the strength of a feeling which he still did not actually describe as love, and wondered at Robin's easy use of the word. She had given her body, but it was pleasure for her as much as for him. Now, she appeared to want to regard it as a sacrifice which evidenced love. This galled him, but he sat down beside her, put his arm around her shoulders, and crushed her against him. He declared his complete dedication to her in a low, determined voice, again without using the word 'love'. She was inert.

"My bottom's cold," she said, standing up, and walked on.

They came to the bank of a fast stream rushing over blue stones. Snowflakes settled in the flow and were instantly lost. He threw stones at icicles hanging on the opposite bank and sent one or two knifing down into the water.

He was finally and reluctantly coming to the words which had been passing through his mind. He had kept this statement in reserve. He always intended to use it, but like a new tool, it had to be deployed carefully.

"Of course we must get married." He made this sound like an unremarkable accomplished fact.

"Of *course*?" she replied quickly, searching his face.

"We really have no choice." Again, he imparted a tone of quiet wisdom.

"Would we have married anyway?" she asked, dully.

"Certainly!" he said, because it was fruitless to speculate.

But it wasn't true that he would marry her if she wasn't pregnant. Did she understand this? Marriage with Robyn, to him, had never been more than a probability. He enjoyed going to bed with her. He enjoyed having his cock in the Ashton family pudding, but *marriage*, despite all the material attractions… At the same time, he had to make this gesture, confident that it would right their troubles; yet she was unimpressed.

To be pragmatic, marriage could be managed without too much difficulty for them and her family. It would involve Ernest swallowing his spittle, but that only pleased Tom; Stuart probably anticipated it.

He patted her hair. She leaned against him.

And the material advantages of joining the Ashton clan

could not be denied. He wouldn't have to work his butt off to secure a partnership; he would bring in valuable business to the law practice and the hearts of the partners would soften. He would be the envy of many of his colleagues.

"I love you, Robyn."

He let the words out at last. What would be the point of withholding them if they were to marry? But it was a struggle to speak. He now felt he had made a very important pronouncement.

She said nothing for a moment, to his chagrin. She seemed to implode. She looked away. "Oh, really?"

"Of course I love you Robyn, you can't believe anything else…"

"Nice of you to offer to marry me," she said in a hopeless tone, still not acknowledging his supreme commitment of love.

"Don't be silly. You're not crying, are you?"

He touched her chin, and tried to raise her face toward him. She resisted. Suddenly she snapped her head back. He was looking at those small features, her eyes dry and hot.

"And do you suppose I want to marry you?" she asked in a ringing voice.

He believed he knew the answer to that. She most certainly did want to marry him, but she evidently wanted a declaration of love, proof of love, first. Instead, in this struggle of wills, he had devalued love by the advance proposal of marriage. In a way, this was what he had wanted to do. But it was so absurd. *If* he was prepared to marry her, why not start with a fervent declaration of love? Bringing love up in the rear, as a consolation prize in what would really be a forced marriage, was simply stupid.

The sound of voices approaching interrupted them. A man and a woman kicked their way playfully through the thin snow on the track, their faces turned upwards, enjoying the flakes filtering down through the trees. Instead of passing, the couple paused and stood aside politely to make way. He made a friendly remark to them about a great day, but Robyn wandered on restlessly without a word or a glance.

"Really, Tom, there are times when I hate you," she said, when he came up to her shoulder. "You don't love me. You don't care about love. Marry you? If you think marriage will cure anything, you're wrong. You assume marriage is the answer. It would be an inextricable botch. Your grand gesture! 'It's the thing to do', you say. 'We have no choice'. Never mind whether you love me! You smugly think you've solved all our problems, and saved me. Fool! My life is already badly enough spoiled by this thing, without twisting it beyond reason with marriage."

"Robyn, I thought..."

"I'm not going to let an ounce of pulp in my belly ruin me! I'll tell you what I'm *not* going to do. I'm not going to tell anybody about this. Not a single living soul. You understand? Have you told somebody? Have you?"

"No, no. I wouldn't tell before I'd discussed it with you. But I thought we might need help, and..."

"No, not one human being. I won't suffer the shame. I won't! I'm not going to let a moment of idiocy between us dictate my life." She hammered on his chest.

"It's more than a momentary thing now. It's a –" he began indignantly.

"A child!" she screamed, "A child out of this nonsense! I won't bow to it. I'm free and I'm going to remain free. I'm not a tearful girl to be saved by a boy play acting as a gentleman. I'll have a child one day, but before then there are so many things I have to do. I'm not made to live my children's lives. I want to live my own life first. I want to travel, get experience, and act in some of the most marvellous roles… You can laugh, but I'll be good. I'll succeed as an actress, no matter what the competition. I can feel the closeness of success with such certainty. I'll marry eventually. Perhaps we'll marry. I'm not going to be tied to you now out of a misbegotten sense of obligation. And I want you to be free too, Tom. I want you to choose your wife because you love her."

She was so assured, standing before him in her dirty white anorak, her gloved hands clenched at her sides, her chin jutting up challengingly. He was swept along by her enthusiasm; he almost believed that she had solved their problems, and he was relieved to be out of the gloom of marriage.

The path led them out of the trees. They parted from the watercourse and went sharply downhill. The stream, now twenty feet above them, fell down a granite face, striking a projecting stone. As they stood below in the spray, he could feel the exasperation of the torrent, beating on the stubborn stone.

6

The cloud had cleared. It was the second day of his quest with Stuart for the mountain man. He could look up over eight thousand feet to the peak of Mt Vogel. 6:30am revealed a pink beak of ice gleaming in the sun, leaning into the bitter southwesterly wind, with lower slopes spreading like the wings of a vast gray eagle. That was the simile Stuart Ashton used once in an article in *The Mountaineer*, but now that Tom looked more closely, from where he was standing, the peak of Mt Vogel looked more like the head of a penis than a bird in flight; a stubby, erect penis with wrinkled testicles flaring out below.

He slipped off his gloves, rubbed his palms together, and lit a burner with the spark from a lighter. An acrid smell of gas stung his nostrils and mingled with the chill of decay in the air. He held his hands over the burning ring for a few seconds and then poured water from an anti-freeze flask into a pan and placed it over the flame.

While the water was heating, he closed his eyes and listened. He could hear the trickle of a stream and the hum of the wind. The mountain, seen when the mind was clear after a night's sleep, was both intimidating and alluring. The prospect of setting foot where only a very few had gone before, and the risk that shadowed every step, still lured him; it lured all climbers. But there was more, admittedly; the distinction of reaching a summit; the knowledge that amongst mountaineers you were one of a small elite band. It wouldn't be the same *if nobody knew* you reached the summit of Mt Vogel. The supreme endeavour concealed a lust for celebrity. Ernest Ashton had achieved celebrity.

He wriggled in the down-padded parka, his skin beginning to warm. He flexed his tingling toes inside his boots, put two tea bags in each plastic mug with powdered milk and sugar, and poured in boiling water. He turned off the burner, replaced his gloves and, with the mugs, headed for the dome tent pitched between boulders encrusted with frost. He kicked at the fabric of the tent, dislodging a shower of powder. "On parade!"

He placed a mug in the hand which appeared through an opening in the fabric; then, bending double, he unzipped the entrance further and eased himself into the blue light, smelling sweat and last night's fried steak. He dug the toe of his boot into the sleeping bag in front of him. "I give you Mt Vogel in all its glory!"

"Shut up, will you?" Stuart growled.

The temperature inside the tent was below zero. Stuart dragged himself to sit upright, sipping his tea with the sleeping bag drawn up to his armpits. "Didn't I tell you I don't take sugar in my tea? I'm not a bloody plumber!"

"And I'm not your valet. Be thankful." He leaned over and pulled the flap of the tent open. "Have a glimpse."

Stuart crouched lower to get a view through the flap, then wrinkled his nose after a glance. "I'll get there or die in the attempt!"

The usually clean-shaven, serious, but not miserable face of Stuart Ashton was beginning to disappear under a brown pelt, emphasising his eyes in their deep sockets.

"Not this trip, mate," Tom said. "We locate the mountain man and return."

Stuart pulled the map out of his pack, an old map of his

father's. "You see the hut is actually marked, here," he said.

"Will the map be accurate now?" He was interested that Stuart was prepared to be open about this reliance on his father.

"Should be on these lower slopes. Up there, things will have changed in thirty years."

The map was one of a set, very large in scale, and embellished with three dimensional strokes. The effect was attractive as well as instructive. "He's quite an artist, isn't he?"

Stuart jeered, "A regular Wainwright. But it's better than the Survey map and a more detailed one doesn't exist."

Later, for breakfast, they made milk with powder and water and mixed it with muesli; they fried sausages and bread on the primus stove. They ate standing, stamping their boots in the moraine valley, as the mist which had covered the lower valleys lifted to reveal cathedrals of rock.

Tom washed the pans in the stream after eating, and then splashed his face and cleaned his teeth. When he returned to the camp, Stuart had packed the tent, sleeping bags and other stores. They hoisted their packs. It was nearly 8am. The mountains had the drenched look of a land that had recently heaved itself up out of the sea. They headed up the valley, picking a course over the smaller stones. Their packs were loaded high and Tom found his footing unstable on the scree slopes.

After two hours of stubborn going, with his head down, sweating, he called Stuart to a halt. He dropped his pack and stripped off his parka. They found a sheltered hollow and brewed tea.

"I need this," Tom said. "You're pushing me, man. We're not climbing Everest."

Stuart took no notice. He was preoccupied with the route. They were ascending a rocky riverbed with steep walls chiselled out by the weather of centuries. The sparse grass and lichens had faded as they gained height. There were no shepherd's huts or animal shelters here. They were at the edge of a lonely world of rock, snow and ice. And yet, if he looked more closely at the ground, he could see tiny sprouts of leaves, with equally tiny red and blue wild flowers between the stones.

They had a short stop after four hours for a lunch of tinned tuna, spread on rye biscuits. After lunch, the occasional chocolate bar followed by a drink of water were sharply pleasurable; the rest was the exertion of climbing or the concentration of descending with their packs wrenching on unstable slopes. They went on until the sun was sinking.

He began to think that they had missed the valley they sought. The area they wanted was a wide basin above a steep fall in the stream – assuming they were following the right stream. Ernest had clearly marked the map showing an old shepherd's shelter, but that was thirty-three years ago. Stuart's enquiries from the local tramping association had revealed that the shelter had actually been rebuilt by trampers in the years subsequent to Ernest's conquest, and used by them as a shelter. The tramping association had ceased to maintain the hut about a decade ago. It was here that Stuart speculated that the hermit lived, or stayed, when he was in the area, and that seemed to coincide with the information they had from the Swiss climbers via *The Mountaineer* reporter.

Soon, they would pass a place where their fathers' expedition had camped. They climbed a steep rock fall beside the stream and came out on a wide moraine of boulders, smoothed by the water to about the size of a football. Before them was a higher level of fine stones, a bank pushed up on a curve by the force of water. They climbed the bank and instinctively headed for a steep wall buttressed by two flutes of rock about a dozen yards apart; it was a natural shelter. The rock face above presented no hazard of falling stones or ice.

"This is it," Stuart declared. "Look, there are a few signs. And I've camped here before." His voice sank. He evidently didn't want to remember.

Tom slipped out of his pack and walked to a pile of rusted tin cans and a gas cylinder. He kicked at the tins and turned them with the toe of his boot, trying to guess how old they were; all that was left to hint at the passion of a climb. On a rock shelf where a stove might have perched, there were black marks.

"These remains could be from passing trampers who only looked up at the slopes of Vogel," he said.

"It's where Ernest and Bill camped," Stuart said flatly.

They pitched their tent. Tom cooked a curry of red beans and tinned beef, with dried apricots as a sweet. Stuart produced a bottle of scotch. They lay in their sleeping bags in the tent after the meal, drinking from plastic mugs with the bottle between them. Stuart was swallowing his slugs in a mouthful.

They talked, at Stuart's inevitable wish, about the mountain. Tom had been able to think a little better of his father as a result of reading *The Fateful Snows* as a child. The practical problem about scaling Vogel was that after you had climbed its shoulders, the final toil was a sheer pinnacle of granite, three thousand feet high. The lower slopes called for ice experience, and the upper slopes required climbing skill of the highest technicality. A summit team would be endangered by ice and rock falls, wind, and changeable weather which could bring snow even in summer. The steep upper slope provided little shelter to bivouac.

Virtually impregnable, Vogel was the target of

mountaineers from all over the world, although only just over twelve thousand two hundred feet high. While Ernest Ashton had been acclaimed for his conquest, a number had died on the mountain; many had been injured or simply been beaten. He had come to think of Vogel as encouraging a kind of madness.

Stuart was beginning to rant. "Do you realise that I've even got a book that's been published recently which holds Ernest up as one of the mountaineering greats? I'll tell you, I was damned economical with the praise when I was writing the section about him, but there is no denying the achievement. And I've written the foreword to the new edition of *The Fateful Snows*! How will I look if…"

He was disturbed by Stuart's intense preoccupation with his father's exploits and simultaneous loathing. The two things seemed incompatible, yet here they were married; tightly, inextricably married.

"That's fine," he said mildly. "Many have climbed Everest, but nobody will forget that Hillary and Tensing were the first."

Stuart was getting drunk. The bottle was three quarters gone.

"The old man's going to look like a rat if this is all a fucking lie. And he'll take me down with him too, that's…"

"You seem to have decided the rumour is true, Stu."

"No. It could be. It could be because Ernest is like he is. Why? Why?"

"I don't know… What I do know is that if I was the first to climb Vogel, I'd have a smile on my face for the rest of my life. Ernest has never been at peace with his achievement in all the years I've known him. Outwardly, to his fellow knights and the people who run this country, he seems to be a scholarly sportsman, and a powerful businessman, but that's not the Ernest we know, Stu. He's a tortured and violent and

79

prejudiced man. He seems to hate himself…"

"And he hates me…"

"Yeah…" Tom had been hearing evidence of this from Stuart for years.

"You think that's true, Tom? A father who hates his son? You've been closer to this than anybody. Closer than Robyn."

"I'm sorry, but I do."

"Remember the fight, when I was eighteen? Well I've told you most everything…"

"You have…" He was going to tell Tom again.

Stuart took another big shot of the whisky. He was on his own trip. "Shit, we had a fight, there in the yard down by the sheds. He ordered me to unload a truck full of stores as though I was a slave. As I walked past him, he struck a blow on my shoulder. We were face to face. I didn't think. I punched him in the face and knocked him down. I was astonished at what I'd done and just stood there, gawking. He got to his feet, and said, 'OK, son.' Quiet and friendly. Then he hit me quickly, and I fell down. I got up and launched into him like a madman. I lost it. The truck driver had to drag me off. He never touched me again."

"You don't need to bring all that into the *now*…" He was tempted to say it was irrelevant, but that would have inflamed Stuart further. And in the sense that Mt Vogel had become part of a battle between father and son, an extrapolation of the abuse, it wasn't irrelevant at all.

Stuart's voice was low and grating. "There were a lot of beatings, but the scar of that one, particularly, has always been with me, and like a scar it's rough, and sometimes inflamed and painful. It marked a stalemate."

Tom thought it was a stalemate with poison swelling on both sides. "Was it so out of the question to get out of Ernest's life after you finished school?"

"I did, I tried, but I've been drawn back. When I first started to do journalism about mountaineering, my father's achievements were draped around my shoulders by others like a golden cloak. I didn't ask for it. I couldn't avoid it."

"I can understand that, and it's been useful to you, but…"

"I thought I was making something of myself, making myself independent of him, carving out my own niche if you like…"

He should have replied, 'You didn't try very hard for independence. You embraced your father's achievements and struggled to better them. You cleaved to him, used him for your own purposes.' But Stuart wouldn't accept or even probably understand this, and to be fair, because the way everything had happened wasn't reasoned, there had been no point where events paused and Stuart could reflect. Stuart probably couldn't help being subverted by the canker inside him.

Instead, tired and a little drunk himself, he said, "You weren't carving your own niche, Stu. That was a mistake…"

The weather became more harsh before dawn. A fierce wind began driving sleet and snow. In the morning, they were huddled in the tent with hot coffee, playing cards. But the weather was not easing, and they would have to face a wet and unpleasant trek. They loaded up and, after three hours, reached a point where they could see a reddish-brown hut clearly against the snow on the far side of a gully. Stuart waved an arm triumphantly.

Melted snow had already begun to find fissures in Tom's borrowed waterproofs. The dampness and chill spread on his arms, chest and thighs. They splashed across a stream which was now running profusely. The hut was below a ridge, protected from the southerly buster which swept up the valley like a harvester.

When they reached the hut, the door swung open in the wind. Tom entered. Inside was a stove with a rusted chimney. The bunk frames had been broken up for firewood by passing trampers; there were old newspapers and plastic packets on the floor; the dust and grime of years coated the walls and windows.

Tom stepped outside the hut. "The mountain man was never here."

Stuart sheltered against the wall of the hut. Agitated, he pulled out the map clumsily, his hand shaking. "We could head south..."

"We're nearly out of stores, and beyond the time we gave Tia."

"We can call her on the mobile. We can do this circuit." He pointed to the map.

Tom looked and calculated. It was perhaps four miles over ridges, up and down valleys. "No, Stuart. It'll take hours. I'm cold and I'm hungry."

Stuart thrust his face close to Tom's; it was gaunt and his eyes were unseeing chips of glass. "You don't understand. You don't *fucking understand!*"

He thought for a second that Stuart was going to strike him.

Tom drove the truck back to Tamaki Downs with a withdrawn Stuart. Stuart hated Tom - or anybody else - having the wheel, but he wasn't fit to drive. He had looked like a person having a fit; his hands were quivering and he was staring and speaking incoherently. Tom had bundled him into the passenger seat. It was past 1am when they reached Tamaki Downs. Stuart disappeared without a word, and Tom stowed their gear in the outhouse and went to bed.

The morning was sunny and calm. Robyn was away from the house, and after breakfast - Stuart didn't appear - Tom noticed that the door of her bedroom was open; it had been hers as a child and was kept for her visits. Curious, he walked in.

The room still had something of the spoiled little girl about it; a faded counterpane on the bed with a fairy motif in pink and yellow which matched the curtains. A more mature sign was the framed coloured poster of *The Importance of Being Ernest* at the Theatre Royal in the Haymarket, London. He remembered buying the poster and taking Robyn to the performance. She couldn't see enough of the West End productions; in this way, she sought to make light of their agonising visit to London, shortly after their Ruapehu 'decision'.

The journey was made humiliatingly for him, mostly at Robyn's expense. He had no money and no settled job. He could hardly remember anything about the night of the performance, or even the details of the drama. Their London days were ugly and blurred as they strived to carry out the plan their febrile imaginings had produced in New Zealand. Robyn was proud and impetuous; she wanted her way and was used to getting it. He was borne along uncritically, fully complicit with her wishes, which became his wishes. His efforts to enlist legitimate medical help were rejected pompously, and he had to grope around in the depths of the city, and by trial and error eventually came to Mrs Rueben.

Mrs Rueben's house in Camden was a tiny end-of-terrace property on a busy road. A narrow path ran down the side of the house, where they had been directed to go; there were two doors along the windowless brick wall. The two doors were ill-fitting, one showing black gaps from the interior darkness; he knocked at the other; it was opened by a bald man of fifty who was preparing to wash, his shirt-sleeves rolled, his waistcoat undone and a towel in his hand. He surveyed them grimly, and then, without remark, led them to an inner room. With an almost inaudible grunt, he left them.

He and Robyn stood uneasily, the floor creaking under the thin carpet as they shuffled. An old black upright piano stood in one corner of the small space, with family photographs on top of it; under the window, were a lumpy chesterfield and chairs with worn moquette covers.

A woman whom he thought was Mrs Reuben, and who looked out of place, sauntered in with a lit cigarette in a long holder between her teeth. She glanced casually at them. Her face must have been smashed in an accident a long time before; a series of fine white scars on the forehead and cheeks suggested that it had been carefully reassembled. Yet she was a woman of sensual attraction, about thirty-five years old. She was dressed to go out – or she had just entered the house. Her thick, shoulder-length black hair was set in waves. Her nails were polished and painted red. A garish imitation leopard-skin coat was wrapped tightly around her body, accenting voluptuous lines.

"All for two hundred quid, kids," she said in a low, throaty voice through a melting cloud of cigarette smoke.

He whiffed the smoke, and suddenly wanted to suck some into his lungs, although he seldom smoked. He gave her the money. She counted it carelessly and slipped the notes into her pocket; then she fixed her attention on Robyn, who looked away.

"It's not so bad, dear." Mrs Rueben smiled faintly, and

spoke with an East End accent. "But you've left it very late. The information I was given was that it was over five months since your last period. Is that right? What have you been doing, making up your mind?"

Despite her languorous attitude, Mrs Rueben appeared to be summing them up. Tom's hand, in the pocket where the money had been, was damp. He clenched his fist a number of times to confirm to himself what they had planned, and what they were now committed to.

"What do I have to do?" Robyn asked curtly.

"I wouldn't worry too much about the details, Miss – what is your name again?"

Mrs Rueben lingered over the introductions, articulating their names as though she was sucking sugar-coated sweets.

"It's all very hygienic," she said, pointing to a large suitcase which she had placed by the door. She opened the case, revealing a collection of enamel basins, red rubber tubes, red rubber bottles or suctions, glass bottles, packs of cotton wool and pills. "You'll have to go to the hospital. I start the miscarriage, and the hospital does the rest. They curette you, stop the bleeding, and clean you up. Get a cab over the road; they're passing all the time. Ask for Camden Trust A&E. Got that?"

"Yes," Tom said.

"Is it dangerous?" Robyn asked unemotionally.

"I've never had anyone die, love, if that's what you mean."

"But it's risky?"

"It's a matter of keeping infection out."

"But there's a risk of infection?" Robyn pressed commandingly.

"I'm no magician, but I'll do my part." Mrs Reuben gave her weak smile.

"Are you trying to put me off?" Robyn maintained her dominant tone.

"I'm trying to get you to face facts, dear. You can't expect a miracle for nothing, can you?"

"I want an abortion, not a miracle," Robyn said, her small face screwing up.

Tom said, "It will be a miracle when our troubles come to an end."

"Sure, I'm a wizard. I wave my catheter and your troubles end," Mrs Rueben said quietly.

"It's no joke!" Robyn wailed.

"You and your big college boy have been sheltered. Let's go ahead, pet."

"She's not scared," he said, angrily.

"Isn't she now?" Mrs Rueben took a folded sheet from the suitcase. "Come on, dear. We'll go out the back. Your man can wait here. I don't want him hanging around on the street."

"No, I want you with me, Tom," Robyn said. "If you don't come, I'm not going to go with her."

"You are hard on him," Mrs Reuben scoffed.

"I don't care. We're in this together."

"I'll come with you." Tom felt sick.

"He doesn't really care about me," Robyn said to Mrs Reuben.

"At least he's here. That's better than most."

"Why do I have to risk *my* life?" Robyn asked feverishly.

"Come on, love." Tom put his hand gently on Robyn's arm.

"*My* life!" Robyn shook his hand off. "All the things I wanted to do. My dramatic work. Marriage. Children..."

"Having children, that's a good one!" Mrs Rueben gave a spurt of laughter which ended in a fit of coughing.

"My career's just starting. It's all good, clean you

understand? But this is bad, dirty. And dangerous!"

"I don't care whether you go through with it or not." Mrs Reuben's patronising tone was almost bored. "You and your boyfriend made a mistake. It's the most ordinary thing in the world. Why don't you go home and tell your mother about it? She'll understand. Women do. There may be a few tantrums, but eventually she'll pat you on your shoulder and call you a poor thing. She may have sailed close to the weather herself, in her day. But you want this pregnancy never to have happened. Just innocent fun in the moonlight. No pregnancy, no miscarriage, no pain, no disgrace. Well, I can almost put the clock back for you, but part of the price is nerve."

Robyn shuddered and shaped her mouth in distaste.

"You aren't taking any notice of me, Miss Pretty. I know that. I can see you don't want me."

"Of course she does," Tom said.

"Oh, do I then?" Robyn bridled, "What do you know!"

"You've decided not to go ahead." Mrs Reuben's voice was flat and dry.

"How stupid. I came here for the operation. Why else would I let Tom hand over all that money? I didn't come here to have my palm read."

"Try letting your mistake grow to life size, and see if it's any easier that way."

"She's right, Robyn."

"You *would* agree. You don't mind if I jeopardise my life in this grot-hole!"

"Sorry about the décor," Mrs Reuben laughed.

"I offered to marry you, Robyn," he floundered, grasping for some words of calm.

"Oh, God! The marriage thing again."

"Then set him free." Mrs Reuben lit another cigarette, enveloping them in a cloud of smoke which hung in the slant of the last sun coming through the grimy net curtains.

"He's free. He can get out of my life any time he likes!"

"No. He's only free if you're not pregnant, dearie."

"What garbage! I'm getting out of here."

"Robyn, are you sure? And what about the money?" he asked plaintively.

"Get your money back, then," Robyn said, stepping into the hall.

"Sure, get your money, big boy." Mrs Reuben fluttered her red fingernails casually in the air.

"Surely you will…" He realised she had no intention of returning the money.

"You've both had two hundred quids' worth of good advice." Mrs Reuben went to the door and shouted down the hall, "Joe, these two want to go."

They were impelled along the passage with Joe behind them, grunting. They hustled down the narrow track to the footpath as though they were being pursued. Outside it had become a chilly, orange-lit half-darkness. A few dark shapes of people moved. Lights were on in the newsagent's across the road. The small and decrepit houses were cluttered around them. On the road, here, everything was normal, under a noise of traffic; boringly, dully normal.

Robyn turned on him. "Oh, you sap! You weak fool! College boy. You couldn't even get our money back. Did you expect me to submit to that painted bitch while you were making eyes at her?"

"That's as mad as… what we've just been through."

So they paid two hundred pounds for good advice. And it was, he reflected long afterwards, good advice.

He walked along Seddon Street, letting the shopfronts

prompt his memory. Jarvis's Milk Bar had given way to Rocco's Coffee, but the entrance and dark interior of The Lunch Rooms seemed the same. This was where he sometimes came with Gladys Botting, the friend of his mother's with whom he lived after his mother died.

Gladys had worked with his mother as a housemaid at the Royal Hotel and retired to an old prefabricated cabin in the town. She was a kindly spinster who cared for him, but could hardly keep up with a half-grown man who wanted to read books all the time. They occasionally had tea and biscuits, or soup and a sandwich here – all that Gladys's purse and his part-time earnings would run to. She died a few years ago, and as he had found when he walked down Copthorne Street, her cabin had been demolished as part of a development of apartments. He never went to her funeral. He was in London, and although they exchanged Christmas cards, there was probably nobody to tell him that she had died. She was one of those unnoticed, anonymous people whom nobody seemed to know. Who would have gone to her funeral?

His was a casual neglect. Gladys was a tiny, shadowy, benevolent figure on the outskirts of his life who gave him shelter when he needed it, and had now disappeared without trace. Perhaps the warm spot she had in his memory was all that was left of her amongst the living on this planet. If he focused his mind on Gladys, he had no doubt of her importance in his life. The trouble was that he rarely thought of her after he left the 'home' she made for him. Her cramped back room with its narrow bed and a vent looking out on a brick wall at 7 Copthorne Street was the first place he called home. The decrepit house on Tamaki Downs was never more than an uncomfortable shack which he and his mother shared like asylum seekers, and to which he never returned after her death.

He had only part of his attention on the chipped advertising board which obstructed the entrance of the Lunch Rooms, promising *All-Day Breakfast and Cream Teas* when he became aware of somebody. He looked up to see a woman with a long neck in a shapeless summer dress observing him. Her cheeks were grey and rough and her dry, straight hair straggled around her shoulders, but in her features there was something familiar. He had an instant of embarrassment in trying to place her.

"Tom Stavely. It's absolutely you!"

"Julie Burrell!"

They embraced, and he thought, 'Do I look as old as her?'

"You're here for the wedding, Tom. How wonderful!"

"The event of the year!"

"Oh my God, yes. We need it. Everybody's going. I'm so pleased you made it. It's bit like old times with you here."

"Not quite."

"No, not quite. We'll just have to pretend. Those days will never come back. Buy me a coffee for Auld Lang Syne."

They talked for a moment about Petra and Darren. Then Julie led him into the depths of the Lunch Rooms. There were three rooms stretching deep into the building, ill-lit, with stained paper on the walls, crammed with varnished kitchen chairs and bare tables. The place was exactly as he remembered it in the past, and no doubt it was still tolerably full at lunch times, despite the advertised breakfast and afternoon tea. Julie tucked herself into a chair in the furthest corner.

"Will a waitress find us?" he asked.

"I don't mind if she doesn't. I expect there's only one girl at this time of day."

Julie settled down to talk, and now her expression was

radiant. "I often think of you, Tom, and the good times we had."

"I know. I was very sorry to hear about Barney. Was that five years ago? I wanted to get to the funeral but I couldn't get away."

"I know. You wrote me a nice letter. It was very sudden. He was mowing the lawn at our place in Taupo. Brain haemorrhage. He was fifty."

"Mowing the lawn?"

'This is how they die,' he would say to Alison, 'Mowing the lawn or cutting the hedge.' She'd probably reply, 'Alcoholism, you mean?'

"He never looked after himself. Over-eating and over-drinking," Julie said. Now that Barney was gone, she could say things she wouldn't have said when he was alive.

"You fed him," he reminded her gently.

"No, Tom, look at *me*. I ate with him." She brushed her hands down her thin chest, sounding disappointed.

He remembered Barney, another university friend who was a high street solicitor in Timaru, with affection. He had met few people who were as widely read in fiction as Barney. Although excessive in everything that he did, work and pleasure, Barney was a sensitive man, one who always had new insights to offer on the human condition. Tom always thought Barney's excesses - which were well known - showed that he didn't care about consequences, didn't seem to care about life. And yet he revelled in life in print.

"And what about you, Julie?"

"I'm a merry widow - well, I have a feller."

"That's good."

"It's OK. The kids like him. You have to settle for what you have."

"Do I know him?"

"I doubt it. Jack Simmons. Owns the bookshop down the street."

"I think Barney would liked to have owned a bookshop."

"You're right. It might have saved him. But Barney couldn't take a step into the unknown, like you, Tom. Sure, he became a steward of the Jockey Club, and the local coroner. These are things he got by running hard on the spot. He couldn't move forward. Barney was even frightened to go on a decent vacation. He always said he had commitments to clients, and we couldn't afford it - which was nonsense. But as a wife, I bought it. You realise these things too late. Do you know, we never travelled further than Norfolk Island in our whole marriage?"

"You had the place at Taupo. I know that's closer, but..."

"An investment, Tom, not a pleasure-dome."

He was thinking that William Shakespeare probably didn't travel all that far in mileage terms, but it would make an unsympathetic comment; it *was* an appropriate thought for Barney who lived in the books he read, and travelled far in them.

"I have the money now, and I'm going to see the world before I die. I was in the USA last year and Jack and I are going to Europe this year. But, about you Tom, those good times we had..."

"A few of years of madness."

He was unable to recall what Julie had been like in bed; undressing her in his mind, as she was now, he found her not repulsive, but asexual. Clasping her would be like embracing a tall bundle of kindling wood.

"I liked you the best of all of them." Her eyes were bright and swimming. "You liked me, didn't you?"

"Of course I did." He spoke affectionately, but the true answer was, 'Not especially.'

"I know you had a lot of women," she said playfully.

"Reputation tends to outstrip reality. And I wasn't alone. I'm sure Stuart had more. Barney had his share. And what about the women? Robyn got around, and a certain Julie Burrell."

"And it was all under the blanket, as it were. Everybody was doing it, but nobody was doing it! It wasn't like wife-swapping or three in a bed. Just good, old-fashioned screwing."

"We were modest in our sins."

"Do you remember the day Barney came home from the office unexpectedly and we were in bed? I ran out to meet him in the hall…"

"Yeah." He had a dim memory of choking in a closet.

"You had to get dressed in the dark. I told Barney I had a 'flu headache, and he got busy looking for papers he had mislaid in the study. I came back into the bedroom and let you sneak out."

Her words unlocked his memory. It was that feeling of being trapped; going out the back door and finding that the only way to get to the front of the house and down the street was along a side path, past the room where Barney was. He had thought of hiding in the garden shed, but instead went over the back wall into the neighbour's garden, explaining to the incredulous woman there that he was looking for a tennis ball.

"Did you ever realise what a bad name we were getting, Tom?"

"Not at the time. I thought we were just having fun."

"What about the time Robyn threw up on the Prestons' hall rug?" Julie laughed.

"Was that a big deal? I don't think I was there."

"You were in bed with somebody else. Robyn was with

that Maurice Hewitt. He was a wild man. I couldn't believe that he became our curate. But you know all about it because of Alison."

"You recall it as though you enjoyed."

"I did. Everything changed when you went away with Alison. Back to dull old marriage."

The tardy waitress appeared and stood mutely in front of the table.

"I haven't got time for coffee now, Tom. I'll see you at the wedding."

They stood up. She pressed her dry lips to his, and pushed her skinny body very close.

7

He arrived ahead of time at the Fontanella, which, according to Robyn, was a fashionable luncheon place; it was in an old farmhouse just out of Springvale town. On looking around the restaurant, he thought 'fashionable' was somewhat excessive. He was lunching with Petra. Robyn also said the Fontanella would be no surprise to Petra, who had been there many times before, thus taking the polish off the venture. He obtained - after negotiation with the head waiter - a table at the front, beside the windows, overlooking a sunny cottage flower garden. He sat down, refused a drink and watched as cars pulled into the parking lot and other diners began to arrive.

He had been trying to get some time alone with Petra, but Darren or Robyn was present at every attempt he made at the Downs, and Petra professed to be very busy; this meeting was his resort. He wanted to see her privately; it seemed appropriate that a father should commune with his daughter before her wedding, and he thought she might be appreciative, if not actually grateful. His absences over the years had disempowered him; it wasn't practicable for him to say, 'Sit down here for a moment, girl; I want to talk to you.'

Petra, ten minutes late, swept in, kissing him quickly on the cheek before he could get up. "Oh Daddy, I'm so terribly sorry. I stayed at the Campbells' last night. We had a party and I didn't get up until late, late, late."

"Where's Darren, at work?"

"Oh no, he's off now until after the honeymoon. He's going to pick me up later."

She sat on the opposite chair. The chair on his left was closer to him. Darren was going to loom up, even here. "Like a drink?"

Petra patted her forehead. "I better have a spritzer, after last night."

"Lots of parties at the moment?" he asked, ordering two spritzers from the waiter.

"Always, I hope!" she laughed.

"How's the baby?" He wanted to encourage some intimacy and this was a natural subject.

She blushed slightly. "Mother told you?"

"No, you did."

"Oh, I see, you're pretty smart. Yes. The baby. I'm looking forward to it. It'll be... nice."

"You'll have to look after yourself, if you're going to have a baby."

Her face went blank. "Stop drinking and smoking, you mean? That's what Mother says. After the honeymoon!"

He hadn't seen his daughter in years and he was trying to proscribe her habits; she was looking at him as though he was a stranger - which he was, virtually.

"I don't mean... I mean... will you manage all right with the baby? You seem to be having such a lot of fun."

"The baby will be fun, Daddy, and we'll have a Karitane nurse."

"Right. Certainly, a nurse."

Petra looked at her watch, and pushed away the menu. "I'll just have a sandwich. Darren will be here soon."

"I was hoping we would have a chance to talk..."

"Hi Bob," Petra said to the waiter. Apparently she knew everybody.

The waiter hung over the table. Tom ordered two shrimp sandwiches on brown, ignoring the waiter's reproachful look, and let the vision of a leisurely tete-a-tete lunch with oysters, crayfish and perhaps a chilled bottle of chardonnay slip away. Bloody cheek, asking Darren to come! Didn't she realise her father wanted to talk to *her*?...Yes, she probably did. She didn't want to talk to her father. That was more like it. Then again, was there anything to talk about?

"There's a cover charge," the waiter said, squinting at the measly order.

"I can afford it."

He tried to engage with Petra now that the waiter had gone, but she was looking around at the other diners, waving to people she knew. This place with its ridiculous name was certainly the local watering hole.

"You've got the honeymoon all sorted?"

"Oh, yes, we're going to Sydney for a week at the Regent Hotel, and then Uncle Stu has bought us a cruise on the Barrier Reef."

"Lovely present. You've been to the Reef before?"

"Oh, sure, but we're doing it in luxury this time."

"Uh-huh. You didn't think of going somewhere different?"

"What do you mean, Daddy, different?"

"Oh, say Tasmania. It's a beautiful place."

She sniggered. "Style, Daddy, style. Monday is washing day in Tasmania."

"Los Angeles?"

"We've both been and the flight is a yawn. The family have a place at Santa Barbara, but no."

He'd be saying to Alison, 'You can't imagine how incurious this girl is. A world to choose from, and she just wants to lie in a Sydney hotel and get laid, and then lie in a

97

luxury cruiser and get laid.' Alison would chuckle and remind him that it was a honeymoon, not an adventure holiday; he wouldn't tell her about the treatment he was getting at this lunch. Soon that big goon would be swaying over them, drooling, and Petra would disappear.

The sandwiches came. Petra nibbled hers and pushed it away. "I'm not very hungry."

"Sure." He could have said, 'Too much booze last night?' but he was uneasy about making personal jokes, or being really candid. He scrabbled around in his mind for a conversational line. This was his own daughter and he didn't know what to say to her! He settled for, "How are you getting along with Robyn and Stu?" Something distantly fatherly.

"Great. Always have."

That was that! He pushed away his sandwich in desperation.

"Is everything all right here?" the waiter asked, peering at the nibbled food and half finished drinks.

"Great, Bob, thanks," Petra replied.

He plunged into feminine territory. "Is the wedding dress ready for its big day?" This was surely a subject where Petra could close her eyes, dream, and elaborate.

"Oh, yeah," Petra said warmly, "It's… great."

"Tell me about it," he asked, immediately galled by his asinine request, and wondering if his waning patience showed, but Petra's attention was on the other side of the room. She fluttered her hand at Darren who was cutting between the tables toward them.

"Hi, Darren." He rose, determined to be affable and unfussy, and offered his hand.

Darren lunged past him and hugged Petra. Tom withdrew his hand and sat down. But Petra was already on her feet, tucking her bag under her arm. Petra and Darren gave him tittering grins as they retreated a step.

"Sorry, Daddy. We've got to go now. Lovely to see you, and thanks... Bye," Petra trailed the last words over her shoulder.

The waiter - it was Bob again - approached and proffered a bill. "You wanna go with them?"

"No. I'm in no hurry, Bob. Bring me a double vodka tonic, and tell me about your wedding dress."

"Whassat?"

He drank the vodka tonic without enjoyment, and leaving the car he had borrowed from Stuart in the park at the restaurant, he walked into Springvale town. He was hungry and had a vague idea that he might buy a pie at Pete's All-Night Cafeteria in Seddon Street, where the local lads used to gather in the early hours of Friday or Saturday morning after a night of drinking. Then it was usually pie and chips or fish and chips, and in season raw Bluff oysters. He hadn't eaten a pie in years, and Pete's stirred his thoughts in an appetising way. He took a shortcut down a side street, and before him on the corner was St George's Church, and the church hall, almost submerged in blowing trees.

The desire for the pie faded momentarily, and on impulse he unlatched the gate in the picket fence and went into the garden. The colour of the trees, the lawn and flowerbeds was less vivid and more worn than he remembered, but otherwise it could have been the day twenty-five years ago when they met Maurice Hewitt here. He had asked to see the bride and groom before the knot was tied. Robyn had wanted Maurice to marry them because he was a friend. No doubt the meeting was an act of priestly duty on Maurice's part, a

99

formality, but Tom hadn't forgotten a moment of it.

Maurice suggested that they meet in the churchyard after the Sunday service, and Tom felt obligated to present himself for the service. He sat in a pew polished like glass by many bodies. The church was about half full, mostly of older people, and the service was a social occasion in the town to be followed by gatherings for lunch.

He found it hard to follow the Bible reading. His thoughts moved to an assessment of the preacher's histrionic gifts. Maurice was dark and soulful, with a deep burry voice and gleaming eyes. His cheeks were pale and hollow. The gist of his sermon was Christ's kindness, but intentionally or not, there was something eerie in his manner, questioning the veracity of the kindness. He might have made a good Hamlet.

Afterwards, Tom eluded the crowd, many of whom he knew in one way or another, or at least recognised. Behind the church was a separate hall set amongst flower and rock gardens. He entered the garden and saw Robyn picking her way along the uneven path by a high, board fence. She paused to consider her footing, and at that moment somebody reached over from the other side of the fence and removed her wide-brimmed, white straw hat from her head. When Tom stepped close to the fence, he could hear the giggles of a number of boys. He wasn't tall enough to see over the top. Robyn clasped her hands over the fence, and demanded her hat back. Quickly, each of her hands was capped by other small hands. Robyn was a slight woman then. Her hands were held fast.

"Y' can have your hat back if you say you're a bum!" one of the hidden boys shouted.

They shrieked with mirth, and Robyn struggled to release herself. Then there was the sound of aggressive intervention by another boy, and she was released. The boy who intervened – Tom assumed it was him – came through a gate further along the fence and returned the hat. The brim was smeared with dirty marks.

Robyn was speechless for a moment. Her palms were red and blue. "Why didn't you help me, Tom?" she complained.

"I didn't have time, Robyn."

"The Dump Road rat!" the boys over the fence chanted.

The boy, who had hard, thin legs and a bare brown chest said, "Don't take any notice of them. They're Sunday School kids."

"Kill the Dump Road rat," one of the boys behind the fence shouted. "Yeah, yeah, yeah!" his companions added, and one of them lobbed over a stone as big as an egg, which struck Robyn on the breastbone. The Dump Road boy dodged back through the gate, apparently in pursuit.

Robyn looked down the top of her low-necked dress. Tom could see an inflamed area, weeping slightly with blood, and swelling.

"You're useless, Tom," she said.

"It all happened so quickly!"

A man in clerical dress appeared in front of them. In the bright light he had smooth, almost girlish features which contrasted with the streak of grey which ran back from the peak of his black hair.

"Maurice! I've been attacked!"

Robyn pulled down the bodice of her dress to show the wound. They sat down on a bench.

"At this time of day? In the churchyard?" Maurice was astounded.

"They were kids. Wild beasts. Seven or eight years old, I guess," Tom said.

"Are you all right, Robyn? We must find them…" Maurice said, starting up.

"No. I don't ever want to see any of them. I was just a chattel in their hateful game."

"We can't have this, not here," Maurice protested.

"We want to talk to you," Robyn insisted.

This was the first hint that Tom had received that Robyn herself wanted the meeting. She had previously described it to him as a waste of time. Maurice abandoned his quest instantly and sank back on the seat.

"How's Alison?" Robyn asked.

"Fine," Maurice said briskly, in a tone to close the subject of his wife.

"We used to have such good times together," Robyn said.

"Yes," Maurice admitted with clipped finality.

"I can't understand how the old Maurice Hewitt could become a priest," Robyn said, not detecting the nuances of resistance from Maurice.

"Well, I have," Maurice said abruptly.

A silence followed, Robyn smiling at memories.

"It's a bit of an about-turn, that's all," Tom said.

"Well, that's the way it is. Now, let's talk about the young couple who have plighted their troth."

"Maurice, I don't think Tom loves me…"

"Hell, Robyn…" Tom moaned.

"It's a bit late to be thinking of putting off the wedding," Maurice said, relaxing back on the bench, unconcerned. "Why not totter on with it, and see how you go? Lots of people have the jitters beforehand. Shall we walk? It's hot out here."

He stood up and shook out the folds of his long black robe.

"No. My chest hurts... I could never marry anybody but Tom. We're fated to be together. I've changed since you and I met, Maurice. I'm not so crazy now. I'm supposed to be... What am I? A young actress and director beginning to make my way in professional theatre."

"An attractive girl on the threshold of marriage." Maurice spoke cheerfully, sitting again.

"I've had a baby." Robyn's contralto tones underlined the statement.

"Robyn, surely..." Tom protested.

"I see... A girl like you isn't alone in that," Maurice said, again unsurprised.

"No, you don't see. I've had a baby and given it away. You can't know what that means."

Again, Maurice was unconcerned. "That's a decision you made at the time, and very often the wisest one. A regular adoption, I suppose. I'm sure the child went to a good home. The authorities are very careful about this, as you know."

Robyn and Tom had already dredged through the emotional agony of her pregnancy, the birth, and the decision to give the child away, a thousand times. All that had shrunk to a speck of discomfort for him, but for Robyn it festered.

"Robyn, you must try to put it out of your mind. It's past. You haven't done anything wrong. Look to the future," Maurice said.

"But Tom is..."

"Tom wouldn't be marrying you unless he loved you. He's a good man."

"Say something, Tom," Robyn said.

"Yes, that's true. Of course I do... love you." At this

point in their relationship, the more often he declared his love, the more real it seemed.

Maurice became more stern-looking. "Robyn, I take it you've closed matters with the father of the child. The child shouldn't be a concern for either of you. The state has taken care of that. All that remains is that you've broken the relationship with the father. You don't see each other, and I mean there's no… remaining affection between you, is there?" Maurice asked.

"Remaining affection? Shit, Maurice, Tom is the father!"

"Tom?" Maurice swivelled his head around Robyn to turn his pitted eyes upon Tom. "Surely not."

"Surely, yes," Robyn said.

Maurice jerked stiff, upright. "But – "

"I never had time to love the child," Robyn said. "It'll turn into one of those devils over the fence. I'm home now from my overseas travels which nobody knows anything about, except Tom. I'll lock that time away secretly and settle down to marriage, with my own home, children, and my husband's career. Never mind my career."

"Children? Your career?" Maurice asked derisively, his ease gone, his eyes searing them both, his cheeks hollowed like the menacing priest in the pulpit.

"I'd like to go on with my career, of course, but…" Robyn went on heedlessly.

"Tom is the father, and now you're going to marry him?"

"For God's sake, yes! Isn't that why we're here?"

Maurice's interlocked hands mauled each other.

"What's wrong with that?" Robyn asserted, her voice cracking.

Maurice was silent for a few moments, stirring the grass with the polished pointed toe of his black shoe. "The family will always be incomplete. You'll realise it every time you look around the breakfast table."

Robyn sniffed. "The child could have been taken away by illness. Many people have spaces at the table, as you put it."

"The point is that you both cast the child out." His eyes, by turn, met their eyes.

She raised her shoulders and dropped them quickly. "We didn't actually cast him out. I don't see what we did as a heinous crime... it was in the interests of the child. We had no home. We weren't married. You think we acted badly? You should face abortion, or an illegitimate birth."

"I'm sure the decision to give the child away was the decision you felt you had to make at the time. I'm not criticising it. I'm not saying you acted badly." His tone was hard and dry.

"What *are* you saying, Maurice?" Robyn asked waspishly.

"I'm saying that it's a bit late to start thinking about marriage now."

"Why, why?" Robyn's theatrically plaintive voice cracked again.

"The missing child will haunt you."

"Oh, come on! We're grown ups. We can live with our past," Robyn snorted.

"Can you? Maybe. But it won't be easy. It won't be untroubled, like marriage ought to be. Was marriage so much out of the question at *that* time – before you decided to give the baby away?"

"Get married pregnant? Everybody knows. And they never forget," Robyn said.

"Plenty of couples have a baby which they keep and marry later. Your appearance in the eyes of others, versus the child's future?" Maurice's lips curled in rejection.

"I don't - didn't - we didn't see it that way... did we, Tom? For Christ's sake, Tom, say something!"

"I agree..." He wasn't sure what he was agreeing with. He thought Robyn's confusion summed up their mental state at the time of the adoption. But Maurice's firm view now was a shock, or at least something he hadn't thought about. The fact of having had the child and given it away was more than a shared and secret experience; it was a kind of bond; a constraint which tied him to Robyn. He hadn't gone beyond that realisation. Now, Maurice Hewitt was purporting to see the future, although in the hot, breezy churchyard at that time, Tom didn't place weight upon Maurice's view, didn't ask himself seriously whether Maurice might be right. He didn't take Maurice very seriously as a person. The man was an amusing amateur actor who might even now be playing a role, a drunk, and a rake - in fact, he had almost certainly bedded Robyn at some stage. Tom couldn't at this time regard him as a seer, merely because he appeared in a black cassock and made a prediction. And yes, it was a prediction.

"What would *you* have expected us to do?" Robyn asked, cuttingly.

"Perhaps before you gave the baby away was the time to make a final decision about whether you were going to marry."

"I don't see it. As if the door shut then, on a room we would never be able to return to? That's nonsense. Tom and I went on together, shared our suffering, and came to realise what we meant to each other. And now we've decided to marry. Haven't we, Tom?"

"Absolutely."

"What was the child like?" Maurice asked softly.

"What's that got to do with it?" Robyn said uneasily. "I

really don't think about him too much. A blue-eyed, fair-haired boy. Tom's colouring. Just a baby. He went to a good family. You can see why I've grown up. And what Tom means to me."

Maurice looked at her sadly.

With a flushed face, Robyn said hurriedly, "Tom's been going around with another woman. I found a woman's make-up in the car."

"Ohhhh! Robyn, why do we have to…" Tom moaned.

Maurice shook his head in bewilderment, and didn't look at Tom. He spoke in a resigned and sterile way. "Tom is obviously going to marry you, and he's a reliable guy. The problem is about you. Your doubts."

"My love for Tom is guaranteed!" Robyn's voice resonated.

"I think it's conditional, Robyn. Conditional on Tom loving you in the way *you* want."

"Oh, Maurice, no."

"Do you have some misgivings about the marriage, Tom? Do you feel that you and Robyn have missed your opportunity to marry?"

"No way. I feel like Robyn said. We've been through a lot, and now we have to get together…" He didn't pause for an instant, because they had made their decisions, but he was professing a clear and attractive view of matrimony, when he *did* feel leery about it. The past with Robyn once had marvellous peaks of enjoyment. Now - at times - the past was like a lacerated body, with wounds that might bleed forever.

"Maurice, that stuff about missed opportunity is just twaddle," Robyn said. "Surely we don't have to talk about things as complicated as that? Please be a priest, and not an amateur psychologist. What about this other woman? Who is she, Tom? She could be my best friend!"

He began to see that this was what was on Robyn's mind, even more than confessing her guilt about the lost boy. It was an attempt to screw information, and presumably a declaration of contrition and love, from him.

"Look, I don't want to go into this." Maurice backed away from intimate details the old Maurice would have been glad to discuss in a farcical way. "It's nothing that will stand in the way of the wedding is it, Tom? You can give Robyn that assurance."

He nodded his assent. He was committed to the wedding. He had been forced into admitting the existence of another woman because of Robyn's discovery – and he supposed she had sensed that there was a part of him that wouldn't mind if *she* wanted to call the wedding off.

"I want to know who it is. It's only fair," Robyn said.

"Nobody you know," he said, as sincerely as he could. "And it's all over. All over long ago."

"You swear it in front of Maurice?"

"I do."

He told these untruths unhesitatingly, because at this time he was beset by uncertainty. The affair – the relationship – certainly wasn't over. And of course it did involve somebody Robyn knew very well, and Maurice knew well too; it was his own wife, Alison. He had considered whether to tell Robyn the truth, but the same uncertainty which made him affirm a proposed marriage he didn't wholeheartedly want, but which had many practical advantages, stopped him revealing a fact which would destroy Alison Hewitt's already damaged relationship with her husband. In the churchyard this day, Maurice was a cuckold.

"What about the cosmetics in your car?" Robyn said.

"They must have been in the glove compartment for months."

Robyn seemed satisfied. She had serenely ignored Maurice's unpalatable advice, and she had wrung enough of an assurance out of Tom. "I'm glad we've spoken, Maurice. It's made me feel better. You haven't persuaded me of anything, and that's good. You've changed, do you know? At one time, we couldn't be together for two seconds without having a joke. Do you remember? Now, neither of us want to laugh!"

"There's nothing to laugh at in what you've told me," Maurice said resignedly. "I do sincerely wish you both the best of luck."

The noisy and salacious humorist of earlier days had become a sombre and cadaverous priest. The wind was starting to blow harder. The trees in the churchyard were shushing. The sun overhead suffused everything with a shadowless, powdery light. They stood up to part.

"If you don't mind me saying so, Maurice, you don't look well. Your colour is... grey," Robyn said spitefully.

Robyn and Maurice embraced slightly. He clapped Maurice on the arm.

"I'm not too well," Maurice admitted.

Robyn didn't stop to enquire into this. She removed her hat, took Tom's arm and shaking her hair out in the wind, headed for the churchyard gate.

He passed by Ernest's bedroom when he returned to Tamaki Downs, having had a steak pie with flaky pastry and brown gravy at Pete's. Pete was no longer there, but the pie was as appetising as it had always been, served with a polite smile by the Vietnamese proprietor. He had also had a beer in the dark, brass-bound bar at the Royal.

Ernest saw him and called his name and Tom went into

the room. The old man had eaten his meal in bed. A tray rested on the counterpane.

"So what did your work on the mountain produce?"

They had reached the stage where they could omit every preliminary, and even every politeness.

"Nothing. We couldn't find the man who has the relics."

"You don't believe this tosh, do you?"

"No, I don't, but Stuart wants to be certain."

"Ah, Stuart…"

"You can't blame him."

"Things might have been different," Ernest said, letting his chin sag down on his chest.

"The world of 'might have been'. Don't let's go there."

"If you'd stayed here, Tom…" He had an agreeable melancholy.

"I could never have stayed…"

"Why?"

"Because of the way you treated Stuart."

He had stirred the old man up. "Daah! You've got a mind like a mincing machine. Measuring every little scrap of life against your swollen ethics."

"And the way you treated my mother."

Ernest was more restive at this. He jerked his body around in the bed. "Your mother? I cared very much for Grace. I let her - and you - stay in the house. I never charged any rent…"

"You never charged any rent? Well, that was generous, I must say. You screwed her at least twice a week, you old goat! I remember you coming around, stinking of liquor, so pissed at times you could hardly stand up. A nice, cheap little fuck-shop in your own backyard."

Grace had always insisted to him that Ernest Ashton was a good man, who treated her kindly. 'Where would we go,' she had asked Tom when he questioned the visits, 'a mother and a young boy, with no home and no means of income?' Besides, he had to concede that she probably got some sexual pleasure from Ernest's attentions, although she would never have admitted it. She had been cruelly beaten as a wife, and while his father's death released her from this, she always retained the refuge mentality of the beaten wife. Bill Stavely had punched the spirit out of her. Her feelings of insecurity were as acute after his father's death as they were before it, and made her a captive on Tamaki Downs.

"Yes, I cared for Grace," Ernest insisted in a heavy voice, not looking at him.

"You kept her in the backyard."

Whatever merits there were in Grace's relationship with Ernest, Tom burned at the thought of the way Ernest had treated her.

"No!"

"She was a skivvy in your eyes. A backstairs job. Never a friend."

"No."

"Did you ever, *just once*, take Grace out, on your arm, to a party or a show? Did you ever have her up to the house when you were entertaining?"

"Grace was always up here," Ernest blustered.

"Yes, in the kitchen, or cleaning the bathrooms."

Tom walked out of the bedroom.

8

He flew up to Wellington for a day with Stuart who had board meetings to attend. Tia was with them. The flight was expected to take about two hours. With Stuart at the controls of one of the Ashton Group's Cessna aircraft, they took off in blustery weather from the airstrip at Tamaki Downs. He was apprehensive at first, although he had flown with Stuart a number of times, but Stuart and Tia were at ease up front, talking about the day ahead, not apparently concerned about the buffeting wind which shook the small plane or the clouds which obscured their vision.

When they started cruising at eight thousand feet, it was clear and calmer. The plane came in over Cook Straight with a southerly tailwind, the sea in serrated white lines below. Stuart had a brief and, to Tom, an unintelligible exchange with the control tower. He circled over Evans Bay and landed at the Aero Club at Rongotai. They took a taxi to the city; all three were going separate ways: Tia to see friends at Victoria University, Stuart his business colleagues, and Tom to a meeting he had previously arranged on the telephone with an old friend, Roderick Crawford, whom he had first met during his ill-fated stay in the law offices of Gottley & Son. Crawford had invited him to lunch at the Wellington Club. 'Where New Zealand is governed from,' Crawford had joked.

He idled through the shoppers walking along Lambton Quay and then climbed to The Terrace, found the club premises, and entered at precisely 1pm. Crawford was in the lobby to greet him, small, effusive, and neat in his black jacket, striped trousers and wing collar shirt.

"I thought you were the doorman at first," Tom said.

"The old uniform, you know. I had a hearing this morning and hadn't time to change, but my time's my own now. We can have a good talk."

Crawford was a warm friend and in many ways a pleasant person, but he had always had an annoying peculiarity. His kind of mind could recall the minutiae of life in detail; a helpful quality in a counsel or judge. He persisted in using the edge this gave him over other people to embarrass them. When you said, 'I enjoyed Provence,' he would ask, 'Where did you go?' You would waver - those difficult French names - knowing he could probably recite the name of every hill town in the province. When you said, 'We had a decent Cloudy Falls white for lunch,' he would ask 'What was it?' When you couldn't remember whether it was a chardonnay or a sauvignon blanc, and chanced, 'A pinot grigio,' he would reply, 'Funny thing. I don't think Cloudy Falls does a pinot grigio.' Crawford got satisfaction from seeing your discomfort. Tom had learned to plead inattention or ignorance to such questions.

"I hear about you occasionally from friends," Crawford said, leading him to a corner of the lounge where two armchairs gave a degree of privacy from the rest of the room. They agreed on two Campari sodas.

"I don't hear about you, Rod. You've disappeared into the priesthood of the judiciary."

"I don't regret the anonymity. It's comforting."

"You've worked your arse off for it."

"I have. It's what I wanted, and… thought perhaps I'd never get. Mind you, I enjoyed the Bar. But it can be a strain. I'm very young to be appointed. I appreciated your letter of congratulations, by the way."

Crawford wriggled, unable to conceal being pleased with himself, despite what Tom knew to be his natural modesty.

"Now you can watch your former colleagues sweating from your eyrie on the bench - and collect your pension eventually."

"You'd have been good at it, Tom. It's a loss to a small country when somebody like you settles abroad."

"On the contrary; I wouldn't have been good at it. It's a vocation. I think you take a lot on yourself when you give judgment. It's not about knowing the law - lots of lawyers are good in that department - it's having the gall to say that the right way is *this* way. It's all the conclusions you draw about people you don't really know and can never know. All done from the point of view of our somewhat imperfect selves."

"You make it sound as though it's arrogant to judge."

"Isn't it, unless you keep an iron grip on yourself?"

"Somebody has to do it."

"We've had some wacky judges and some not very choice characters."

Crawford's eyebrows rose. Tom didn't care. They talked of colleagues and the politics of the country. When they went into the dining room, he could see that Crawford was nettled that he had been less than gushing about Crawford's judicial appointment. As they passed through the crowded lounge and dining room to their table, he saw some faces peering at him, trying to remember who he was; some were people he recognised, now politicians, diplomats, businessmen, and he stopped twice to shake hands and say a quick, jocular word.

"Well what's so great about your career, anyway?" Crawford asked irritably when they sat down. "You married money, but that didn't seem to work."

"You're right. I got sick of being welcomed everywhere effectively as Mr Robyn Ashton. As though I had no skills of my own, and only a big portfolio of shares and lots of financial influence."

"You could have made it on your own merits without any help, Tom."

"Sure, but to answer your question, I didn't see my working life as a career. You know, where you start on the bottom rung and climb up. Okay, I have a good job now as head of risk for an insurance group. Quite a number of people work for me. Employing and organising managers is interesting, and I'm left with some big decisions. I see myself more as adventuring in a very complex world. I've had several jobs. I even spent nine months in chambers for the Bar in London; most of that time was out of court in coffee shops, gossiping about the judiciary and my colleagues to be. Didn't like it. And solicitors' practice, it's the same as here in my experience. You know, solicitors aren't bad people; they're like everybody else. It's just that their natural human mendacity spoils partnerships. The solicitors' firm that is even-handedly - fairly - managed is rather exceptional."

"Memories of Gottleys," Crawford said, leaning back in his chair and tasting the wine he had ordered.

"Gottleys was Dickensian, and primitive. Fairness, or even employment procedures, didn't come into it. Gottleys was the embodiment of the ego of Reginald Clyde Porter."

Crawford, who had done very well there for a few years, smiled but didn't comment.

"I flirted with the newspaper industry - as a lawyer. Libel law mostly. Found that I liked the corporate environment. Now I am where I am. I've had plenty of time to travel and consider the ways of others."

"I admire your free spirit."

"It's chancy 'out there'. You're snug in your judicial seat."

"It was chancy getting to the judicial seat."

"Yes, but it wouldn't have been that painful, would it, to see out your time earning big bucks at the Bar?"

"You're suggesting my career was win–win. I don't think I'm all that complacent, Tom."

"I'm sure you deserve your post. And I'm sure you're a credit to the bench, but you've bought what I regard as the myth of the ascending career, Rod."

"It's not a fucking myth." Crawford leaned over toward him, slopping his wine on the white cloth, speaking in a low voice out of the corner of his mouth. "All round us are the people that make this country." He gave a quick glance behind him as though he might be overheard. "These are the people in politics, business and the law, that call the shots. I think I've had a pretty decent career; yes, a distinguished career. And it's not over yet."

"Not at all over. Court of Appeal, Supreme Court, all that."

"I have my hopes. And what's wrong with that?"

"Nothing. Your choice. You've simply had your head down since you came out of university, heading for the New Zealand judiciary. You've made it. I hope it's worth it. There's a big, nasty, complicated world out there. Ever get curious about it?"

"I think I know what it's like…"

"Television news and trips to Raratonga aren't –"

"I've been to bloody England!"

"Staying for a week at the Park Lane Hilton, with your judicial umbrella at home for safety? You have to get out there and survive."

"I'm happy with my choice," Crawford huffed. "I'm making a contribution to this country."

"You sound a bit like Stuart Ashton and my dear ex-wife. They are 'somebodies', or they think they are."

"Do I detect sour grapes?"

"I told you I wouldn't be a good judge because I'm not a good enough person, but that apart, I wouldn't mind the comfort, intellectual interest and security of the bench. But I wouldn't have been prepared to wager my life for it, Rod. That's how it looked to me after I'd been in practice for a couple of years; a life dedication, a long road *maybe* leading to a judicial post or some other public appointment. I'll grant you that bits of the road would have been interesting, but very limited."

"Limited?" Crawford frowned. "I don't see it that way. The whole of a country's life passes through its judicial system in a sense... Every human contortion you can think of."

"Yeah, and you pronounce judgment on it, but it's a voyeuristic position –"

"Hunh!" Crawford growled. "Tom, that really is balls. I – we judges – make a rational analysis of the people and the facts we have to deal with."

"I agree. I also agree that your motives and moral standards are high, and that there probably isn't a better way of fitting you for your task than the Bar. But, and it's a very big but, you see life across three feet of oaken bench. And before that, you saw life looking up at a man in a wig behind three feet of oaken bench."

"And you live it, I suppose," Crawford said, with a sarcastic inflexion in his voice.

Tom nodded. "Yes, in a relative sense."

Crawford watched his wine, twiddling the stem of his glass. After a short silence while they concentrated on the asparagus vinaigrette, Tom steered the talk toward their exploits of the past, mutual friends, and their families. The conversation about careers remained merely a grain of grit in the warm belly of their relationship.

Petra and Darren were at breakfast when he went down from his room. It was Sunday. Breakfast was served from a buffet kept alive by Beryl and her helpers for a couple of hours every morning, and the inmates of the house, except Ernest, attended at their whim. Darren was wearing a suit with a tie, and Petra a modest dark blue dress.

"You're going to church?" Tom asked, surprised.

"Yeah," Petra grimaced, and Darren chuckled.

"It's not a habit?"

"Oh, God, no. Mother insists. Just before the wedding, you know. A couple of visits. To please her and Reverend Beck, and maybe some of the other old wrinklies."

"We'll be going down to the Hardie's in Fairlie for elevenses," Darren said.

"Well, you have to pass the church on the way, don't you?" His voice sounded weary.

Conversation with Petra and Darren was like trying to light a wet match. Instead of turning his attention to the wad of Sunday newspapers that he had taken upon his knee, he remembered a windy afternoon at St George's - it would be twenty years ago - when he and Robyn arrived with Petra.

"Ah, Mr and Mrs Stavely with their... child," Maurice Hewitt said, appearing to grasp bitingly for 'second child' and then omit it as he greeted them in the vestry. Maurice made notes in a huge ledger, sitting at a small spindly-legged table, like a schoolboy's desk, his robe spilled out around him on the floor. He asked about godparents and allowed that

Stuart and Michael Curran could be named without being present. Out of the narrow gothic windows of the vestry, Tom could see, in the distance, the yellow scar of the highway through the forest of pines on the hillside.

When the notes were complete, Maurice led them to the christening font behind the pews at the rear of the empty church. He transferred water to the font, a stone bowl sculpted by a Maori craftsman. Petra started to become restive. Tom could hear the wind outside, the engine of a car, the brushing of a tree against the building. It seemed that Maurice, too, was listening to these noises.

"Is nobody else coming?" he asked.

The idea that the Stavelys could have a ceremony without a party was unusual.

"No. It's not necessary... Not what we want," Robyn said.

Maurice turned the corners of his mouth down and began to read the service, chanting his lines mechanically. With surprising agility, he took Petra from Robyn and tilted her over the font, wetting her head. He said, "*We receive this child into the congregation of Christ's flock, and do sign her with the sign of the cross...*"

Petra mumbled a few friendly sounds to Maurice who hustled on.

"*This child has promised by you his sureties to renounce the devil and all his works, to believe in God, and to serve him; you must remember that it is your duty to see that this infant be taught, so soon as she shall be able to learn, what a solemn vow, promise and profession she has made here by you.*"

Petra was back in her mother's arms, with her head being wiped. In the vestry, Maurice completed the certificate, and Tom handed over a donation in an envelope.

As he and Robyn walked down the path afterwards, she said, "You weren't even listening."

"I heard every word."

As they settled in the car, and Robyn made the child comfortable, she said, "Do you believe that stuff?"

"No. Do you, Robyn?"

"Yes… I've never asked you. Were you baptised and christened?"

"Not to my knowledge."

"You're a savage, Tom. Why did you agree to Petra's baptism, then?"

"Because it places her socially; baptised and presumably later to be confirmed. She's got the option to go on later if she wishes. It's convenient but not essential."

"That's false," Robyn snapped.

"She's joining a club."

"Anybody would think you were her business manager. Petra is my idea of reaching out beyond my life."

"What about the other child? Are you immortal through him?" he asked. In their most raw discussions, the lost child intruded inevitably.

"He's part of me. The part that wanders at night."

"What a fantasy. We should have separated long ago." He was exasperated and no longer shy about referring to the roadblock he could see ahead.

"I married you because I loved you, Tom."

He could be candid now. "I think I was very confused."

"The child linked us," Robyn said, appearing to see their marriage in the past tense. "It's a secret we share."

"You're wrong to think of the child as a link. Or Petra. And neither are extensions of you. They're just separate people."

"We married because of the lost boy."

"No, we married in spite of him. Don't you remember what Maurice Hewitt said, 'The empty space at the breakfast table?' The ever-present reminder of our folly and loss."

"I never believed Maurice."

"I never forgot what he said, Robyn."

"Then why in hell did you marry me, Tom? It was a doomed marriage."

"At the time we married, I suppose I hoped he was wrong."

"You're just ignoring your own failings as a lover, and seizing on a crazy voodoo pronouncement by a mad priest."

"Maurice isn't mad, Robyn."

"He's eccentric. He's an actor."

"Don't you remember what Mrs Rueben said, long before Maurice Hewitt?"

"She wasn't an abortionist, Tom. She was an extortionist. She gulled you out of your money."

"She said we wouldn't be free if we had a child."

"That's the link between us, as I said. Painted bitch."

"No. She wasn't referring to us sharing a hidden peccadillo. She was saying it would tie our future relationship, and it did; it tipped us into marriage."

"I don't remember her as a philosopher. And I intend to find the lost boy... some day."

"That's a very bad idea, Robyn."

The hut came into view over a rise. Stuart charged wildly down the slope towards it, sliding on the rough footing. A thread of smoke came from the chimney, torn away by the wind. It was padlocked on the outside.

"This is it," Stuart said, his face dark.

"The man can't be far away."

They walked around the hut, Stuart cursing their bad luck and kicking the door angrily. The noise echoed in the narrow valley.

"Where are you, you sodding little man!" Stuart shouted.

Then they heard the crack of a rifle, and the almost simultaneous whisper of the bullet as it passed near them.

"Shit!" Tom yelled, and held his arms above his head.

About fifty yards away, a man with a grey ponytail in a black poncho was leaning on a rock, resting his gun.

"Shoot me, you cunt!" Stuart roared, slowly raising his arms.

The man made no immediate move. The wind dashed rain in their faces.

"We've alarmed him. Let's cool it, or we won't get inside the hut, Stu."

"I'll get inside if I have to choke the bastard!"

They waited for a few moments, and Tom said loudly, "Can we talk?" He moved slowly along the path towards the man, to a point where he could address him more easily. "My name is Tom Stavely. The man with me is Stuart Ashton. I've come to ask you to show me the things you found on the mountain. We don't have any weapons."

The man didn't move or speak; he had all day to pause, and eventually Tom said, "Look, I'm prepared to pay you, if you have anything we could use. Can't we sit down like mates and have a drink?"

The man never moved.

"What's your name?" Tom asked.

No answer.

"I have some whisky, mate."

The man seemed to be impressed by money and whisky, and lumbered forward. He was about fifty, but that could have been the hard life. He had a long gray beard to go with the hair. His pink lips ringed a huddle of green teeth, his eyes cloudy and yellow. His ungloved hands were brown and metallic-looking, like excavator grabs. He surveyed Tom for a moment, and then, apparently satisfied, came closer and examined Stuart.

"Get the door open, man, and let's see the stuff!" Stuart snarled.

"You want me to blow your head off?" The man replied.

"Shut your mouth and cool it, Stu, or we'll get nowhere."

"Yeah, nowhere. That's you," the man said, baring his teeth.

Stuart backed off, his face contorted. The man took his time while they waited in the lashing rain, then lowered his rifle, unlocked the door and nodded them both inside.

The interior was filthy; it stank of stale food. The floor was covered by damp newspapers and the four, two-tier bunks were strewn with dark items of screwed-up clothing. A pot-bellied iron stove occupied part of the space between the bunks, radiating some warmth and creating a haze of smoke in the room. The only sitting place was on the edge of the lower bunks.

Tom slipped out of his pack straps and parka, delved into his pack and produced the bottle of whisky; he opened it and handed the bottle to the man. "Have a go, mate. I'm Tom. This is Stu."

"Charlie," the man said. He had two or three swallows and passed the bottle back.

He and Stuart followed suit while Charlie watched them dully.

"Let's get on with it, for Christ's sake!" Stuart said.

"We heard that a Swiss climbing team came here, and you told them you had found equipment from earlier expeditions," Tom said.

"Naah. I didn't tell 'em. They reckoned what it was. But what's here is mine."

Actually, the Swiss, according to his information, were more precise; they told a reporter from *The Mountaineer* magazine that they had seen a cache of articles which appeared to be from the 1967 and 1972 expeditions, and they mentioned documents.

"That's OK, Charlie. Look, my father Bill Stavely was killed climbing here in 1972. He was with Ernest Ashton. You could have something belonging to him."

"Ernie Ashton, huh?" The man approved; he pulled a canvas bag from the top of one of the bunks and tipped the contents out on the floor; a collection of gloves, leather cases, a camera, a compass, binoculars, and a canvas wallet.

Stuart fell down on his knees over the articles, shouldering Tom aside, pawing them with shaking hands.

"For shit's sake, Stu, what're you doing? I'm in this too!" He stood up, put his boot against Stuart's flank and shoved him away. "Get out!"

Stuart glanced up at him, frantically, with a beaten dog look, and moved away. They fingered the items, but had no way of telling who had owned them. He opened the wallet. Inside was a small leather-bound book, which he removed.

"Let me see it!" Stuart tried to grasp the book, but Tom swung away possessively.

He opened the book cautiously. It was scrawled in English. Some of the pages had been torn out, and others, where ink had been used, were blurred, but there were readable pages in pencil. Stuart reached for the book again.

"Let's have a look," Stuart said, with a note of hopelessness.

"We might be able to identify this," Tom said, disregarding him.

Tom began to read a few words of the close pencil writing which straggled over the pages; then he saw the inscription written inside the front cover. He was conscious of his heartbeat. He looked at Stuart, and pointed to the inscription: 'W Stavely, 1972.'

"Your father's!"

"He must have lost this when he fell," Tom said.

He and Stuart squeezed together on the bunk, ignoring the man, the smell, and the darkening shadows in the hut. The last words of a climber who had died on a mountain were of special significance. Death was always near on mountains like Vogel, but you could never tell how near, or precisely how it might come. Both of them were absorbed.

The early part of the notebook had reminders about the route and lists of stores. Bill Stavely had made checklists of tasks he needed to perform, some written in an uncouth hand when he was preparing for the expedition. It looked as though the book had lain open in the snow or rested in a wet pocket.

From what he knew, his father was a relatively uneducated man. Bill Stavely was used to farm accounts and invoices, but had seldom been required to write a letter; he wouldn't have had the introspection or the vocabulary to be a diarist. However, in the sleepless hours, huddled in a tent waiting for the weather to change, he had evidently found something to do in scribbling comments about his condition. Tom wasn't able to separate in his imagination, the words, however awkward, from his fore-knowledge of the impending tragedy, the searing cold, the shock of falling ice, and the pain of the fall.

When the pages were readable, Ernest Ashton and Bill Stavely were at ten thousand feet, within a day or perhaps two days of the peak, in good weather. He lived the climb himself as he followed the scrawl on the discoloured pages. His father sparingly detailed their uncomfortable arrangements to sleep that night, on an ice ledge, with a steep slope above and an abyss below. They had managed to ascend a near vertical wall, and roped themselves and their packs behind a safety fence, precarious but secure enough in their bivvy. The weather, their fitness and their spirits seemed to be in order for a dash to the summit in the morning.

The next entry was more wavery, and the shape of the wording uncertain. It was dated the 12th. He felt horror rising in him as he read. It was an event known to him from Ernest Ashton's chronicle, written at leisure at Tamaki Downs. Bill's comment, made within hours after the event, was as fearful as the words he used were prosaic. Tom could hear the ice crack as his eye passed over the faltering pencil lines on the faded page.

About 3am ice ledge broke. No warning. Fell. Hit end of line hardly awake. Swinging. To ice-face. Drove spike. Sharing weight till dawn. Both unhurt. Up sheer 100 ft & over cornice to slope.

Now the weather was threatening, and Bill made another of his sparse references to Ernest after what must have been a crucial conference.

Ernie shocked. Wants down. Risk both ways. E final on descent. I summit. Row. Chance weather. Visib 10 yards.

Tom put his finger on the page and looked at Stuart, shaking his head. "We've never heard of this."

"It's years since you read the book."

"No, I skimmed a copy in your library the night before we left."

Ernest's story of *his* solo Mt Vogel conquest was well known, and written with verve, a classic of mountain endurance that had been in print and selling steadily since the time it was first published. The fall which Bill described in a few words, and the tense discussion afterwards, was a major chapter of the book, and no doubt had helped to make it a bestseller. What was in the book was a very different account of the discussion; the fateful moment when the threat of extreme danger separated two men; the moment when master and man parted.

Ernest's account in *The Fateful Snows* purported to be a factual assessment of risk, but as Tom remembered from his recent rereading, there was a whiff of condescension. Bill Stavely was said to be 'brave and resourceful', but by implication didn't have the gumption of a leader like Ernest. Bill had made 'a reasonable decision' to give up, but Ernest vowed to dare the elements. If what the notebook said was true, the facts were the reverse.

Stuart was shaking his head in disbelief. "That's a screwed-up version."

"Why shouldn't the notebook be true, Stu?"

"It's just… comment, not what actually happened."

He tried to think what that moment might actually have been like. If Bill's account was correct, Ernest would have detailed the risks in his hectoring way, and most likely ordered Bill to accompany him down the mountain; that Bill had the nerve to oppose must have seemed monstrous, and had a suggestion of the impetuosity which some mountaineers experience at heights, not that the air at ten thousand feet was particularly thin. And there was a hint of the nature of the exchange between the pair in Bill's cryptic note; both men were *final* - Bill's word – on their decisions. And they had a *'row'*. Mt Vogel was a great prize, and that Bill Stavely, a nobody in Ernest's calculation, should desire it against Ernest's judgement, must have been explosive.

Stuart's head hung down.

"It's a shock for both of us, Stu."

Bill had made an entry marked 1300 hrs the next day: *4hrs. Solid ice. 60 deg slope. Visib 20x. Light sleet impvg. 8hrs summit?*

"What the notebook is implying is that Ernest is going down the mountain at this point. Bill is on his own, Stu."

"We don't know that," Stuart said. "They could be together."

Bill's next entry was joyous, given the whole page, and clearly readable through the brown stains. He had over-pencilled the words to make them plainer.

Summit! 1700hrs. Slow prog up soft snow west ridge. Clear, sun above clouds. SW wind vicious. Plant flag. Photo. 2 mins!

"He knocked the bastard off!" Tom said.

"It's not clear," Stuart insisted feebly.

"Only one person made it, Stu."

Stuart seemed to lose interest and deflate. He grabbed the whisky bottle and swallowed heavily while Tom read on.

Slow descent 1500ft. Gusty wind. Dig ice hollow before dark. Exposed face. No choice. Roped in. Biscuits. Chocolate. Orange juice. Freezing. No sleep. Stiff at dawn. No strength. Try north wall now. Trav to west ridge too long and windy.

"The north wall is quicker," Tom said. "Yes?"

"I don't know."

"Ernest said my father was good on rock and ice."

Avalanche on ice-face. Fall/slide 2000ft? Conscious. Ledge. Secured. Move to eat. Snow & sleet. Leg broken. Hip? Hoping for E.

"Hoping for Ernie!" Tom burst out.

Charlie giggled and swigged the whisky, watching the pair. Stuart was silent, his face full of dark hollows. Tom focussed on the small stained book. The damp had wrinkled the leather and left surreal makings on its brownish surface.

The next entry was the last and was written with a shaking hand: *Weak 24hrs. Sighted E! Movg strongly. Seen me. Arr 2hrs?*

Tom thought he could see part of the sequence. "So Ernest found him. Ernest must have hung about to see if Bill was going to come back. He found out about the conquest. The weather wouldn't have been clear enough for Ernest to have followed Bill's climb with his glasses after eleven thousand feet. They must have met. What happened?

We don't have any story about Ernest leaving his injured buddy on the slopes and coming down the mountain for help, or trying to help him down."

"Stop speculating about something you know nothing about! They still had a lot of dangerous work to do to get down. Bill could have slipped while the old man was helping him. Bill could have slipped off that ledge. We can't know."

"What we do know is that Bill Stavely went to the top alone."

As they sat in Charlie's hut, trying to absorb the implications of the notebook, he began to see himself elevated to the position of judge of his friend's fate. Stuart might want to bury the truth deep, but Tom had the notebook. *He could tell the story - or destroy the notebook.* He imagined he was invested with an awesome power - to drag the Ashtons off their perch, or save them.

He and Stuart sat quietly, engrossed in their private thoughts, while Charlie grinned and slurped the whisky. Then Charlie produced a folded paper, inscribed *To Stu Ashton*. Stuart read a short handwritten note on a small page torn from a notebook, and it dropped from his fingers.

Tom retrieved the note. *Stu: After our chat on the phone, we thought at the office, that the story was too good to lose touch with. So we've come up here. Charlie would only show us his stuff guardedly and wouldn't part with it. We have a video of him and the hut etc. We will be in touch with you for comment. We take it you will let the Stavely family know. Best, Bob Drake, Chief Reporter.*

"The bastard never mentioned coming up here when we spoke," Stuart said.

"They don't know much more than they did before their trip. But we do." Tom reflected that if Drake had at least been able to photograph the pages of the notebook, the story would have been out, and his options as arbiter of the

Ashton's fortunes would have been snatched away. He would have been reduced to what he had been before this climb, a spectator of the festering hatred between father and son. As events had happened, the notebook was still, it seemed, a hidden and explosive secret between him and Stuart.

He started bidding with Charlie for the notebook. "I'll give you $100."

The man grinned cunningly. "No way."

"OK, $200."

"Wait a minute," Stuart interrupted. "I'll give you $300."

"What are you saying, Stu? It's my father's book, surely..."

There was a long moment of silence, Stuart's face red, creased, his breathing heavy; Charlie simpering and gulping; the wind crying.

"I could outbid you every fucking dollar of the way, Tom."

"Are you going to do that?"

Stuart plunged his head into his spread hands. He howled like a kicked dog.

"Two fifty's the limit, Charlie. Take it or not," Tom said sharply.

Charlie's amusement had gone. They closed at $250 which Tom produced and tucked the notebook into an inner pocket.

Stunned by their discovery, both of them donned their parkas and packs in silence and resumed their descent. When they were a few hundred yards from the hut, Stuart suddenly rounded on him.

"What about the photograph?" he said fiercely.

Tom had studied the photographs when he was looking again at *The Fateful Snows*. Ernest had produced a shot of the flag and the summit view, and a blurred photo of what was said to be his own head and shoulders. From the look of the open sky and surrounding peaks, Tom concluded that they were authentic summit shots. But he had already worked out the answer to Stuart's query.

"I think you'll find you really can't tell exactly who the person swaddled up in in all that gear is, Stuart, but the photos were surely was taken at the summit."

The shot of the climber had been taken by holding the camera at arm's length; it was evidently taken in a wind which swirled snow powder around the lens and the subject. The snow goggles were barely raised above the eyes. The head was enclosed in a padded hood. Below the eyes and covering all the lower face was prolific ice-encrusted hair. The only human feature exposed, apart from hair, was a pair of almost closed, deep-set eyes, and a blob of nose.

"I don't believe that's necessarily a photo of Ernest. Both men were wearing much the same gear."

"Well, how did Ernest get the photo, Mr Smartass?"

"Bill must have been alive when Ernest arrived at the place where he was lying injured. That's how he knew that Bill had summited, and he took the camera. He had a bit of time to consider the story he was going to tell the world. He would have had the opportunity to look at a print before he released the photo."

"It's all supposition."

"Is the notebook supposition? Is Bill's declaration in it that he had achieved the summit supposition?"

"Why didn't Ernest take the notebook and destroy it?"

"He may have known that Bill carried and used a notebook. Would he have thought about it in the agonising circumstances of their last meeting? Would he have expected that Bill would have been able to make blow-by-blow entries? I doubt it."

"More supposition."

"Stu, the point where Ernest conceived that he could steal the conquest wouldn't necessarily be when he found Bill. Bill may have died shortly after. Ernest left him and mulled it over on the way down. He had plenty of time to think. I expect his mind was in a turmoil. He'd failed."

"No. The only time he had was until he got to the lower base camp…"

"Hours; long enough to mull over the possibilities."

Stuart said, "The team was waiting for him. He announced his victory straight off to them. We know that independently. He didn't go home and think about it."

"Not quite right, Stu. Ernest wrote that when he got to the camp, the very first words were from *his* team; *they* congratulated him because the spotter pilot had called them on the radio to confirm the victory. They assumed Ernest was the one. He was the big man. Ernest knew for certain at that point that Bill had made it to the top, and he must have known that there was nothing to stop him stepping into Bill's shoes. What was to stop him? Bill must have been dead to his certain knowledge. Nobody could contradict Ernest. Later, there were Bill's summit photos which were so ambiguous that Ernest could claim them for himself. An additional piece of luck."

"You're making up fairytales."

"I agree we'll never know the full story, but the bare fact remains that one man summited, and it wasn't Ernest."

Tom felt simple shock as they continued down the slopes. His mind moved slowly over the evidence which would have enabled Ernest to decide to steal Bill's achievement; to steal it, and be hailed as a great mountaineer… And he was concerned about Stuart, who was like a man concussed.

The way down was trackless but not difficult and they made good speed. When they had several miles yet to cover, they were overtaken by a heavy snowfall. Stuart, who was leading, stopped.

"What's up?" he asked, as Stuart turned to face him.

"I want the book, Tom."

"What do you mean? It belonged to my father. I bought it from that guy."

Stuart came very close. "Give it to me. I should have bought it and I could have. I want it now. I want you to hand it to me voluntarily."

"No way, sorry." He tried to make a joke of it, pushing Stuart away, and stepping to go round him.

Stuart caught his arm. "Give it to me or I'll take it."

"And what will you do with it?"

"Destroy it."

"Why try to destroy the truth?"

"You're going to ruin me and disgrace my father with lies and innuendo."

"Stuart, the truth is clear."

"And you're going to blab to *The Mountaineer*. You're going to ruin me."

"I haven't said anything about blabbing. Let's get home and think this thing through."

"No!" Stuart said, throwing his weight against Tom. "If they can't produce the book, if the book doesn't exist, all they'll have is a few photos of a rotten hut and a recluse and some gobbledegook from the Swiss."

He stumbled over in the snow under Stuart's thrust. "Have you gone mad?" He spoke lying on his back in the snow, his arm up for protection.

"Give me the book!"

Stuart bent over and wrenched at his parka. Then he straightened up and aimed a blow with one of his poles. Tom deflected the blow with his forearm. For a moment they were stilled, Stuart dazed by what he had done.

"You're crazy, man. Get hold of yourself!" Tom shouted, struggling to his feet.

Stuart suddenly went limp and sobbed.

They slowly resumed their walk in silence and did not speak for the remaining distance. The silence was heightened by the snowfall which enclosed them, each man in a separate world. He remained a safe distance behind Stuart and gripped his poles, ready to defend himself, although he thought that Stuart's breakdown had passed. They were in the truck before Stuart spoke.

"You know I'll be ruined by this. Everything I've worked for is in sports journalism."

"It's not as bad as that," he said, trying to make light of it, but thinking it couldn't be worse.

"What are you going to do with the notebook?"

"I haven't thought about it. I need to take time."

"We've been friends just about all our lives..." Stuart began.

He'd talk to Alison about this. 'He's going to lean on our friendship for help. But what help can I give? What help *should* I give? After all, the aggrieved party here is my own long gone father. I've always felt with Stuart that the warmth of years of friendship and shared interests heavily concealed deeper feelings, conflicts which have never surfaced overtly. For me, what is down deep is a simple difference of position which nothing can change. Boss boy and farm boy; master and serf.'

Alison would say, 'It's your own sense of inferiority.'

'No, It's a sense of what is real. Stuart really is my master *in his own mind* and it's always been like that. But I feel I'm as good a man as he is.'

Alison wouldn't let this pass. 'Tom, don't close your eyes to yourself. You've ridden a long way in the Ashton Rolls-Royce. You never were merely a bright little urchin.'

'I was Mr Robyn Ashton,' he'd say.

'You've used them, Tom. Recognise it!'

He responded to Stuart, "We've been adversaries, at times."

"We need your help now."

Tom said, "You, Stuart, and Robyn are two of the biggest pieces of furniture in my life, for your own separate selves. My feelings for you both are difficult to define, but they are warm and benevolent. And what about your feelings for me, the farm boy given a coat of varnish by a university?"

"I've never thought of you like that," Stuart choked, as he began to throw the Land Rover carelessly around the bends in the gravel road.

He didn't challenge Stuart, although he didn't believe him. He clamped his jaw and looked at the road ahead. "Steady, man, steady."

It was incredible to him that a notebook which had been abandoned in snow and ice could reappear and explode more than thirty years of history and a proud human conquest. Now, the notebook had opened a void which could be filled by a new, stark reality. He believed that there could be no conceivable reason why his father would fabricate the notes he scribbled in his last hours. The prop for Stuart's reputation had gone. It could be shored up by Tom, but if not, a bad smell around Mt Vogel would haunt Stuart for as long as he chose to be a climber-journalist. 'You know he's the son of Ernest Ashton, don't you?' people would say when his name was mentioned.

Amongst mountaineers, there are many stories of cowardice and neglect of human duty on the slopes, but the truth about Mt Vogel, if it became known, would surpass them all as utterly vile, the theft of another man's conquest. In the mist would hover questions about Ernest's implication in Bill Stavely's death, questions which, thankfully, that at this time didn't trouble him.

As he was jolted around in the cab of the truck on their journey, he had a desire to interrogate Ernest, to plumb the depths of his perfidy, the lie of that heroic book *The Fateful Snows*. The impulse which guided him to the red couch with Robyn taunted him now. If the desire to strike squirmed in him like a live animal, at least age had tempered it with an understanding of the corrosive effects that hatred could have upon him. Stuart too was fuming about his father, and Tom feared that such was their history, words would not be a sufficient weapon.

9

Tia met the Land Rover as Stuart drove it to the back entrance of the house at dusk. "Stuart, there's a call for you from *The Mountaineer* magazine."

"I won't take their calls."

"They also want to speak to you, Tom," Tia said.

"Tell them I'll call them back."

He really meant this as a polite code for 'don't bother me', but Stuart was boiling. "What are you going to say to them? Whine about the great wrong done to your father?"

"First, Stu, we ought to talk about this and decide together on the best way to handle the press. After we've had a chance to shower and get a bit of rest."

"What's happened?" Tia asked.

There was a moment of silence and awkward stares.

"Nothing as far as the world's concerned!" Stuart shouted, "just surmise and... lies!"

"I can't believe this," Tia said, "Ernest is..."

"Somebody?" Tom said.

"He may be an unpleasant man, Tom, but surely-" Tia began.

"Unpleasant? Understatement of his lifetime! Say nothing to *The Mountaineer* or the press. Nothing!" Stuart was adamant.

"Not necessarily, Stu. Maybe we can use them to throw a different light on things," Tom said.

"Only if you're prepared to deny the authenticity of the notebook, Tom."

"We can't fly in the face of facts, but we can – "

"I'm going to get a party together to climb Mt Vogel!" Stuart burst out.

Tom looked at Tia.

"This isn't the time," Tia said. She clutched Stuart. "I see the idea of vindicating yourself, Stu, but you can't rush it. You know better than anybody that it takes planning and planning takes time." Tom spoke in a level tone.

"Planning, normally, yes. But this is different!"

"In what way different?" Tom asked flatly.

"My fucking reputation and everything I've worked for is in jeopardy."

"Listen to Tom, please Stuart," Tia begged.

But Stuart didn't appear to be listening to either of them.

"I could be ready in four weeks and I can count on a couple of climbers. Will you come, Tom? That would be the imprimatur that I need. "

He couldn't help thinking this was far-fetched, if not irrelevant. "No. I've told you the climb is beyond me now. And I have commitments at home in England."

"Christ man, it's my life, my reputation in issue here!" Stuart bellowed, the vein on his forehead standing out.

"You and I can talk about this. We can work something out. I'll talk to Ernest."

"*Work something out*? When my future is in the hands of a bloody reporter?" He dropped his parka and pack on the tiled floor of the porch and disappeared upstairs.

"I'll go up to him," Tia said. "Oh, Tom, what's going to happen?"

"Try to get him to stay away from the old man. They'll have to talk ultimately, but not at the moment. Stu will calm down. He's tired. He hasn't had an opportunity to think."

Tom went up to his room, but paused long enough only to splash his face with cold water and remove the notebook from his pack. Then he went to Ernest's bedroom. Ernest was awake and reading a magazine. This was the moment when Tom had the metaphorical dagger in his hand, and it was exhilarating. He didn't have any wish to justify his father. It was as though Bill Stavely was an unlucky player in this, rather than his kin. His entire focus was on Ernest and himself. He would have cared if Stuart, who seemed crazed, had run upstairs and got to Ernest first; he wanted to get to Ernest first himself. He wanted to prick the bladder of arrogance and see that toxic fuel leak away.

Ernest dropped his reading and removed his glasses when he saw Tom. "Ah, the fact-finder's return. Well, you've got it all sorted now, have you, or have you been listening to fairytales?"

"Bill Stavely's notebook isn't a fairytale, Ernest." He waved the notebook in his hand.

"Notebook? Let me see." He lifted his claw of a hand. "Arrgh! Stavely could hardly read or write!"

Tom avoided his reach and read, "*Summit! 1700hrs. Slow prog up soft snow west ridge. Clear. Sun above clouds. SW wind vicious. Planted flag. Photo. 2 mins!*" He pushed the book under Ernest's nose, and dodged his attempts to grasp it. "You can't deny that!"

"It's probably one of my notebooks. Where did you get it?"

"No, Ernest, no. You know it isn't. It's Bill Stavely's notebook, rescued from the glacier by a mountain man. Your notebook in which you recorded your fraudulent conquest is in the Canterbury museum. Remember? You never recorded that priceless moment of arrival at the summit of Mt Vogel twice in different notebooks."

"I didn't steal anything from Bill Stavely, but supposing I

had? Who did I hurt? It was an achievement running around like a chicken without a head. Stavely was dead."

He wasn't expecting this piece of Machiavellian pragmatism. "Is that what you told your conscience when the mountaineering world was patting you on the back, and saying what a great man you were?"

Ernest Ashton rested his head on the pillow and turned to face Tom. The tissue on his skull had tightened to reveal a tall, square structure as his face, like a closed door; still a touch of superiority in the design, and draped across it like a rag was a cynical smile. "I was a bloody fine mountaineer. World class. Everybody knows that. Everest, K2. And Bill Stavely was shit."

This barb drew no blood from Tom. "That's what you thought of your climbing buddy?"

"Climbing buddy nothing. Your father was my sherpa. Not even a sirdar. He carried the kitchen. He was dirt."

"In your book, Bill Stavely is a brave companion."

"Poetic licence," the old man breathed. "He robbed me. Took money from the Downs' accounts for gambling. He beat your mother. He was well capable of pencilling up a lying notebook."

"If he was so bad, why did you take him as your companion?"

"Because he was available, fit, and had some experience - more than any other member of the party - and most important I needed a mule to carry my load. Do you get it? A mule, not a companion."

"You despised him. And, if you both succeeded, you wanted somebody whom you could upstage as a servant."

"I despised him. I shed no tears when he died."

"Tell me how he died."

"Read my book. He fell on the ascent and I went on alone."

140

"I prefer Bill Stavely's notebook."

"What does *he* say?" The old man asked this question scornfully.

"That you parted after a fall on the way up. He went on, and you went down. He summited, and fell on the way down. We don't know any more, but evidently you found him and plundered him like a pirate."

"The man was a fantasist." Ernest turned away dismissively.

"You know you've screwed up Stuart's career. I wouldn't be surprised if he didn't come upstairs and throttle you."

The old man looked apprehensive, then oily. "I'll be ready for him. I always have been."

Tom was annoyed and couldn't resist striking again. "I don't think I ever told you, Ernest, that when I first screwed your daughter, on the red couch in the drawing room, it felt like I was sticking a pine cone up your bum. Being here now feels the same."

The old man stared at him, calculating the enormity of this. "I've never thought much of you Tom. You're a quitter."

"Do you realise this, Ernest? The Mt Vogel story will be plastered around this country – and overseas. It's the kind of story the newspapers and magazines love – callous, chillingly evil, and a bubble of reputation pricked, not to mention the shame of a high and mighty family. When it happens, and it'll happen soon, it'll be like the red couch feeling for me."

"I'll deny it. I'll sue you. And my pockets are deeper than yours."

"*I'm* not going to tell the story. *The Mountaineer* are already fishing for it. They'll syndicate it to the newspapers here and abroad. Parliament will take your knighthood away if you live long enough. *The Fateful Snows* will be trashed by every library and bookshop in the world – or maybe collected as a tangible example of a monstrous lie."

He wasn't going to tell Ernest that he had just about decided, in Stuart's interests, to keep quiet about the notebook.

"A scabby little hack tried to talk to me on the phone. I hung up." Ernest rested his chin on his chest, seemingly beaten.

"It's too late for you anyway. You're nearly in the grave. If there are any mourners at your funeral, they'll need pegs on their noses to stop the stink from your coffin."

Ernest reared up, his eyelids fluttering, his voice phlegmy. "Bill Stavely, that drunken hobo as the conquerer of Mt Vogel? While I, with my mountaineering expertise and my conquests was on the lower slopes? Never. No, never that! That would be an arse-up world."

"That's it, isn't it? It wasn't just a simple matter of stealing a companion's victory. The celebrated Ernest Ashton *couldn't* be bested by his servant. *You'd* have died of shame if Bill Stavely climbed Mt Vogel and you failed! You had to step in. Your reputation demanded it!"

"You're like your father, a turd. Smarter and more sober perhaps, but a turd."

Tom couldn't help deriding the man's agitation. "Sir Ernest Ashton, renowned climber, author, landowner, and Prince of South Canterbury. What an illusion! I'm not a very good man, Ernest, but you are a villain! A man like you doesn't commit just one villainy. What else have you done, Ernest, apart from attempting to destroy Stuart?"

"Are you going to sanctify Bill Stavely at the same time as you are ruining me?"

Ernest had suddenly headed in another direction. He now seemed to be looking at Tom's assertions as facts which would be accepted.

"Why not? Just a little. He'll have his name in the record

books, after all. The drinking and wife beating and gambling and petty thievery will be forgotten."

"I won't forget."

"You'll be dead. But that's beside the point. We're talking here about you and my father in the eyes of the world. And we're talking, much more importantly, about Stuart. The story will virtually ruin him."

"Drivel! Stuart will have to find his own way. He's never taken any advice from me, or given a damn for what I think."

"The one thing he did give a damn for is your conquest of Mt Vogel and your book about it. He built his career on it. I don't know why your lie hasn't crushed you, as it's about to tarnish him."

Ernest spurted a short sound from his throat that was his laugh. "Not everybody has your infantile Sunday School morality."

"The smell of you, the putrid smell, will be on Stuart's skin for as long as he pens a word about mountaineering."

Ernest dismissed him like an irritating courtier, with the flick of his waxy hand.

He left the bedroom, realising that a storm was rising. The wind was whipping the leaves threateningly. He went down to the study and poured himself a whisky. He gulped it and it burned. What had been said was there to be said; no shocks, and no sense of personal offence, other than the deep and old abrasion of the Ashtons' imagined superiority. What was left, like two rocks on the sand after the tide of abuse had run out, was Ernest's utter disdain, and Tom's hatred of him - dislike was too feeble a word; he had to acknowledge it was hatred.

Alison's parents lived in Geraldine where her father, a former architect, and her mother, were happily spending their retirement years. Visiting them was partly duty, but also a pleasure because of their cheery relationship and equable lifestyle. If he could have chosen his parents, Geoffrey and Helen Fuller would be the people. He sat on a deck chair in the sun in their garden, drinking tea, and felt that he was accepted as 'family'.

Helen Fuller said, "I can't understand why Alison didn't come with you, Tom. It would be wonderful to see her. And we really won't be able to go to see her for… for a while, anyway. "

"She doesn't want to attend an Ashton celebration. She really couldn't have come with me and avoided the wedding."

"No, that would…" Geoffrey began.

"So it's not true, Tom, that your boy isn't well and she has to be at home?"

"Not really. Nick wasn't well, but I don't think she wanted to get into the Ashton thing, and she didn't want to talk about why."

"We understand the sensitivities, Tom," Geoffrey said.

Helen nodded, and cupped her hand around a rose in the nearby bed in a preoccupied way. Her leathery smile could not hide the angst of being separated from her only child and two grandchildren by vast oceans. Geoffrey Fuller, a surveyor in local government in Bath, had wanted a better existence and found one in local government in Christchurch. Now retired, he and his wife had good health, a pleasant home, and an adequate pension; everything they wanted – except the company of their daughter and grandchildren. Alison, Tom knew, felt more distant about it. She was happy with telephone calls and occasional visits. Helen, like other grandmothers, would have liked to pop in on the grandchildren every week.

"You'll bring her and the children back to see us soon, won't you, Tom?" Helen said.

"Sure."

"Is there any chance that you'll come back permanently?" Geoffrey asked in a wistful tone.

Tom supposed that Geoffrey must have thrashed around the possibilities that might put them physically closer to Alison. The most obvious one was to go back to Blighty, but they couldn't face that. Well, Geoffrey couldn't. Yet he wanted to grant his wife her dearest wish. He wanted her to stop yearning. It grated like sandpaper on his nerves when he saw her sitting in the garden, staring at the flower in her hand without seeing it. He had never thought it conceivable that Alison might settle in England. Inconceivable. He and Helen came here for peace and security and found it, and Alison rejected it all! She *liked* it in England. Tom was Geoffrey's only chance. The long strands of silver hair fell over his tanned forehead despondently.

"I can't say," Tom replied gently and sympathetically; it was the seemingly unsquareable circle for him and them.

"You must have a lot of opportunities here, Tom," Helen said softly.

She didn't blame Tom as the man who took her daughter and grandchildren away, but she fervently hoped he would bring them back. She had been married happily for forty years and she understood that these decisions to stay or go were reached in a composite marital brain whose workings couldn't be unravelled by an outsider - even a mother or mother-in-law.

"Yes, I do have some opportunities."

"And wouldn't it be better, in the long run, for Alison and the children to be here? This is God's own country, after all." She mentioned God with a lilt; he knew this expression had nothing to do with religion.

"I don't fault the country in any way. I guess in terms of beauty and freedom it isn't bettered anywhere…"

"So what's keeping you away, Tom?" Geoffrey cut in.

Tom thought that Geoffrey was firmer now. Geoffrey's anxiety seemed to Tom, like a headache that wouldn't go away. This couple were not going to let Tom go quietly, and he considered that maybe he owed them an explanation – at least as far as it was explicable. "Have you ever been in, say, Lambton Quay in Wellington, on Saturday night at about 10pm or Sunday at noon?"

"Not much happening?" Geoffrey asked.

"I have a lonely feeling."

"You forget, we come from Bath where it gets quiet, like countless towns in Britain. You're really saying *you* want the buzz of a big city," Geoffrey said.

"He's saying it's more interesting in London. They're a young couple, Geoff."

"We like the entertainments and diversity of London. Alison does, certainly. But that isn't it entirely. I work in a profession. If I worked in the medical profession, or in a branch of academia, it would be the same. In a population of four million, probably the same size as a pair of London boroughs, these professional groups are small…"

"No room for promotion, you mean?" Geoffrey asked.

"No. It's not promotion or money or opportunity to exercise your expertise – it's the small-town hothouse of peers. Everybody looking over everybody's shoulder, and the gossip and prejudice that goes with it."

"Oh!" Helen was surprised and a little shocked.

"I think I understand," Geoffrey said. "Life in a goldfish bowl."

"Yes, in the same sense that families who have lived in

146

Coronation Street for a few generations live in a goldfish bowl."

"Some find that reassuring, Tom," Helen said primly.

"They do, but I don't. I find it cramps me. But when all this has been said, Geoff, neither Alison or I have definitely decided what we're doing. It's a very, very difficult question."

"It sounds as if you may never make a decision. Inertia will keep you where you are," Geoffrey said.

"That's true."

"I know that Alison is having an immensely better life with you than she had with Maurice Hewitt, and that's a relief," Geoffrey said.

"Maurice seemed such a nice person when we first met him. Alison never thought she'd be a parson's wife," Helen said.

Tom didn't understand Alison's attraction to Maurice. It wasn't a forbidden subject, just something that he never mentioned and that she never volunteered. Maurice was darkly handsome, agreeable and witty when Tom first knew him, and that may have been the sum of it. When Tom met Alison, she was, with Maurice, one of the party crowd. In the licentiousness of that time, she had struck a spark with Tom that didn't die, as every other relationship he had with a woman did. Where and when the spark was first struck was lost in time now; it may have been in the shadow of a dawn over twenty-five years ago when he woke up beside her in bed.

"Maurice changed. He didn't like the life he was leading. He thought it was bad." Geoffrey spoke resignedly.

"Yes, but if that was so, why did he become so grim and unhappy?" Helen asked.

"Maybe he took a path that didn't yield the consolation he expected," Tom said.

"His illness was the ultimate burden," Geoffrey said.

"In her devotion to Maurice at home and in the hospital, Alison was a model." Helen said.

Tom remembered that as Maurice's illness progressed – it was leukaemia – he became more curt and sarcastic. He laughed only at the misfortune of others. Alison told Tom that Maurice seemed to delight in the long silences which fell around the hospital bed. If she showed pity, he began to sneer and become vituperative.

Tom used to visit Maurice very occasionally when he was in a hospice in Timaru; he saw it as supportive of Alison. On one occasion they had a conversation, which he had later described to Alison as nonsensical, but had never forgotten. Maurice, with strange perspicacity, had portrayed him in a way he was always earnestly seeking to deny.

Alison was there when he arrived at the bedside, and shortly excused herself.

"I'll leave you men to tell some yarns for a while."

After she left, Maurice said, "What would the world think if she did anything less than crucify herself? It's not the 'flu I've got, you know. I have to lie here and watch her charade…" He sighed and closed his eyes.

Tom would have liked to leave too, but he had only just arrived, and he stayed, a prisoner of his sense of duty.

Maurice marshalled his strength. "We've both been caught by a different kind of ill fortune, Tom," Maurice said, looking at him piercingly from under heavy eyelids.

"My misfortune has been to receive an unexpected and deadly blow. My mechanism's gone wrong. I've been unlucky. I've lost on a chance in ten thousand. You're different; you've invited your troubles in the door like old friends. And yet I'd change with you. That's the part that hurts, to see you floundering deeper and deeper into a filthy bog – you must be blind – and yet be willing to change places with you, because at least you'll be alive. Your folly won't kill you. You may come as near to suffering the agony at the thought of death as a live healthy man can, but you won't die."

Maurice rubbed his face with a blue hand. "Look at me! I can feel my empty cheeks, my hollow eyes. My skull feels thin. I've no hair. But you! You've changed too. I can see! Your face is shrinking. There's a blotchiness about your skin. And you have staring little eyes. You're oppressed too. You're beginning to show the misery of loathing your wife, and being loathed by her, of continual arguments that seep into every moment and poison them. You're in hell, my friend, and I would change places with you just to breathe and go on breathing."

Tom didn't want to argue. "OK, I'm a sinner."

"I don't know anything about sin, Tom. What I know is that you're a wrecker, dragging everybody down. Your wife, your kids, your friends. You're the Pied Piper. You came out of a shack at the Ashtons and you're going to ruin them."

"Isn't that a bit of an exaggeration?"

It was true that at that point, his relationship with Robyn was shattered, but he had never seen himself as a leader in family disruption; merely a man who was careless about whom he cuckolded.

Maurice paused, and again concentrated his sharp gaze. "Can you understand what I feel for my wife? Her smile that turns up the corners of her mouth. A demure confidence. She appears to be holding something back, and peeping at my confusion. Is Alison concealing something from me? No. There is nothing behind that self-satisfied smile. It's a foolish mask. I know her; the line of her thoughts, her manners and her moods. I know her interests and her accomplishments. Nothing about her is hidden from me. I've even reflected on her death. In that case, I would lose her as one loses a piece of paper with writing on it; one remembers only the tenor of the words. I'd be free of her. I'd have used her up."

Hearing this description of Alison, which he thought showed that Maurice didn't understand his own wife, made him less concerned about being described as the Pied Piper. He believed that illness had made Maurice cranky.

Maurice began to quiver and sweat, and stared at the ceiling. "It's the side effects of the drugs. I'd change places with you, Tom, yes. I'd swap my death for a living hell. Does that surprise you? I should be calm, resigned to my end, saying prayers. Instead I'd exchange with a wreck like you. I don't know what to believe anymore, but there's surely no peace in dying."

"Can't you get some solace from your... calling?"

"That farce? Don't be ridiculous!"

He didn't feel guilty - or wounded - at the bedside of this harmless near-corpse, once a delightful companion. He wondered, without being truly concerned, whether Maurice knew or sensed anything about his association with Alison, but it seemed that he was convinced of her virtue; contemptuous of it, and of her meticulously performed wifely duty. Maurice must have assumed that when all the hectic partying finally faded away, so did all the affairs or associations to which it gave birth.

Tom thought that Alison couldn't disguise in her husband's presence the enigmatic satisfaction of a woman well-loved, and Maurice, who had been so prophetic about him and Robyn, couldn't see that the *nothing* that he supposed was behind Alison's mask, was actually something which was living and growing joyfully.

Alison rejoined them for an awkward fifteen minutes at the end of the visit. When they left the hospice together, subdued, it was dark in the street. He crushed her to his side as they came down the steps at the entrance to the building, almost lifting her off her feet. They went to a restaurant where they had a steak and a bottle of wine. They talked about everything but Maurice. Later, they drove to Maurice's house in Springvale. It was very late. They had a cognac from Maurice's liquor cabinet, before going to bed in Alison and Maurice's marriage bed.

10

He borrowed a car from Stuart and drove to Christchurch to see Len. After a beer and sandwich in a pub he went to the neurological disability centre in Riccarton where Len lived. Len was a handsome eighteen year old boy with honey-smooth skin, and rich yellow hair, but his body was now fat. He had a comfortable room with a special bed, and although he spent his waking time in a wheelchair, he could not perform any task himself; he could not eat, wash or move without help. He could not speak. He was doubly incontinent. He received twenty-four hour attention from specialist carers and medical staff. He had to be swung into his bed on a hoist, and showered lying on a tray. Whenever Tom saw him, he appeared to be in a good humour, but he couldn't recognise Tom or, Tom thought, anybody else.

He greeted the staff, some of whose faces he remembered; they permitted visitors at any time. He settled on a chair in Len's room and chatted to him for a while - although Len couldn't reply, or understand. He talked about Len's sister, and his half-brothers in England. He asked Len questions, and answered them himself.

On the hour, he switched on the television. The news included a short piece on the so-called mystery of Mt Vogel, referring to Sir Ernest Ashton and *The Fateful Snows*, and very guardedly mentioned that a Swiss team were raising questions about what happened on the mountain when Sir

Ernest's climbing partner was killed. The soundbite implicitly promised that more was to come.

He switched off the television and resorted to a DVD of Abba which he found amongst Len's collection. It pleased Len, who drooled and made a low noise.

When Len had the accident, his care was discussed on the telephone with Tom in London. Tom assented to the doctors doing 'everything', and the result, very creditable in terms of medical science, was this; they created a semblance of a human being out of a heap of bruised flesh and broken bones. He had appreciated since then that Len had only a minute quality of life, and ought to have been allowed to die; but here Len was, a creature with the kind of consciousness which could only show pleasure and discomfort.

That morning, before he left Tamaki Downs, Robyn had said to him, "Of course you'll make arrangements for Len to be at the wedding."

He hadn't expected this. "But Len won't know what it's about," he protested.

"He's part of the family and he should be there."

"On show, you mean? So it looks right?"

"His sister's marriage is an important family event."

"Are we a family?"

"Stop picking holes. You know what I mean."

"It's ridiculous, wheeling him in like an ornament."

"You don't know what he feels or knows," Robyn said tartly.

"Do you?"

"I give him the benefit of the doubt."

Petra came in and immediately sensed the tension. "What's the matter?"

"Daddy doesn't think Len should be at the wedding."

"Why? I want him there. He's my brother." Her face had

a smooth petulance; a way of transmitting her disapproval without moving a muscle.

"Of course, darling, so do I," Robyn pronounced and stared at him balefully.

"Len may be too… you know… to come."

"Don't be mean, Daddy."

He conceded weakly. "I'll have to check with the doctors whether he can travel. It's a long way. We'll have to have a nurse. And don't forget, Len wears a nappy and that'll have to be changed."

"Then get two nurses and an ambulance." Robyn forced her advantage sternly.

"It's a hell of a long way for Len to travel for –"

"For what, Tom? His sister's marriage? And before you tell me that a Christian marriage ceremony is tribal trumpery, remember that *you've* come twelve thousand miles for one!"

"Oh, Daddy, you don't think that about church weddings."

"Doesn't he just, darling! You don't know the half of what he thinks."

"I'll see the doctors." He retired meekly from the fray.

He spoke with the doctor on duty when he left Len, saying that he was prepared to meet the costs of staffing and transport to get Len to Springvale and back for the wedding.

The doctor looked at him closely, as if examining an unusual species. "Come into my office, Mr Stavely."

Tom followed the white coat into a small cubicle. The doctor hunched over a desk and pushed up his spectacles to his hairline. "Let me ask you a question, Mr Stavely. Would you take Len to a performance of the *Merchant of Venice*?" He dropped his spectacles back on his nose by a movement of his brow and looked at Tom critically over the rims.

"No."

"No indeed, Mr Stavely."

"But it's no use telling my ex-wife that Len wouldn't have a clue where he was or why. She's not interested in what he can understand. She's interested in what the guests understand. She wants him at the wedding as a necessary exhibit, a family artifact."

The doctor was amused. "Sure, I've met Mrs Stavely. She has her reasons, but there's a risk. Len has epileptic fits. Did you know that? He could have a stroke or a fit in the ambulance, and the nurses might be in difficulty in those conditions. It's going to be an uncomfortable, risky and unnecessary ride for him."

"OK, I'll call Robyn now and I'd like you to speak to her, doctor."

"Surely, Mr Stavely, you can talk to your own ex-wife…"

"Surely I can't. My ex-wife will only accuse me of misrepresenting what you say to get my own way. You can help Len - and me - by talking to her."

The doctor reluctantly agreed.

Seeing Len nodding in his chair, so fair and yet so damaged, made him think of Len's older brother, the lost boy, whom Robyn tracked down about three years ago through the Camden local authority in London which handled the adoption. The boy was nineteen at that time. Robyn had telephoned Tom and written about her plans, wanting him to be involved.

He talked about it to Alison. She said, 'I think it's something you ought to face, and understand, rather than leave as a dark hole full of bad dreams, or worse, hear about from Robyn's point of view afterwards. Go along with Robyn.'

The visit was agreed, against his instincts, and handled in

the way that he and Robyn had developed since parting, with paper-thin courtesy over a cauldron of conflict. Alison felt constrained to invite Robyn to the house for a drink when she arrived in London - tea, as it happened. This was polite recognition that at one time they were all friends together. Robyn chatted charmingly, giving no sign that she was measuring and assessing their Fulham semi-detached, a comfortable but not luxurious home, against her own superior standards of space and décor.

The next day, he met Robyn at the Camden underground station and they walked to the meeting room at the Camden Social Services Department, Robin swaddled in a thick overcoat, her cheeks mottled red, and her eyes very wide open and glowing. He knew the signs. She had been drinking heavily last night, and had swallowed a handful of painkillers this morning.

They were late for the meeting and were shown in quickly. A young woman social worker greeted them. "Peter is in there now," she said, pointing to a door. "My advice is that you try to start very quietly. Just go in and chat."

Robyn rushed in and tried to get close to the boy, but he had hemmed himself in on the other side of a table pulled close to the wall, with chairs on either side. Robyn had to give up and squeeze into a chair opposite. The boy stood, slouched against the wall, almost out of reach. Tom hesitated, standing by the open door.

Peter really deserved to be called a young man, but Tom could only think of him as a boy. The room was white and brightly lit, the furniture white plastic. The boy's head was bent and he looked up slowly, straight at Tom. Tom took the few steps across the floor and held out his hand across the table. The boy touched his hand before sliding down on to a chair. The boy's hand was rough.

Tom had thought of many possible openings for this meeting. He didn't want to be here, had almost feared it, and yet he had a sickly fascination with what this product of his genes was like. Would the boy be like a young version of him? Or would he be like somebody in the street whom you might walk past without a flicker of recognition? Would a subterranean current of recognition flicker between them? Or would the betrayal of parenthood have hardened into a concrete barrier? Would the boy want to partake of the Ashton-Stavely life in some way, visit New Zealand? Would he ask for money? There were a myriad of uncertainties. Tom mumbled an indecipherable but friendly greeting and sat down on one of the flimsy chairs.

"We wanted to see you." Robyn spoke with a softly sympathetic resonance.

The boy looked at her casually and paused. "Why?"

This bald question, in the boy's dry voice, silenced the room.

"Because -" Tom began.

"Because we wanted to know you are... alright," Robyn interjected, her eyes moist.

"Bit late for that, isn't it?" The boy gave a weak smile at Robyn's answer.

Tom noticed how much like him Peter was; the same honey-coloured hair - which was sticky - blue eyes, and a prominent jaw line; none of Robyn's dark looks; unmistakably his son. But Peter's clothes made him look different; the jeans, with dirty training shoes which Tom had noticed under the table, and the shapeless woollen fleece jacket flecked with white paint. Peter hadn't dressed up for them. He looked like a tradesman. He was a painter and decorator, they had been told. His hands were bony, the fingernails broken, with dirt in the quicks. He spoke a burred kind of

English which Tom supposed was a provincial accent, but Tom couldn't identify which province.

"I thought you wanted to see us," Robyn said, with a hint of a whine.

"I went along with it," he said unemotionally.

"Curious?" Tom asked, trying to make light of it.

"He has every right to be curious," Robyn said.

"Sure he does. I didn't mean – "

"Yeah. And you're curious too," Peter said.

Tom was relieved as the boy appeared to want to head away from childish regrets into a more rational exchange. He may have been unschooled, but he had a sharpness about him.

"True," Tom admitted.

"It's not true at all," Robyn said. "It's so much more than curiosity. I think about you often, Peter. I wonder what you're doing. I feel that part of me, part of my life, is moving around out there in the darkness. There's an empty space in my life. We've… been haunted by the empty chair at the breakfast table."

Tom had a pulse of annoyance. Robyn had unbelievably reached for the Hewitt metaphor, one they had both used in their arguments at different times, flopping open a compartment of her being which was damp and dreary inside.

"You wanted it this way." The boy's lips curled slightly. He was cold – and factual.

Robyn crumpled. "I know, but we…" She suppressed a sob.

"What's the 'we' business? I thought you weren't married now?" The boy had the edge.

"No, but we were." Robyn tried to give the words significance, but they sounded plaintive.

"Are you saying you made a mistake – about marriage?"

Tom had to come in. "Yeah. I think so." He couldn't contain a short, painful laugh.

"Shit. You guys make mistakes, don't you?"

"That's true, and – "Tom said.

He had in mind trying to explain the pressures on him and Robyn, inexcusable as they may have been, simply as a matter of candour, but Robyn cut in.

"It's not true, about our marriage. It was loving and decent until – "

"Until you decided it was a mistake." Peter put in boredly.

"I was going to say – "Tom tried to get the initiative.

"How are your... parents?" Robyn sliced through his efforts again.

"They're OK. Been good to me. "

"That's good and..." Tom was going on to try to say something sympathetic about Peter's family life, ask whether he had brothers or sisters, but he began to see how inquisitive anything like this would sound coming from him.

"Is there something we can do for you, Peter?" Robyn asked.

"Whaddya mean?"

"Like, well, like money. Do you need money? Would you like to meet our family in New Zealand? What about your education? We could help..."

"You want to kinda take over as my parents again?" He had a chilling cynicism.

"We want to help." Robin supplicated with her two palms raised.

"Shit, I've got all I want," Peter said. "It sounds like you want me to change tracks. Become your son. Enter your life. What makes you think your life is so good that you can make mine better?"

Robyn couldn't find an answer. Tom was embarrassed for himself *and* Robyn. "We didn't mean to put it that way," he said. If only the kid knew how grotesque the Ashton-Stavely family life was!

Tom could admire the distantly measured way Peter was dealing with them, realising that they were crassly offering material help from a desert dry of real affection, but welling over now, at this moment, with sugary emotion. He thought Peter didn't want them or need them, and Peter certainly – and quite naturally – didn't take to them. They were, after all, gratifying their aching curiosity, and trying to apply a soothing poultice to their own dereliction of duty. Tom accepted the way Peter was rejecting – and humiliating – them, and shut up.

The talk spluttered on, with Robyn unable to justify herself under the boy's cryptic questions. Finally, Robyn asked, "Shall we meet again?"

"I don't think so." The answer was quick, dismissive, with even a touch of contempt.

They all stood up and Tom took the calloused hand again, which was grudgingly extended. Robyn got in front of Peter, trying to propel herself into his arms, but he half-turned away, fending her off with his forearm. She gave a moan and ran out of the room.

"Best of luck, Peter," he said, turning away from Peter and raising his arm in a salute as he went.

He followed Robyn, who had already disappeared. The social worker stood by a desk with a file in her arms.

"How did it go, Mr Stavely? Mrs Stavely was upset."

"Not well," Tom said, "but thanks for your trouble."

The social worker nodded as though that was to be expected. And wasn't it? Tom thought.

He caught Robyn up in the street. They went into a

Starbucks. By the time he had brought two hot cartons of Americano to the table, Robyn had recovered herself.

"We got what we asked for," he said. "It was a stupid and very embarrassing enterprise."

"If you hadn't kept interrupting all the time – "

"*I* kept interrupting?"

"We had to see him," she insisted.

"Our curiosity and guilt. I don't blame him being touchy."

"He's a workman, Tom. A bloody paper-hanger. So different from us." She said this as though it was a fault of Peter's.

"Peter isn't so different."

He didn't say why. Sure, he, Tom, had the lawyerly veneer; he spoke and dressed like the middle-class business executive he was, but he was still the son of a flunky. He had had twenty or more years of this polish, but he could still feel that it was wafer thin. Of course Robyn was more remote; neither she or her family thought much about tradesmen.

"Oh, don't be silly," she smiled. She had played out the scene and moved on.

Tom realised that the meeting had provided her with the insight she needed. He could almost see her neurotic concerns fading. She could now regard Peter as a lost cause, a person who was irretrievably committed to a course that was different from hers, and somehow less worthwhile. Her thoughts about the part of her that was loose in England would be correspondingly feebler. For himself, he was deeply depressed by his part in the massive change that they had wrought in Peter's life.

"We've created a painter and decorator, Robyn."

"He likes it. That's what he wants."

"No, that's what he got. We dropped him in a slot; it happened to be a tradesman's slot. It might have been an academic's slot, or an artist's, or a civil servant's, but it wasn't. There's nothing wrong with his trade, but just think how different his life would have been as our son."

"Well, he can get out of it. I offered him money, education…"

"Oh yeah. *Now,* she says. You've given him all the wonderful opportunities, haven't you? Don't you see, he's a fucking house painter? He paints houses. He'll paint houses all his life. He'll get up early in the morning before his kids are out of bed, grab a piece of toast and jump into his white van, with a ladder on top, and drive for miles. He'll paint and paint and drink milky tea sitting on a cold stone wall in the drizzle. He'll hang wallpaper and some old cow will say to him, 'There's a wrinkle over here… Do this bit again.'"

Robyn was actually grinning – which emphasised the wrinkles forming around her mouth and on her cheeks. "It's not so bad. He can take his family to the Costa del Sol in summer and eat fish and chips on the beach."

He couldn't summon anger in his clashes with Robyn any more; she was as distant as a short-tempered taxi driver, or a woman ramming her baby carriage through a supermarket queue. Seeing the reality of Peter's lost possibilities, and understanding his part in them, was a jolt as hard as a blow on the head. He had participated in the theft of Peter's options in life – as he had suspected long before this meeting – but now he would continue to see Peter when sleep departed at 3am; a fleshed out person with a ladder and splashed overalls.

He kept his promise to himself to call Patricia Hedley and

she invited him to visit. He did so in part because he was curious to see how she was faring, and partly in memory of George. He had been George's best man at his wedding. George had died in New Zealand when Tom was in London, and he hadn't seen Patricia since a year before that time.

The Hedley home was a bungalow in a quiet and prosperous street in Geraldine. Patricia, who was working in the front garden, pulled off her gloves and welcomed him at the gate. She was exceptionally well-groomed for a gardener. They hugged sedately and, as with so many of his meetings with old friends, they studied each other across a chasm without saying more than a few words of greeting.

"Nice car," she said, looking at the vehicle he had parked opposite. "The Ashton Bentley?"

Odd that she should know that, but it was a showy car. "Sure. I've never driven or even ridden in a Bentley or a Rolls before. You have to try everything, if you get the chance," Tom said.

"And?"

"A bit gross and quite unnecessary."

She hesitated. "Oh, I don't know."

"I like the new house," he said. It looked modern and confident, expensive; architect designed, he guessed.

"I sold the farm after George died and bought this place," Patricia said, leading him to a seat in an orangery overlooking the garden. "It was nearly new and one of the couple who built it died, so…their retirement dreams ended."

"The girls don't plan to take up the plough?"

"Hardly. They're at uni and after that I suppose they'll be travelling abroad or living in the city. They're doing cityish things, you know, computers, finance, and they have cityish boyfriends – not like George."

"What about you?"

"I'm stuck here," she smiled, serene but not enthusiastic. "And not uncomfortable, by any means."

"But stuck. I see my sister. We don't holiday together. You know, she's a nun. I see the girls, but they don't want me hanging around their lives except at Christmas. Maybe a weekend at Queenstown with one or other of them. But that's it."

"You don't get away on a holiday on your own?"

"I keep thinking about it."

"What do you actually do when you're here, Patricia?"

"Oh, all the usual things. I play tennis and bowls. Walk. Voluntary work for a charity. I'm on the church committee. There's plenty to do."

Patricia would be about forty-five, perhaps a few years older, and she seemed to regard herself as old, or at least retired. And yet she was a comely woman of good, even voluptuous shape and obvious good health. With her cashmere sweater and tweed skirt, she wasn't sending any sexual signals, but she must have had the scope if she wished. Her hair was carefully cut and combed, and probably dyed that straw colour; her complexion was pale and smooth. She had a natural smile.

"It sounds as though you think of yourself as seventy," Tom said wryly.

He had a long draught of the lime juice Patricia had given him and surveyed a scene of domestic comfort, the couches and chintzy curtains, the bookcase, the wide window sill with its vases of begonias, the spaniel asleep on a mat. Everything was in its expected place, a version of what everybody strives for. And yet he had a sense of waste. This woman with half her life before her seemed to have stopped living. She was in a mausoleum surrounded by her comforts. The spaniel might as well be stuffed; the flowers, wax.

"I don't think of my age very much, Tom."

"I hope not. You're a young woman with many miles to go."

She was evidently embarrassed that he had touched a nerve. "And you, Tom, are a young man. You look very fit. I know you must be happy with Alison."

"Yes, but I have to work for my living, bringing up children while you are… at leisure."

"You're having a second run with Alison, which is marvellous. You deserve it. You know I never was very keen on Robyn myself. You've got a new life with all the striving and stress of any family life. I don't want a second run. I feel that what I had with George was enough for me. I can't imagine starting again, because that's what it would be, getting used to somebody else, accommodating them…"

"Comparing them with the past." He thought of the difficulty of getting used to somebody who held his spoon differently, who changed his socks only when reminded, who farted in bed, and forgot to put the garbage bins out. A new irritant in your life.

"I suppose so. George wasn't perfect, but at least he never upset me."

"George was a good man, and I can understand he's a kind of roadblock in your life."

"No, Tom. He was my life. What I have left is just… the rest, the fag end."

"No, Patricia."

"It's very quiet and also very pleasant. I count myself lucky." She was still smiling.

"Surely some local beau pursues you?"

"Yes, but I draw the line at men who are married, and those who haven't a bean."

He wasn't surprised at the bar on married men. She was

a moral kind of woman, as well as being a practising Catholic. She and George had been two swans, never part of the party set in the past. The indigent male was an understandable problem too. She had money, so how could she ever get a guarantee that it wasn't her main attraction?

"Understood," he said. "That means you're still alive. There is a niche. An umarried man with a bean or two."

"It's not a very big niche and I don't think it can be filled in Geraldine."

"I hope you don't mind me saying so," he said, laughing, "go to Christchurch. Go and stay in Sydney for a while. Take a cruise with a singles company. Do some computer dating!"

"Is it as easy as that?"

"Have you ever tried?"

"I've read the 'man seeks woman' ads in the magazines and I get a bit cynical when I read about so many attractive, unattached and solvent males who strangely have to seek a companion through a dating ad."

"Sure, there's a lot of creeps, male and female, out there, but you can't just moulder away here for the next forty plus years. Give yourself a chance."

She was silent for a moment. "You're right, Tom. You come through the door after however many years and put your finger on the tender part of my existence. I don't talk to anybody about such things, not even my sister. But you're right."

"I'm not a stranger. Remember your wedding day? Your sister Kate, forgive me again, is unlikely to argue against celibacy. The point is, you shouldn't just sit still whether you hook up with anybody else or not. Try it. Experiment. Have some fun."

"I'll think about it. Come and see the garden. The fruit

trees are lovely. You should see the colours in the spring."

She showed him round the garden in a withdrawn manner, and when he declined to stay for dinner, she brought him back to the orangery. He felt she wanted to say something to him, but couldn't quite bring herself to speak. He sat down after mixing Southern Comforts with ice for them both.

"I'll have to get away soon, Patricia."

"Oh, I love this drink," she said, "and I wickedly have one when…"

He wouldn't have thought of her as a solitary tippler. She was so neat, tidy, well-controlled and thought out. "When you have a problem?"

"It's to do with what we were talking about before, Tom. Me, sitting here."

"Afraid to go out and meet the lions."

"Yes. I'd like to tell you. You ought to know. I trust you, Tom. Did you hear about the circumstances… the events around George's death?"

"Not much more than you told me on the telephone. All I heard was that he died suddenly from a heart attack or seizure, and in some ways I understood because he always seemed to like to do hard, physical work. But he was relatively young."

"It wasn't a heart attack, but I suppose that was broadly the story that got around."

"What happened?"

"Suicide."

All his fixed ideas about George lurched. "I'm surprised to hear that. I always regarded George as one of the few people who was unreservedly happy with his lot. I couldn't have done what he did on the farm. It would have been like a sentence in a prison for me, but he loved it."

"He did love the farm, and I believe he loved me. There was a lot of doubt about the cause of his death, but I know it was suicide. Whisky and sleeping pills in a snowstorm on a remote part of the farm. The pathologists report said he had a bad heart, which could have been the cause."

"Health troubles?"

"No."

"Why did he do it, Patricia?"

"He was apparently being questioned in a police enquiry."

"You're telling me something that doesn't seem possible. What was the enquiry about?"

A whole spectrum of possible offences ran through his mind without any one of them associating itself with George. George had a persona that didn't even faintly suggest the possibility of criminality. He even drove his car within the speed limit.

"A sex crime, I suppose you'd call it." She looked pale now, drained.

"That's a big category." He prepared himself to hear about the other woman. Not very likely a man. George was as macho as they come. Certainly not a child; not in the case of George Hedley.

She put her empty glass down on the side table and straightened her shoulders. "Indecent assault on a boy."

Ten guesses might have got him to indecent assault, but not on a boy. Yes, this was the countryside where tough, fit men, sometimes men who were starved of women, wrestled with sheep and cattle. Adrenalin and testosterone pulsed. And so sex happened in odd ways. Rarely? Frequently? How could anybody know? And it was a crime.

"That's incredibly out of character, virtually unbelievable."

"I know."

"Who was the other party?"

"A boy of fourteen who was in care. Somebody George was supposed to be mentoring in farm studies for a charity."

"And the discovery was enough to cause George to...?"

"I believe so, Tom."

He found it hard to understand why a man should value a spurious reputation for probity enough to kill himself. But shame could burn in some people like sulphuric acid. Stuart felt shamed by his failures on Mt Vogel.

"There's no doubt is there, Patricia? You know, proof..." He was thinking as a lawyer.

"I don't think there's any doubt. I don't even have that comfort. There's a public track which crosses the farm to the north. I understand George was seen with the boy by two trampers, strangers to the district, who were using the track. They complained to the police, and they produced a photograph taken with a telescopic lens, although I've never seen it. I got the impression that there wouldn't have been a complaint, but for these witnesses. The boy wasn't complaining. An enquiry, not limited to George, had been going a while, but I never knew anything about it until after George's death. I probably would never have known, but the local police sergeant thought I might be worried that the enquiry would continue and awful things would come out. He wanted to assure me that the file was closed, and that there would be no mention of the complaint at the inquest."

"And mercifully the newshounds never got wind of the complaint."

"The police were pretty good about shutting it up. George was a Mason and so is the sergeant and the coroner. The verdict was death as a result of heart failure. He was buried as a highly respected person."

He lay back on the cushioned couch and contemplated

this abnormal but virtually private stain on what must have been two near-blameless lives. Was Patricia blameless? He could hardly ask, even assuming there was a certain aridity in her relationship with George, why George should prefer a boy to her. That's how it would sound. That would be a question too far. The reality for him wasn't too hard to imagine. A sudden surge of sexual feeling in the heat and imagined solitariness of the farm. He'd had the feeling himself, the erection. There was surely something sexy about the lonely outdoors, with the wind blowing the grass and trees gently in the sunshine. What happened may have had little to do with the relationship with Patricia.

"Well, Tom?"

He could see from the stiffness of her jaw and the way she was braced in the chair how hard it had been to talk, and that the complexities of her sexual relationship with her husband were beyond mention even in their frank talk.

"It's not a big deal, and you shouldn't let it shock you into immobility – as I think it has," he said.

She thought about this and seemed to accept. They finished their drinks and promised to meet at the wedding. "Petra's a lovely girl, Tom. I hope she'll be happy," she said. But when he closed the front gate of Patricia's cottage, his vision of the Hedleys was reeling.

After dinner that night at Tamaki Downs, Tia and Stuart went to the study to work on one of his scripts and Tom was left with Robyn. He mentioned his visit.

"What did you make of Patricia?" Robyn asked with a self-satisfied smile.

"A little bit lost after her husband's death and unable to move forward."

"She's too perfect, isn't she? I only hope Stu doesn't go on with her. I want Tia to have a fair chance."

"What are you telling me? You mean she's one of Stuart's...?"

"Sure. Didn't you know? Quite a few people know it. Not George - in his time. If he did know, he didn't object."

"How long?"

"Oh, years, I suppose."

"Years! Do you think it's still going on...?"

"Could be. I hope not, for Tia's sake, but..."

He thought of the composed, even slightly prim woman with whom he had spent the afternoon, so convincing in her quiet solitariness and rigid social morality.

"I'm astonished. I can't reconcile that with the Patricia Hedley I know. I always thought of her as the devoted Catholic wife. Even today..."

Robyn brushed this aside. "She has a brilliant act. She'd be quite good on stage. She might have been hurt by the fact that she had become available for marriage and Stuart chose Tia. But I don't think she's given up on Stuart. She's waiting quietly in Geraldine." Robyn clamped her mouth shut confidently.

"But Stuart had others..."

"Certainly. Who knows whether she was number one or number three?" She made a blasé gesture with her hand.

"And George. I always thought of George as a devoted family man."

"Didn't you know that George was gay?"

"No. Not a clue. He and Patricia seemed very happy with their girls. No signs I ever saw. How do you know?"

"He was always involved with so-called charitable work with boys. He wasn't a Catholic himself, but he was pally with the Catholic priest through Patricia. There were complaints and rumours that boiled up more than once, but nothing ever came of them, until just before he died. The police had a case involving several boys, the priest and George, and were about to prosecute. You see the excitement you miss in moving away from here, Tom?"

"How did he die?"

"The official verdict was heart failure due to exposure, but there was a lot of gossip…"

He would be saying to Alison when he called her, 'You can't imagine what I've learned today. Remember George Hedley who died a while ago, and Patricia? I couldn't have been more wrong in my assessment of that couple. I sat and listened to the perfect Patricia this afternoon… I'm giving her a lot of crappy advice as a big brother, all about finding another bloke, and I learn from Robyn that she's always had somebody around the corner and probably still has! What an arse I am!'

Alison would probably observe, 'Robyn has a tongue like a razor.'

But he was in doubt whether he would mention that the bloke was Stuart, or refer to the possible cracks in Stuart's union with Tia. It was a subject Alison would find distasteful, and it would be a slight against his friend.

11

He lay on his bed at Tamaki Downs and talked to Alison in London the day before the wedding.

"Everything ready, Tom?"

"Formally, yes. The marquees are up on the lawn. The delectable food and drink is arriving. The weather report is good. Robyn says everything is going to plan."

"You sound doubtful. What's wrong, then?"

"This Mt Vogel business has cast a shadow. Petra and Darren don't seem interested or concerned, but the old man and Stuart are so much at odds that it's unsettling."

"The news must have travelled around South Canterbury. The guests will know, won't they?" Alison asked.

"Oh, yes, but they won't quite know what to make of it at this point. It's one of those stories which will gather momentum and excite more interest."

"Tom, *The Times* has a story today about Mt Vogel, what a difficult mountain it is, and the history, and what a distinguished climber Ernest is. It talks about the Swiss report, but it's all queries."

"If the full story comes out, it's going to be widely reported."

"Will it come out?"

"There's nothing much to go on if the notebook isn't seen by anybody. You remember I told you Bill Stavely's actual declaration that he made it?"

"Who knows about the notebook?"

"Only Ernest, Stuart and me. But we don't know if the Swiss team photographed any of the papers they saw."

"What does Ernest actually *say?* You're with him."

"It depends when you talk to him. One moment it's absolute denial, and the next, a kind of acceptance, but with complete contempt about any efforts to get at him. He really is a wicked old bugger. What I found in speaking to him was the absolute impossibility of their problem on the mountain. I'm not talking about how or when my old man fell, or what Ernest might have done or not done – we'll only be able to surmise that. I think it just could not be, it could not happen, that Ernest was bested by his bag-carrier. Ernest would have been destroyed by that. His whole future depended on stopping that. There were only two possible outcomes in his mind; either they both climbed the peak, in which case Bill would play Tensing to Ernest's Hillary, or Ernest achieved it alone."

"Is Ernest *that* hubristic?"

"I believe so. That's what it is, hubris. He's mired in it. I'd guess his mood when he descended the mountain was near suicidal until he was gifted with a way to claim the victory for himself. When he left my father for dead and descended, he must have been seething in confusion. He never radioed his base camp, claiming his radio was broken, and the first words spoken, according to his own account, were from his team when he arrived – fulsome congratulations, based on the radio message from the spotter plane, and the arrogant assumption that the spotter must have seen Ernest. He didn't have to claim a victory; it was given to him. And perhaps, in a flash, he thought, why not?"

"What does Stuart say to him?"

"They keep apart. Ernest more or less lives upstairs. Has his meals brought to him by Beryl."

"She's still there? I remember her."

"Yeah, crusty old stick, fawning over Ernest."

"Is Stuart still going to climb Mt Vogel?"

"Yeah. He's busy with preparations."

"It seems like an illogical reaction."

"It is, but it's his way of engaging with the problem. Better than going upstairs and choking his father."

"Say he succeeds on the mountain, would it make that much difference?"

"Well, he would join very select company... Yes, it would redeem *him* in a way. It would, at the same time, focus public attention more closely on what happened with Ernest."

"Can he succeed, Tom?"

"All the odds are against him, if you look at Mt Vogel's record."

"A kind of do or die effort?"

"I think it is. Sadly. He's fit enough physically, but I don't think he's well enough to make the judgments the climb will involve. He'll be risking the lives of his companions."

"Can't you talk to him?"

"I've tried. It's no good. He won't listen to me."

"What about Tia? She has influence with him, from what you've said."

"She has, but no."

"Then he won't listen to anyone. It sounds awful, and I'm glad you're not involved, even in a supporting role. Nobody should encourage him. Is Stuart making too much of the damage he's going to suffer?"

"No, I don't think so. What's happened is a stain on the kind of life he wants - the brave climber-journalist, the cultured adventurer, the man of the outdoors. Whether the facts come out or not, Stuart is already undermined. He knows the truth, knows that the whole *Fateful Snows* thing is

175

a fraud. Nobody could forget this taint. Stuart has tied himself up with his father's following, and with *The Fateful Snows*. He did it, I think, in the belief that he could best his father in both mountaineering and writing. Besting his father has become a kind of mania. Now he could be notable because of his father's wickedness, instead of being seen as the son of a hero, who is himself a hero. You know how people behave over this sort of thing. They don't say anything, but back off after a while. Stuart could find he's not the sought after celebrity *he* thought he was in mountaineering."

"It sounds like the same disease as Ernest has. Hubris."

"Ernest has always been bigger than Stuart and Stuart has always played the 'son

of Ernest' prominently as part of his game. Now, by this monstrous act, Ernest has increased his shadow, which we find is very ugly. A vital point is that you and I might not think it's that important, but Stuart *feels* it deeply as a betrayal and a potential public put-down."

"Stuart can turn his journalism to another field, or work in the family business."

"Of course he can! He has the ability, the financial security and a world of other opportunities. But he wants what he wants."

"Come home soon."

"You'd be interested to see all this, Ally."

"Hearing from you is enough. I don't want to participate in the orgy. I know what it'll be like. Everybody will arrive, decked out in the latest fashion, and in three or four hours they'll be throwing up over the roses."

"It won't be like the old days, Ally."

"We'll see. You take care when you meet the scrawny crows of yesteryear. And tell Petra I'm thinking of her, and wishing her the loveliest day in a long, long marriage."

He had seen the guest lists. The wedding was to be a great dynastic event, with Ernest's younger brothers and sister, and their children, plus two hundred and fifty guests from all over New Zealand and abroad. Petra and Darren were like dolls in this ritual; an essential, but not a talking or feeling part. If Stuart cheated his father by marrying on the marae, that situation was to be reversed now. The preparations had been going on for weeks, as the Downs was made ready.

He viewed the event, as Robyn envisaged it, as embarrassingly excessive; more an excuse for the Ashtons to celebrate themselves. Petra and Darren were pleasant young people, but their wedding wasn't exactly a noteworthy union, and they wouldn't know many of the people present. It was Robyn's show, and in her mind seemed to be just that - a show. She was very good at organising shows. He had never questioned her motives behind this one, or even intimated his feelings; to do so would only evoke a rebuff. 'You'd deny your daughter the best…'

Robyn hoped that the weather would permit a reception in marquees on the lawn, but plans were laid to move the whole party under cover in the house if necessary. Rooms that had been virtually unoccupied over recent years had been thrown open and redecorated. The guest wing, usually cold and deserted, but luxurious, had been made ready.

In all this, Beryl Dilsey, the housekeeper, had been pushed aside. He had seen her tight-mouthed submission to the director whom Robyn had employed to organise and manage the party. He was a bustling young man in a dark suit with thick spectacles who was always moving, not looking at anybody, but speaking out of the corner of his mouth.

The director had brought caterers from Christchurch and a 'television' chef was in charge of the menu and wines. In the last few days, trailer trucks had unloaded a huge variety of local and international seafood, meats, fish, game and poultry to be stowed in refrigerated cabins, and an elaborate camp kitchen at the rear of the house, discreetly hidden from the view of guests.

As he strolled around the manicured grounds and through the refurbished reception rooms, he couldn't help thinking that this could have been his wedding to Robyn in 1984. Nothing was very different; the lawns, the gardens, the marquees, the chef, the musicians, the complexion of the guest list – even many of the guests, businessmen, politicians, a sprinkling of judges, senior civil servants and military men. Tomorrow, when the tables were laid and decorated with flowers, he expected this eerie feeling to be confirmed. The bid for the 'wedding of the year' status was as evident now as it had been when he and Robyn married. He wondered if in some strange way Robyn was trying to recreate the event, with Petra playing Robyn.

The morning of the wedding was clear and calm. A perfect blue dome topped South Canterbury. Order had returned to the Downs overnight. All the ropes, ladders, electric cables, toolboxes, paint pots, platforms and planks had been stowed away. The florists arrived at 7am with profuse bunches of flowers; rooms and marquees were decorated. The tables were laid with an array of silver and crystal on the starched white cloths. Small huddles of waiters and managers could be seen conferring discreetly in one tent or another. At nine in the morning, all the exquisite presentation lacked was guests.

He breakfasted with the morning-suited Stuart in the dining room. Robyn and Petra were engrossed in their preparations, and ate upstairs, if they ate at all. Ernest had never joined them in the dining room for any meals, an effect which reduced the amount of argument and recrimination, and even produced an uneasy armistice.

He rode to the church with Stuart and Tia in the Ashtons' Bentley. He hadn't bothered to arrange for a morning-suit when he knew he wouldn't be giving away the bride; the navy blue tailored suit he had was smart enough, and when Robyn, meticulous in her survey of detail, had asked him a few days ago what he would be wearing, he pointed out that he wasn't part of the official wedding party. "Second order may dress second order," he said. "You can't expect me to walk around looking like a penguin without a pond." Robyn crimped her mouth together and said nothing. If Alison knew what he had done, she would say it was pusillanimous, but he couldn't resist it. However, he found an immaculate morning-suit with a quiet brocade waistcoat lying on his bed the evening before the wedding. He took pleasure in not wearing it the next morning.

The Springvale Anglican Church was small and the guests overflowed to stand in the aisles and at the back; about fifty could not get in and were on the steps outside, watching a television link. Stuart waited outside for the bride. Tom went inside with Tia and squeezed into a reserved place at the front. Darren and his best man were before the altar, twitching their heads and shoulders like a couple of nervous colts.

Ernest Ashton, jaunty in a grey-tailed coat, orange brocade waistcoat and striped trousers looked proudly around the crowd; there must have been people there who were wondering if he was the man they thought he was. Tom could see the hard brightness of his eyes and teeth. The skull effect of his head was obtrusive, the high forehead, deep eye-sockets and jutting jaw, but age and illness had shrunk his bullock shoulders to a coat hanger. 'The man has a nerve,' he had already said to Alison. 'He seems to be utterly untroubled by the story in the papers, as though he's in another reality, and everything on the Ashton plate is spotless.'

The cranky organ music sent a pulse through everybody as it switched from Mozart and boomed 'Here comes the bride...' rising to split the roof beams. The bride, slim as a child, despite the potential child wriggling in her loins, had a cream silk designer dress with a long train carried by two bridesmaids, and a gossamer veil held in place by a silver tiara with diamond and pearl droplets – an Ashton heirloom. Her mother, in contrast, wore a confection in yellow which sloped from her shoulders like a tent, topped by a wide straw hat of the same colour loaded with imitation fruit.

He'd comment to Alison, 'Petra looked as beautiful as the traditional bride, no baby signs, but Robyn had fallen into the hands of an eccentric, and also no doubt expensive, designer.'

Reverend Beck, the parson, a short, avuncular man with a permanent smile, began the service enthusiastically. How different from Maurice Hewitt who officiated at his marriage to Robyn. Maurice, pallid, almost powdered white, had gabbled the service in a dry voice, seeming to watch Robyn and him sardonically. Maurice could have been saying, 'I've already told you that this marriage is going nowhere, but you haven't listened or understood, so I'll treat it as a formality.' Tom didn't think that at the time of course; he merely regarded Maurice's performance as lacklustre.

When the parson asked who would give Petra away, he

came back to the present and felt a jab of wrath, but he was close enough to see how preoccupied Stuart was; he was collapsed and grey. 'I didn't give a damn, him giving Petra away,' Tom thought he would say to Alison later. 'After all, it's part of a meaningless medieval ceremony, and what does it matter?' Of course he *did* give a damn, but he had to retain a shred of self-respect. Instead, he would tell Alison about Stuart: 'He isn't the urbane adventurer this morning. Not at all. The Mt Vogel poison is in the air.'

He didn't go into the vestry with Robyn and Stuart when the couple signed the marriage register; he waited outside with Tia under the trees. Mark Curran approached them. He greeted Tia and then put a hand on Tom's arm, drawing him away.

"What's going on, Tom? This stuff about Ernest on TV and in the *Christchurch Sun?*"

He thought Mark would be the first of many who would approach him today. "It's true that there's some question whether Ernest climbed Mt Vogel."

Mark's breathing surged. "Jesus, that can never be! What's going to happen?"

"I don't know. It may go away." That was a less than honest opinion; it would never go away, but he didn't want to feed Mark's fears.

The sun, coming through the yellowing leaves of the tall beech trees, dappled the happy crowd. The conversation was abruptly ended when the bridal couple emerged from the church in a furious peal of bells, a cloud of confetti and warm cries. A guard of honour had been provided by members of Darren's team. Tom noticed a missing member of the guard seated on the kerb fifty yards away, with his hungover head between his knees; it was another curious parallel with his own wedding, when one of the kilted Black

Watch guardsmen from his territorial regiment collapsed in the sun on the steps from the after-effects of stag night. If Darren had had a hard stag night too, it didn't show in the rubbery youthfulness of his face. Tom must have been the tenth or fifteenth person in the rush to kiss the bride, but she was oblivious.

The reception at the Downs would not begin for two hours, giving the guests plenty of time to drive there. He travelled back to the Downs in the car with Robyn, Tia and Stuart.

Robyn relaxed confidently on the cushions. "That was really perfect, and very touching, wasn't it?"

He and Tia agreed, but Stuart looked silently out of the window.

"What's the matter with you, Stuart? You're so glum. It's a great day!" Robyn said.

Stuart swung round to them. "You realise what's happening, don't you?" he said fiercely.

Robyn looked alarmed at his tone and pointed guardedly toward the back of the driver's seat. The driver was Ted Cross, a gardener-handyman at the Downs.

Stuart's face collapsed into deep rifts. "OK," he sighed.

They were silent for the rest of the journey, except for Robyn's occasional and trivial comments on the guests at the church. When they arrived at the Downs, she insisted that the four of them go into the study.

"Now, what is it, Stu?" she asked, closing the door.

"While we're bumming up Petra's wedding, and performing like lords of the manor, feeding all these prats with every conceivable delicacy and drowning them in the best Bollinger, this vile story is seeping into every earhole here and in the country. The implication is that Ernest is a fucking liar and fraud, and maybe even a killer. And his son who climbed up on his back? He's a - "

"We'll come through this. It'll be a nine-day wonder. Don't you agree, Tom?" Robyn said briskly.

"Sure."

Stuart turned on him. "You're not saying much, are you Tom? Because I'm right. It's not going to snuff me out, because people are too decent for that. I'll just wither on the vine. Less offers to do projects. Less offers to do TV programmes and write articles. I'll be the son of the infamous Ernest Ashton. And how infamous will he be shown to be? Fraud and lies are one thing - we see plenty of it - but the theft of a dead man's achievement on Mt Vogel is about as low as anybody can go. It's a kind of desecration of the corpse. Ernest will be long remembered for being uniquely vile."

Robyn seemed unimpressed. "It's not *that* bad, Stuart."

"It's the end for me!"

"No, Stuart," Tom said, in a flat tone of disbelief.

"What do you mean about Dad possibly being a killer?" Robyn asked. "I mean, surely Tom, you don't think your father was murdered?"

"No, I don't. It's not even an issue; it's an innuendo in the newspapers."

He had thought about murder, and while it was a possibility, it would always be impossible to know. A man capable of basing his reputation on a fraudulent claim had an unusual mind, and could perhaps be capable of murder. But he had tested himself by asking what he would do if he learned conclusively that Ernest killed his father. The answer was ready and simple: nothing. And what would he feel? Nothing different, because his feelings against Ernest had always been at high tide. He had long ago worked out that his own future was improved by the death. Perhaps he would puzzle the causes more deeply, dwell on the connection between his mother and these two men, and whether that played a part, but he would never fathom it.

"There, you see…" Robyn said, trying to sweep away problems before the reception. "And why can't we sue for libel? All these innuendoes."

Stuart stared at Tom. Tom was immobile.

"All right!" Stuart began when he saw Tom wasn't going to answer. "We're not suing because we can't."

"Why?" Robyn wailed.

There was a pause. Robyn looked from her distraught brother to Tom, and back, and, Tia, with tears in her eyes.

"Because it's fucking well true! Our shitting father never climbed that mountain!"

"But how do you really know?" Tia asked softly.

"Ask him," he said, pointing at Tom.

"Tom, tell us, for God's sake," Robyn said.

Tom moved his shoulders and furrowed his brow but didn't speak.

"Oh, Tom, don't let us have any of that noncommittal lawyer stuff from you. Not now. Not on this," Robyn, with two bright red spots on her cheeks, shrieked.

"Leave it where it is, Robyn," Tom said. "No lawsuits." He thought Stuart might have taken some heart from his omission to mention the notebook.

"You know what these hacks are, Robyn," Stuart said. "As soon as they've got a story, they deconstruct it and pitch in a few new theories. They don't have any evidence. They won't say Ernest killed Bill Stavely. They'll say a cloud hangs over Bill's death. They'll invite you to speculate. They're already doing it. The only witness to what happened is utterly discredited. They can have a ball!"

Tom thought he needed to remind them of something unpleasant. "I think you ought to be prepared for a police enquiry…"

"But why, Tom?" Robyn wailed.

"Because once the police hear that Ernest may have told lies about an event involving a death, they'll be bound to enquire. There's probably sworn evidence before the coroner's court giving Ernest's view of how my father died. If events now throw that into question…"

"Oh, hell!" Robyn said.

"I don't think an enquiry will get anywhere. It'll just be an unpleasant formality, but there'll be publicity."

Stuart was looking at him darkly. "And can you imagine where this thing will go if the police find out that Ernest had been fucking Tom's mother *before* the Mt Vogel climb?" Stuart said.

A silence fell for a moment.

Tia, her face stony, had been watching them, round-eyed. "Oh, Stu…" she said quietly, slipping her arm around his waist.

"You mean a kind of motive of Dad's to kill… Was he… doing that?" Robyn asked, although she must have heard gossip over the years.

"I believe so," Stuart said, looking at Tom.

Tom managed a rueful grin. "I won't be saying so. It's past and it's gone."

"It just gets more and more dirty," Tia said.

"And it's that man up there," Stuart said, pointing to the ceiling.

"Please. Let's put on a good show for Petra," Tia said.

At the reception, he was redeemed by Robyn, who allocated

him a seat next to her, despite her disapproval of his dress. "You look as though you just walked out of your office," she said. There was no way he could say a sane word to his daughter, one place along the table. She was greeting the onslaught of remarks from everybody with a vacuous smile. Tom faced the many ranks of excited people across the tables, gabbling and quaffing champagne, while the waiters hovered above with their laden trays. In this position, he was safe from enquiries about Ernest by the curious. Ernest had been tactfully placed at the other end of the table well separated from Tom and Stuart. Tom drank little himself; he enjoyed the Maine lobster (specially flown in, as though the native crayfish was not good enough) and listened attentively to the speeches and toasts. The ceremonies were mastered in a low key by a cousin of Stuart and Robyn. The best man was as eloquent as he was athletic with a perfectly memorised collection of jokes; Darren's few words were, to Tom, surprisingly apt, as were all the toasts; they might have been taken from a manual on etiquette.

Behind the wall of chatter, he rehearsed in his head what he would say to Alison. 'Oh, hell, Ally, it was so desperately predictable, and boring, and false, from the parson's nonsense about being grateful for the food – as though we were starving – all these overweight, red-faced people who couldn't wait to gulp the oysters and tear into the beef fillet. But nobody vomited, told a dirty joke, forgot their lines, or shed a tear. In Robyn's word, perfect. All caught on camera and video too, for the society columns and mags.'

Robyn interrupted his thoughts as they ate. She put her head close. "Reminds me of our wedding, Tom. You know, the marquee, the lovely day," she said quietly and with the fluidity of at least five glasses of champagne. She sighed.

"I had noticed. In some ways, a remake."

"Yes… I tried to remember everything about our beautiful time, and make it the same. Even the flowers and decorations, get the colours right…"

"You certainly succeeded." It was something he didn't understand about Robyn. Their marriage was a crashing failure, and she wanted to imitate the pomp that started it.

"I wish things had worked out differently, Tom." She placed her fingers affectionately on his wrist, on the bare flesh below the cuff, and turned her big, sore-looking eyes on him.

"So do I, but we have to accept…"

The current of rose-tinted retrospection changed direction when she heard his arid words. "You never fought to save the marriage."

"Robyn, surely this isn't the place…"

She turned away. Her eyes were wet.

The guests drifted away in little knots after a couple of hours to sub-parties in other marquees, and the bride and groom made slow, kissy-huggy progress through them, into the house to change. Then, an hour or so later, many guests reassembled in the hall and the porch; the word had spread that Petra and Darren were leaving. More cuddles and cries of affection, and the two young people, flushed and fresh, settled into Darren's silver Mercedes for the journey to Christchurch and beyond. This was where Tom's wedding day with Robyn took a different track. Yes, the reception was similar, but the party…

All he could remember of the post-reception party at Tamaki Downs, was the dancers circling in a darkened room like scraps of bright coloured paper floating in a bowl. Then he was lying on the bathroom floor, his eyes not quite closed and his hearing working perfectly. A crowd had gathered outside the bathroom door. Robyn leaned on the door frame.

"If you've come to see him, then have a good look," Robyn said, standing aside and gesturing to the people behind her. She was dressed in a tailored costume, ready to travel. "Sober him up if you can. But it doesn't matter. I'll drive."

One or two people bent over him. Stuart pushed them away, seriously trying to revive him, but he was covertly conscious.

Alison Hewitt sat on the edge of the bath, her dreamy face disturbed. She looked down sadly at him, and then spoke to Robyn who still stood calmly by the door. "Look what you've done to him…"

"Listen to her. What will she say next? Don't have any more champagne, dear."

The stupid giggles and comments from the onlookers dried up.

"You better go home to your husband. I'll get somebody to drive you." Robyn's voice mounted in volume suddenly, like an actor beginning an important speech; it had a commanding effect, a masculine quality.

Alison, sobbing, was helped to her feet. Her coat was passed to Robyn, who threw it over the edge of the bath carelessly. "Take a couple of aspirin."

He sat up, mumbling, feigning more incompetence than he felt because there was no intervention he could usefully make in this hysterical scene. Alison, crying, was being led to the door. Somebody made a comment to Robyn that wasn't audible to him. She rounded on the speaker harshly.

"What? That stupid dough-face? And my husband? He's *my* husband!"

She stalked away into the reception room where there was still music in the darkness, leaving him on the floor with those ministering to him.

"There goes your daughter, Tom," Robyn said triumphantly, squeezing up beside him as they watched the car ease down the drive and disappear behind the hedges.

"I hope they make out all right," he replied, wanting to say, 'This is all completely wrong, you know, and Petra hasn't given herself much of a chance.'

"Why shouldn't they make out? You always were cynical and negative, Tom. And don't forget that if Darren goes astray, Petra always has the independence that money brings. She'll divorce him and get somebody else."

"Sounds… easy." The silly cow didn't realise, after all the pain she'd suffered, that it wasn't easy. It was a train wreck, every time.

'Yes,' he would say to Alison, 'This is quintessential Robyn. Buy another husband if the old one sods off.'

'Robyn hasn't found another, though,' Alison might say.

'She only has to snap her fingers, Ally, to get a man. All that money. But it isn't easy to fit somebody else into your life, not a life as fancy free as hers.'

"Anyway," he said to Robyn, "I congratulate you on directing another first class performance. Absolutely what I would expect from somebody with your talents."

She looked at him with a flicker of confusion, unable to tell whether he was serious. Then she put her arm through his and walked him away from the others. "I'm worried about Dad and Stuart. They seem to have been… I don't know … watching each other… waiting."

"Until Petra and Darren are out of the way?"

"What do you think? Am I imagining it? I've been feeling the friction between those two for thirty years or so. I tend to ignore it; we have calm periods, but the clouds have built up so horribly over this Mt Vogel business."

"I don't think either of them would have wanted to disturb Petra's wedding."

"And now?"

"I don't know."

"Aren't you going to tell me now why you're so sure Dad is -"

"No, I'm not going to tell you."

"But -"

He heard raised voices in the hall. He identified Stuart's voice. He and Robyn moved into the hall to find a circle of guests around a young man whom Stuart was pushing into an armchair, his fist crumpling the man's shirt and tie. With his other hand, Stuart was wrenching at a video camera that was secured by a strap around the man's neck. The man himself was choking under the pressure of Stuart's fist. Stuart dragged the strap over the man's head, flung the camera to the floor and stamped on it. The crowd were silent with amazement. He hauled the man to his feet and bundled him out of the front door.

"Ted!" he shouted at the handyman who was on the path. "Get this trespasser off the property!" He pushed the man down the steps into Ted's arms and stood panting. Ted walked the man away down the drive.

"Bloody creep!" Stuart said, as he faced the guests. "Snooping around here taking pictures and asking questions."

"This is it. The press are here. It's Mt Vogel," Tom said to Robyn.

12

The party had started to wilt soon after the bride and groom left the table in the afternoon. The dark mood of Stuart and his father had infected the gathering. The guests knew from the newspapers and television that a scandal was brewing, enough to set them on edge, but little more. Many guests approached Tom privately, and all were bemused by the prospect that Ernest's greatest achievement was a fiction; it was almost more than they could believe. Tom gave no support to the stories, but neither did he refute them. He was aware that his failure to deny the truth of the rumours tended to give them credence, but he thought that was just too bad.

Ernest had coasted around the groups of guests, being received on the rim of various parties as the paterfamilias he was, and in no cooler fashion than he was accustomed to. People had heard but could make no judgement. Tom met him as he was leaving the dining room, rocking unsteadily.

"You've got your little girl off, have you? What a very good job you've done," Ernest slurred.

"Thanks, Ernest. Praise from you is indeed praise." Tom was equally cold.

"I was pleased to see you didn't try to give her away at the church. Not your place, as I told Robyn long before the wedding. Not you, not the vanishing man."

"That was helpful and well-meant advice I'm sure. I've always thought of you as the guardian of propriety."

"And fortunately there wasn't a space for you to jump up and make a speech and tell us what a splendid chap the father of the bride is, ha-ha!"

"You, at least, Ernest, already know how splendid I am. Sleep well. Be wary. As I've hinted before, take care your son doesn't come in the dark to kiss you goodnight."

Ernest's alchoholic jollity froze. His lips parted as though he was going to take a bite. "I'll take care." He swayed through the door toward the stairs.

What had been planned by Robyn as a banquet with unceasing hospitality lasting late into the night had become a desert of scattered tables and chairs by early evening, with dirty dishes, twisted tablecloths and table napkins collapsed on the floor like dead doves. The string quartet had played ever more quietly in the late afternoon and ceased when they had nobody except waiters to play to. The catering staff moved in to clear the tables and the air resounded with the warlike crashing of crockery and the rattle of cutlery. The marquees and rooms became desolate. Those who might have stayed to party preferred to go to friends in Springvale, or Geraldine.

Tia appeared to have summed Stuart up as immovable in the evening when he was in the library, drinking. He refused her invitation to go upstairs with her and she whispered to Tom, "I'll leave him with you, Tom. He needs looking after." Even Robyn, before she left for the Currans' party in Springvale - to which Tom had been invited - made him promise to stay with Stuart.

"I'm very worried about those two," she said, "and it's spoiled the wedding party. I was hoping we would have a wonderful time *here,* but it's dead."

Tom had this duty put upon him, but it was one he would have performed anyway, without the requests.

He and Stuart continued drinking in the library when

the guests had gone and the housekeeping staff had been banished from the room. Tom put aside his abstemiousness of earlier in the day and they consumed beer and a large part of a bottle of whisky. Their talk was drunken and desultory, memories and trivial argument, and Tom would have been glad to have retired at about midnight, but for Stuart's morose focus on his father, to which the dialogue always returned. He listened to Stuart's rambling monologues of hatred and despair, only to be sure that Stuart would eventually go safely to bed. It was 3am when he levered himself upright and tossed down what was left of his drink, his patience gone.

"I'm for sleep, man. What about you?" he asked.

"You haven't mentioned the notebook," Stuart slurred.

"Let it rest. This isn't the time."

"Ish time."

"Let it rest then, forever. Let's think the notebook doesn't exist, Stu."

"You mean that?"

"It's the way I feel."

"But it does exist, and if you want to forget it, give it to me."

"Resting forever isn't enough? You have to ask for more?"

"I'm a supplicant at the altar of Thomas Stavely. I beg for more. Please answer my prayer and give me the notebook."

"It's my father's book, the record of something he did in life. Can you understand as a creative and sensitive man, knowing my history, that the notebook is something I would want to keep?"

"Your very fine feelings! What about my feelings, having you holding my neck under a guillotine, the guillotine of loss of reputation!"

"You don't trust me to keep the notebook privately?"

"No, I don't. Would you want your reputation in somebody else's hands to destroy at a whim?"

"You're my friend. I don't act on a whim. But I'll think about what you say."

They both stood up. Stuart managed a cracked smile and put his arm around Tom's shoulders. "I ought to beat your head in and take the notebook, but I'll think about what *you* said," he laughed.

They both left the library and stumbled up the stairs, supporting each other.

When they reached the landing, Stuart turned in the wrong direction. "No, this way," Tom said.

"I'm going to talk to Ernest."

"Not at this hour." Tom pulled him back.

"My house. My father, Tom." Stuart pushed his arm away.

"You're not capable of talking to anybody." He grabbed a handful of Stuart's shirt, stopping him.

"Piss off and leave me alone!" Stuart fended him off.

"Don't go there, Stuart. Give up these mad dreams of celebrity. They've possessed you. Your father is a truly vile man. Just let him be that. You can't punish him; he's beyond punishment. Old and diseased. You can't get a reckoning from him. He won't be held to account. If your reputation is lost, it was founded on a lie – his lie, not yours. You have to find a new direction. There's no other way."

"You don't know what it's like to be publicly known for... something considerable... and honourable... and distinguished, *"* Stuart hissed.

"What's your reputation but what you think other people think of you? You yearn to be famous and well-regarded, and you have been. But you haven't any particular *right* to celebrity…" Tom realised his liquored tongue had perhaps flapped too much.

"Rights? And will we have claims and tenure? You sound like a lawyer. Don't lecture me on celebrity when you know nothing about it!"

"Yours is built on your father's lie. That's a fact. You're right that I don't know anything about the adrenalin which puffs you up, but an idiot can see that you have to accept what can't be changed and get beyond it."

The words were said, but he hadn't meant to hit Stuart this hard.

Stuart swayed close to him. "I think you're enjoying this, you faceless, legal scribe!" He shoved Tom, who staggered away.

Tom lost any restraint. "You're a dick, Stu! A huge erect, scarlet penis, bigger than a Ferrari!"

Tom took a few steps toward his own room and stopped. He turned to see Stuart's swerving path down the hall toward Ernest's room. Even in his inebriated state, Tom thought that the confrontation between him and Stuart, despite the passage of years, was still between a son of the manor and a farm boy, just as that between Ernest and his father on Mt Vogel would have been the confrontation between master and man. No matter how deeply overlayed by friendship and even love, who he and Stuart were was wrought in steel in their minds.

As Stuart departed, Tom was left with enough regard to be fearful of what might happen and he tried to decide whether he should shout and make a fuss, or shut up and go to bed. If he made a noise, who would come? Tia was the only other person upstairs in this part of the house. Would she be able to control her drunken husband? Never. And the half dozen people who had stayed over from the wedding were in the guest wing.

On the instant, he compromised and turned to follow Stuart. By the time he had lumbered to Ernest's door, Stuart was inside. The room was lit only by the moonlight, which drenched the cold downs and illuminated the room through the open curtains. He stumbled into a contortion of shadows and human cries.

Stuart and Ernest were on their feet, locked together, groaning, cursing and struggling. He had a picture from the doorway as they clinched. He knew this could only last a few seconds, because although Ernest looked strong, he was frail and no match for his son. It seemed harmless and pointless.

"Break it up, you stupid buggers!" he shouted, and stepped forward to separate them.

At the same moment, there was an explosion which plugged his ears and cut off his hearing. A hot shockwave hit his face and shoulders and peppered his eyes. He fell to his knees. Stuart's head was snapped backwards at an impossible angle and he collapsed to the floor. Invisible to Tom at first, but apparently tangled between the bodies of the two men, was a shotgun which thumped on to the carpet beside Tom. The old man fell back, half lying on the bed. Tom forced himself up from the floor, his mind gyrating crazily, and flicked the lights on.

The shot, which must have come from under Stuart's chin, had blown away all the front of his head. The old man was blue and panting like a dog, his eyes fixed on the body, while a scarlet fringe spread out like a halo around what was left of the head.

"You've shot your son, you evil bastard!" He bent down and touched Stuart's wrist, but there could be no pulse.

"Haaah. I was ready for him. He was going to kill me. I had my faithful Purdey ready."

The old man glinted with triumph, then flinched. The

flame in his eye sockets flickered. His chest heaved. He tried to turn his head toward the table by the bedside.

"The pill – there…"

A white pill, placed on top of its packet in readiness to relieve the seizure, a water jug half full and a glass all waited for this emergency. Tom reached for the pill instantly, and then his eyes met Ernest's eyes, pools of mud and green weed.

Ernest's pathetic look said, 'After all that's been said and done, you're going to save me, aren't you?'

His thoughts in response were as clear for Ernest to read as if they had been written or spoken. 'Do I really have to help a swine like you?'

"I know, you're not prepared to help me. I expected that," Ernest gasped in a moment's hopelessness, and then, when he must have read the drooping lines of Tom's expression correctly, he had a different message, silent and sneering. 'No, you haven't the guts to do what I'd have done. You'll save me!'

Tom's fingers curled slowly around the cold glass handle of the jug. He raised it and poured water into the glass, delaying while the level rose.

"Hurry, Tom…" Ernest croaked.

Only a drop was necessary really.

"Please, Tom…" Ernest's breath rasped in his throat; he had turned a dark, bruised tint.

Tom stopped now, straightened up and looked again at the drooping figure on the bed paralysed in pain, and Stuart's faceless body on the floor. He picked up the pill between finger and thumb, following it with his eyes as it travelled over the small distance from the table, to the gullet which hung open expectantly. Then, instead of dropping the pill in the orifice, he slopped the water in. The old man erupted in a choking convulsion.

When Ernest's spasm had subsided, Tom held up the pill before him.

"Please, Tom…" His voice was faint.

Tom dropped the pill on the carpet and kicked it under the bed. "How do you like that, Ernest?"

Ernest was choking, his chest heaving. He couldn't reply. He tried to rise. It wouldn't have taken much for Tom to put his fingers around Ernest's throat and restrain him. A gentle gesture would do it. He had the thought, but dimissed it. His brain was curdled. After a couple of surging breaths, Ernest was unconscious.

Tom replaced the water glass, stepped carefully over Stuart's body and went out of the door.

He was not reeling drunk now, but scarcely sober; the events of the night were churning their confusing possibilities in his head. He went to his room and splashed his face with water in the bathroom. His body had the heaviness of metal. The destruction of Stuart was an event too monstrous to grasp. He hadn't looked after his friend. He had let Tia and Robyn down. The lawyer in him warned that he had just witnessed a brutal crime, and may, in his passion and drunkenness, have committed a crime himself; there would be consequences.

What *he* had done hadn't been thought out. It had happened. He slumped on the bed for a moment, while he tried to order his thoughts. He had a desire to black out everything that had just happened, the memory of that charnel-house room, but he had to tell Tia now, and call the police. No, call the ambulance service, that would be would be smarter…Why disclose that he knew they were both dead? Why…?

13

Moments later, he awoke with a leaden head, nearly deaf, his eyes glued shut. He opened his eyes. It wasn't moments later; it was dawn!

At first he thought he had awakened naturally, but then he realised that somebody was knocking insistently at the door. He sat up. The door opened before he could speak or get off the bed; it was a young uniformed policeman.

"Mr Stavely? I'd like to talk to you."

His vocal cords were slimed and slack. "By all means... but give me a chance to..."

"You're already dressed, I see."

"Sure... The wedding party..." He coughed.

The constable moved into the room and looked around, examining. "And you haven't slept in your bed."

A new constable from the local station. He couldn't have been more than twenty-one.

"Do you know what's happened, Mr Stavely?"

"I'm not sure... I had a lot of drinks." His mind had no traction, but at least he realized that he should keep his mouth shut for his own protection.

"You've got blood on your shirt, I see." The constable's voice moved up a few notes.

He looked down. The chest of his shirt was flecked with a fine spray of blood. The memory came back. He was sickened. The cop was going to shove him into a hole, a prison hole. "Will you get out of here? Give me a chance to get up, go to the lavatory, if you don't mind, have a wash, and then I'll go downstairs to talk to you!"

The constable, unabashed, looked at Tom curiously. "You haven't answered my question, Mr Stavely. Do you know what's happened?"

"Do you have a warrant, officer?" The constable's keenness was blunted by this random shot. "Breaking into my bedroom, asking questions like the Gestapo!"

Tom didn't think the constable needed a warrant, but the constable was uncertain; it was probably the biggest case in his experience. Tom stared him out. "Remove yourself!"

"I'll see you downstairs," the cop said abjectly as he retired.

Tom's head boiled. It was 7am. He had to think out his story. He tore off his shirt and stuffed it in the laundry bag. He dropped the rest of his clothes on the floor and soaked for a couple of minutes under the shower, trying to blot out Stuart's bloody body and the old man's blue corpse. No time to shave. He pulled on a clean shirt and trousers, then brushed his fingers through his hair.

Who found the bodies? Almost certainly Beryl Dilsey, who prowled the halls before breakfast. Did nobody hear the gunshot last night? That was possible. The house was built like a castle. And what of poor Tia, whom he had meant to see, and really intended to see last night? Beryl Dilsey would have broken the tragedy to Tia as if she was announcing dinner.

He couldn't go down to meet Tia and Robyn without going to Ernest's room first. The hall was empty and quiet. Robyn's bedroom door was open; the room was unoccupied, the bed undisturbed. She hadn't returned from her party. The door of Ernest's room was closed. He opened it, and went in, expecting to find a cop on duty, but there was nobody.

The room had a heavy, sickly metallic smell. The gun was on the floor where it had fallen, a web of blood on its mother-of-pearl inlaid stock. Stuart's body was still on the floor, but covered by a stained white sheet. Ernest's bed was empty; the covers thrown back. He lifted the sheet on Stuart's body; it seemed to have partly sunk into the carpet, distorted in death, the head unrecognisable. His stomach heaved. He dropped the sheet back over the body.

Assuming that the crime scene had been left until a forensic team arrived, the empty bed could only mean that the old sod had survived and been taken to hospital. That was a complication. What would Ernest say about the pill? What would he say about the encounter? He closed the bedroom door on a scene which was as confused as a partly-arranged stage set.

At the foot of the stairs he met a red-eyed Beryl. "Where's Tia, Beryl?"

She marched past, her white face puckered. "Don't speak to me!" she said, and hurried on.

He was alarmed at her remark and would have called her back, but a man he recognised came toward him down the hallway. It was a cop he'd known as a young constable.

"Tom Stavely. Haven't seen you for years. Terrible things, Tom, terrible things." He shook his head hopelessly.

The corpulent Fred Bostock was now a sergeant and probably in charge at Springvale.

"Glad to know you're here, Bossy. I want to talk to Mrs Ashton. Where is she?"

"She's in there, poor lass." He pointed to the study and Bostock made to follow him.

"I'd like to see her alone… You understand?" Tom went in and closed the door on a surprised face before Bostock could work out whether this was right or not.

Tia, her cheeks swollen and red, was sitting straight-backed, open-eyed, frozen on a chair. He rested his hand on her shoulder. She responded by placing her hand over his but remained silent, staring. He didn't have any words to offer. Condolence wasn't enough and this was not the time to try to explain what he knew. After perhaps a minute of silence, he whispered that he would come back and he left the room. He found Sergeant Bostock in the hall using the phone. The constable who had come into his room was standing nearby.

Bostock finished his call and said, "This is Ian Mackie, by the way."

"We've met." He nodded minimally at the expressionless Mackie.

"Ian and I will be holding the fort quietly while a homicide team come up from Timaru. Should be here in about…" Bostock looked at his watch. "Aw, maybe an hour or so… I couldn't believe it when I got a call from old Beryl this morning. Just couldn't believe it. Sir Ernest's gone to the hospital, but I must say he looks bad. And Stuart… it is Stuart, isn't it?"

"Yes."

"I've known Stuart since he was a boy, as long as I've known you…"

A key scratched in the lock of the front door and Robyn came in. Her hair was wild and her complexion yellow. But she smiled.

"Bossy," she said. "What's the problem? Stock on the road? And Tom. You look as bad as I feel. I stayed over at the Currans'–"

She was halted by their staring eyes and immobile faces.

"You better explain, Tom," Sergeant Bostock said.

Bostock was a likeable man, but he was also a cop with

cop instincts. Friendly or not, Bostock would register every word. Robyn was looking at him expectantly, and he could see could see the tiny pulses and tensions massing in her face, her realisation growing that something was badly wrong.

"It's not Dad and Stu is it, Tom?" she whispered.

There was no way he could soften this. "Yes. There's been an accident, Robyn. Stu's been killed, and Ernest is in a bad way."

'Accident' came out quite naturally from the turmoil of light and shadow, and the clash of bodies, and the deafening noise.

She uttered a little cry, and put her hand against the mahogany panelling for support. "Tell me."

"Why don't we go and sit down?" Bostock said.

They went into the library and Robyn collapsed in a chair, head in hands. Bostock and Mackie were looking at Tom, waiting. He didn't know what to say. His thoughts were stumbling. If he said he knew what happened... On the other hand, could he deny that he was there?

He tried to gain more time. "Look, Bossy, I think it would be best if I spoke to Robyn on her own at this stage. It's a very, very…"

"Oh, it's all right, Tom, just tell me," Robyn said, dabbing her wet face with a handkerchief.

The woman didn't see that he wanted to work out his story with her first. He was constrained to go on, or deny that he knew anything. "I think it was a terrible accident... What little I know points to that," he said in a rush.

"Accident?" Robyn echoed, as though it was a strange word in this context.

His mind was focussed on the stark event which actually happened, but in spite of that, the word 'accident' came out again, as he suffered the numbing pain and grief of what had happened to Stuart at the hands of his father. Something inadmissible had happened, something which his dulled mind could hardly grasp, let alone reveal and attempt to explain. Father kills son.

Robyn was waiting, agonized, and the two cops were watching intently, the way that cops do, anxious to get a sight of their prey. He could keep quiet now, claim ignorance, or perhaps there was an opportunity here...

"Stuart and Ernest were evidently talking about Ernest's gun. You know, the one with the inlaid stock. In Ernest's bedroom. They had both had a few too many. The gun must have gone off."

Talking about a gun. Thus the fantasy about the gun was born. He thought he'd taken a protective step for his dead friend, harmless but helpful, the only thing he could think of under the urgent eyes of the watchers.

Robyn's expression showed suspicion, and then as she eyed the two cops, became calculating. "Stu and Dad, talking about the gun...?"

Here they were, talking in front of two cops. If only Robyn had had the sense to see he wanted to talk to her first! "You know how keen on the gun Ernest is. The Purdey," Tom urged, embroidering frantically.

Robyn had her eyes fixed on him mesmerically, trying to work this out. The idea that Ernest and Stuart would be discussing a gun was unlikely and probably ludicrous to her. But she moved her head to assent cautiously. "Sure, very keen..." she whispered, sensing that she ought to be following Tom's lead.

"Father and son," Bostock said matter of factly. "Of course."

"But did they get on together?" Mackie asked.

Robyn looked at Tom.

"Sure," he echoed, as though it would be foolish to suggest anything else. He had to bolster up what he had already said.

"Well enough," Robyn eked out the words.

Mackie now took a step forward. "Mrs Stavely, you asked when you came in whether it was 'Dad and Stu', sort of indicating there was an issue."

Robyn got the point now. "If anything's wrong, why not mention the two men who are dearest to me in all the world?"

Mackie twisted his head to one side. "That isn't what Mrs Dilsey says. She says –"

"Oh, come on, old Beryl…" Tom said, raising an arm to fend the words away. "Lay off the Sherlock Holmes act, will you?"

"Beryl's dotty," Robyn said, her voice shaking and her cheeks puce. "I'd be glad if you'd leave me alone for a while," she said to the police. "I must see Tia. How is she taking this, Tom?"

A police forensics team from Timaru arrived by 2:30pm. He watched from the windows of the drawing room as they extricated themselves and their luggage from their two cars. He could see immediately who was in charge. A man, compact, short, in a tight blue suit, stood away from the others with a briefcase in his hand, watching them, and also scanning the house, appraising it. For a second, his eyes rested on Tom in the window. Then he strode ahead of his team with a duck-like swagger toward the front entrance.

Tom went through to the hall. Bostock had opened the door. "This is Inspector Christopher Stelios, Tom Stavely," he said.

Stelios, was about thirty-five, cheerful, with an olive skin, short black hair and big brown eyes with black eyebrows that met at the bridge of his nose. They shook hands. Tom felt like the proprietor.

Stelios had a low-voiced discussion with Bostock and Mackie and they accompanied him with other officers on a tour of the house. Tom followed the crowd, not party to the conversations, but concerned to get a feel for how the investigation would go. The forensic team were given their orders, mainly for work in Ernest's Room: photographs, scrapings, fingerprints.

Stelios noticed Tom listening and broke off his instructions to approach him. He drew himself up to meet the difference in height of four or five inches. "You needn't bother to be with us, Mr Stavely. When we want you, we'll come and get you."

He emphasised the 'we'll come and get you' with a display of teeth.

"Just in case you wanted any help…"

"We'll let you know. Why don't you wait downstairs?"

Stelios interviewed the housekeeper and staff, the remaining guests, and Tia and Robyn before coming to Tom. Tom took a walk and read in his room while the two or three long hours elapsed before his turn. He couldn't talk or even be in the same room with Robyn or Tia. The events had shocked each of them into a paralysed silence and they stayed apart.

His head was still drumming and he thought it best to say as little as possible when Mackie summoned him to the study to meet a buoyant Stelios.

"Come and sit down, Mr Stavely. It's not often that I have the pleasure of doing my work in such elegant surroundings." Stelios spoke very much like a New Zealander born and bred. When he had finished contemplating the oil paintings on the walls, he arranged a recorder on the coffee table between them.

"I want to help all I can, Inspector, but I have to get back to London. I have plane tickets from Christchurch for the day after tomorrow."

"You can't go, Mr Stavely. You're a material witness in a homicide case." Stelios leaned his head over to one side, pleased to reveal an amusing aspect.

He had expected this. "How long is it going to take?"

"I can't tell you." Stelios waved his hands at the impossibility, "a week, a month, who knows?"

"That's not very helpful, can't you - ?"

"It's the nature of the beast, Mr Stavely. You must let me have your passport and stay either here or in the area at a known address." Another wide grin. His soft brown fingers beat out a rhythm on the coffee table.

"Oh, come on, Inspector..."

"Do you want me to arrest you?" Stelios drew back in mock horror at the unthinkable.

"Hell, I just want to go home after my daughter's wedding."

"You'll be free to leave in several days, or you'll be under arrest, accused of a crime," Stelios said with enjoyment.

Tom was stifled, his dry throat contracted

"We need your fingerprints."

"But surely, Inspector..."

"Routine."

It was not until the evening that he was able to speak to Alison in London. The news that Stuart was dead shocked her, however much he tried to soften it. He gave her a sketchy account of the previous night to spare her, omitting his action with Ernest's pill. "The truth was that although I knew I had to tell Tia and ring the police, I fell asleep on the bed."

"You must have been very drunk to pass out after…"

"I was in a funk too, not about what I had to do, but what was going to happen."

Alison was silent on the line for a few moments while she absorbed the impact of his words. "What did you tell the police?"

"That it was an accident."

"But you were there."

"I didn't tell them that."

"Oh, Tom. You've always said to me that the only safe way with the law is to tell the truth."

"I know, but…"

"Why do you want to protect them - the Ashtons - Tom? That evil old man."

"I feel protective about Stuart, killed by his own father. What a way to go. He deserved better. He may have been diminished in future by the old man's fraud, but he didn't deserve to be murdered by him."

"But a fact is a fact, for God's sake, Tom. You can't rewrite history because you want to. It's all over now. Stuart doesn't need a reputation."

"He needs a memory."

"You need the memory, and Robyn and Tia. You're not thinking straight… I know Stuart means a lot to you. Did you think he was going to kill Ernest?"

"No, but I thought the old man, so fragile, could be harmed in the encounter. I didn't care if he was. I didn't want Stuart to get himself into trouble, that's all. I don't

know precisely what Stuart was going to do. I don't think
he did either. He wanted a showdown, a reckoning. Which
was completely impossible when he was sober in daylight,
let alone drunk at 3am…"

"Couldn't you stop it?"

"No way. I tried. I grabbed them both. I didn't realise in
the dark that they had a gun. I'd had too many drinks. I left
the old man semi-conscious and went back to my room.
When I woke up, the housekeeper had already found Stuart's
body and called the police, but if you can believe it, that old
shit was still alive. His miserable, diseased heart was still
beating. They called an ambulance and took him away."

"What will Ernest say to the police?"

"I have no idea. He's a vicious old bastard and I think
the Mt Vogel affair has deranged him. If he lives, he may
blame Stuart - or he may even blame me."

"But blaming you is ridiculous, Tom."

"I was there, and I had what could be seen in court as a
motive to kill Ernest in revenge for my father. I didn't have
any motive to kill Stuart, but I suppose one could be found.
Perhaps the fact that he gave my daughter away at her
wedding."

"I'm glad you haven't lost your sense of humour."

"It's not funny here, believe me, Ally. If you were here…"

"I wish I was too, now, to see you through this. Tom,
listen to my advice. You've told the police you weren't there.
Don't you see that you're involving yourself in murder? I
understand why you want your friend to have a sort of clean
death. Being murdered after Ernest has been revealed as the
rat he is, is awful. But you can't have it the way you want it,
Tom. You can't get involved in a misbegotten crusade that
could cost you your liberty… and everything else. Don't do
it. The Ashtons aren't worth it."

"Stuart's worth… a lot."

There was a long silence on the line. He could hear Alison's uneven breathing. "All right," he said, "what do you say, my dearest?"

"Go to the police, Tom, and tell them the absolute truth, and tell them why you've told lies. You'll do it, won't you, Tom?"

"I'll… think about it…"

"What's the, you know, the tone of the enquiry. I mean, is it…?"

"The guy conducting it – Inspector Stelios – is a bumptious little rooster who seems to think it's fun, so it's not really threatening."

He couldn't be candid with her that he thought that Stelios' joviality was a cover for a hard, aggressive core.

"Good. You'll do as I say, won't you?"

"I'll…"

He heard her sobs as they said goodbye.

He would rather have been at home in London, but had it not been for the threat of a criminal prosecution, he could have enjoyed the days at Tamaki Downs. He spent them walking and reading and thinking about Stuart. Tia had returned to her family in the Banks Peninsula. Robyn had disappeared to Christchurch for her play production. At times, he imagined what it would be like to be the master of Tamaki Downs. The surly Mrs Dilsey served him in the dining room, where he sat alone amid the silver and crystal and mahogany. Mark Curran had arranged for a temporary manager who lived and dined in the guest wing. Apart from the housekeeper and her staff, he had the Downs to himself. He had to repel newspaper and television reporters who called continually on the telephone, and occasionally doorstepped him. That was easy but irritating.

He telephoned Stelios in Timaru and Christchurch every other day after the meeting, but his calls were not taken personally by Stelios or returned, save for an answer from an officer that the investigation was proceeding. He also talked to Alison every day on the phone.

To stop her mounting anxiety, he lied – yet another lie – that he had told the police the whole story and that they seemed to accept it. In truth, he was now agonised by the thought that it was too late to retreat as Alison had suggested. The shock of events had skewed his judgment, as she said, but if he told the truth, he feared he would lose credibility and increase the risk of being implicated. Every day that passed without a decision hardened the plaster around his lies, and made it more difficult for him to own up.

It was four days before Stelios came back to the Downs. He was brusque but good-humoured. His self-confidence unnerved Tom. They went to the study and made themselves comfortable with the recorder between them.

"Lovely house this, Mr Stavely. Must be one of the best in South Canterbury," Stelios said, looking round, appreciating again the furniture and the view of the lawns. "Superb. You're very comfortable here for your enforced stay, aren't you? Let me ask you about your relationship with Stuart Ashton."

"We were close friends."

Stelios turned his shoulders this way and that, enjoying his work. "That's what I hear, very good friends."

"What do you mean?"

"You know what I mean, Mr Stavely." His head was on one side with a simpleton's grin, waiting for the answer.

Where had Stelios got this remnant of prejudice? Ah,

there were plenty of rats around, waiting to squeak, knowing little and adding a lot of smelly droppings. Robyn herself at the time of their separation had hinted at his friendship with Stuart as a cause, and doubtless had not been secretive with her views. It was Robyn's second self-justification. The first, of course, was a predatory Alison. Even Tia, on the day he first arrived at the Downs, seemed to suggest his relationship with Stuart was unhealthy.

He had told Alison a long time ago, 'Robyn always approached my friendship with Stuart on the basis that he was taking me away from her, and that went way back into the woods when we were kids. The wives or girlfriends of other friends of mine seemed to have the same feeling. These are all women that would go off without their men to a hen party or a weekend's golf without the slightest guilt.'

Alison accepted this calmly. 'Woman are selfish with their man's time. It's as simple as that.'

He said to Stelios: "Ask straightforward questions and I'll do my best to answer. If you want to proceed by innuendo, don't expect me to help."

"There's no need to be offended. It's nothing to be ashamed of." A big grin and wide open eyes accompanied this.

"I'm not going to comment on stuff like that."

A silence fell in which the two men stared at each other, Stelios sardonic, Tom trying to hide anger and communicate boredom.

"Mr Stavely, when I interviewed you the morning after the event, you told me you last saw Stuart Ashton in this room in the early hours of the morning, and that this was where you parted. That's not true, is it?"

"Ah, well, I think so. I was pretty drunk at the time. In

fact, when I spoke to you I was still feeling the effects."

"You want to excuse yourself as being drunk?"

"I'm fairly sure I last saw Stuart here."

"The truth is that you were in Sir Ernest's bedroom at the material time."

"No. I was very drunk, but I don't believe I was..."

Stelios didn't show any annoyance, only the blandness of a clerk shuffling papers.

"You don't believe you were there? Even if you were drunk, you'd remember a gunshot going off in the room you were in."

He had put himself in a corner and he was going to have to brazen it out. "The events of the night are not all that clear to me because I'd had a lot to drink."

"We have evidence which places you in the room." Stelios watched for the effect of his words. A faint smile curved his very pink, small lips.

Tom tried to fix a slightly questioning look. He shook his head negatively. For the sake of the recorder he said clearly, "Quite wrong."

"Your prints are on the water glass by the bed."

He had already thought of this. "I've often handled the glass."

"The housekeeper says a fresh glass of water was placed by the bed at eight o'clock that night. The glass had been through the dishwasher."

He hadn't expected this refinement. "I may have called in there during the evening when I went up to the lavatory. Yes, I think I probably did."

"There's more than one lavatory on the ground floor."

"I can't explain why I prefer to piss in one hole rather than another, Inspector, but I also went back to my room during the evening and previous evenings because I suffer

213

from hay fever, and I need fresh tissues and occasionally medication."

"But you've already told me that on the night of the death, you last saw Sir Ernest Ashton in the early evening when he retired upstairs."

"Yes, he was going on about the gun. What I meant was, that was the last time I had a conversation with him. As I've said, I probably called in later to see if he wanted anything."

"You were in the habit of calling in, to see if he needed any help?"

"He was a sick man. I did what anyone would do."

Stelios was quiet, considering this. His plumpness and the tight buttons on the waistcoat of his blue suit made him look trussed up. "Mrs Dilsey says you had an argumentative relationship with Sir Ernest."

He had already anticipated what Beryl would say. She was a sycophantic fan of Ernest's and an assiduous listener at keyholes. "How would she know?"

"She says she heard you abusing each other."

"She's never been in the room when I've been chatting with Ernest. Never. Ernest and I had a robust relationship. Differences of view, but you don't get entry to Sir Ernest's bedroom unless you're a trusted member of the family."

Stelios opened his eyes wide and pursed his lips sceptically. His large teeth were a contrasting white against the grey-blue shadow of his cheeks. "Housekeepers hear things, but let's get on. Your fingerprints are on the gun, Mr Stavely."

He didn't expect this. The big eyes were drilling into him. "Ah, yes, well I used the gun to shoot rabbits in the evening – not of course on the evening of the wedding, but other evenings. Stuart and I would walk after dinner. He carried the 22 which is kept in the gun closet, and I think I borrowed Ernest's shotgun on the last occasion. Occasionally the reverse."

"Sir Ernest's precious shotgun to shoot rabbits?"

"We weren't shooting for the pot. The main purpose was to have a walk."

"Doesn't elementary gun security apply in this house? A loaded gun in the study and the bedroom?"

"The guns are cleaned by one of the staff, I believe, before they're put away, and obviously wouldn't be loaded."

"So who put the cartridge in?"

He knew he had to be wary here. "I don't know the answer, but it's possible the cleaning had been deferred. Dirty guns could have been put away in the gun-case pending cleaning. If they were, I suppose the possibility is that they would be loaded."

"We can check this with the staff."

Another silence from Stelios, during which he glared at Tom. He had abandoned the amused superior investigator role. "I'd be glad if you'd explain this to me, Mr Stavely. There is blood on the body of the shirt which Mrs Dilsey recovered from your laundry. The laboratory has checked. It's the blood of Stuart Ashton. Constable Mackie says you were wearing a blood-stained shirt the morning after the death."

He had remembered the shirt too late after the confusion of the morning. The laundry bag had gone from his room, and he couldn't risk asking Beryl Dilsey or the staff for it. "I was in the room in the morning before Stuart's body was removed... very early."

"Why?"

"I got up to go to the lavatory and I went to see if Ernest was all right. I always did that. Nothing special about it. But he wasn't there. I removed the sheet and realised what had happened."

"You touched the body."

"I don't know what I touched. I may have touched the gun. I uncovered the body, which had a stained sheet over it. I probably hugged the sheet. I was shocked. Nearly ill."

"Constable Mackie says you were sound asleep when he went to your room, and you were wearing the shirt at the time. How could you have visited Sir Ernest's room?"

"After I visited the room, I felt so ill that I came back and lay on my bed to try to get to grips with what had happened. That's where I was when Mackie came barging in."

"Mackie says you were asleep when he knocked. You went off to sleep after seeing your friend had been killed?"

"Mackie is a young man who I'm sure will eventually make a competent policeman, but he ought not make suppositions through closed doors. I was in shock when Mackie came in, and scarcely able to talk."

Stelios weighed up what had been said. He searched Tom for a flicker of uncertainty. "I don't believe you. I think you were in the room at the time the shot was fired. The forensic experts say your shirt was sprayed with blood. It wasn't merely stained. It's consistent with you being close to the weapon at the time it was fired, or even firing it."

"No." A blanket denial was all he could manage. But he took care to show as little emotion as possible. He tried in his manner to shrug this off as utterly impossible. He exhaled heavily and spread his palms. For the recorder, he said calmly, "What you're saying is unworthy of serious contention. This concerns my best and oldest friend and a sick old man."

What must have been buzzing around in Stelios's head like a wasp was Tom's centrality to the crime. Stelios was obviously sure it was a crime and not an accident. It was so easy to cross everybody except Tom Stavely off the list of suspects – the staff, including Beryl, seemed remote, as did the bemused guests in the other wing, Tia, a small wilting flower, and Robyn, who was out of the house. Only Tom Stavely was left, and Stelios could easily have picked up enough intelligence from the others to realise that Tom, a former relative himself, was in the turbulence of the family relationships. Stelios must have been pondering how to deal with Tom's denials. He had to work out what the circumstantial evidence like bloodstains and fingerprints really meant. Tom thought Stelios was worrying that there was some family feud he didn't know about.

Stelios had a resentful look, perhaps disappointed that the fingerprints and the bloodstained shirt might not be such decisive evidence as he had thought. "I don't believe you, Stavely. You're in serious trouble." He stood up and repacked his briefcase with the recorder.

"Where do we go from here, Inspector? I need to get back…"

"Forget about leaving the country, Mr Stavely. In all probability, you'll never leave it for a long time…" he said, with a cold smile, as he walked out of the room.

14

Tom looked at himself naked in the bathroom mirror before he dressed to answer Stelios's summons. Stelios had telephoned the night before, after a space of three days, telling him to report to Timaru police by 9am. He had been awake all night, and the ache in his mind was joined by an ache in his body. Was he going to be charged? When he had asked Stelios what the meeting was for, the derisively amused reply had been, "You know what it's for." When he protested, Stelios cut him off. "Be there," he said, "or we'll come and get you."

He hadn't been carrying any extra weight, but the person he saw in the mirror seemed thin. His complexion, even after a close shave, looked sickly and wrinkled. His cheeks were flabby, his eyeballs yellow. There hadn't been much to do but read books and drink in the long dark lonely nights at Tamaki Downs. The dread of what might happen that morning suffused every vein in his body like an agonising slow-acting poison.

He was on the road early and in Timaru at a quarter to nine. He identified the police station, parked and waited numbly. It was like being poised on the edge of a high cliff and imagining the fall. A few minutes before the appointed time, he walked through the door into a busy office where he attracted no attention. He had to interrupt the duty sergeant who eventually directed him to an interview room. He sat down on a plastic chair at a plastic table under bright lights.

After five minutes, Stelios appeared, immaculate in a white shirt and plain dark blue tie, smelling of bath salts. He sat down with a mirthless smirk but without a word. Tom thought there were only two possibilities. Either he was going to be charged, or the call last night, with its deliberately vague explanation, was part of a campaign on his nerves, intended to weaken him. He did his best to look unconcerned, but his haggard face must have betrayed him. Stelios took a leisurely moment to contemplate him.

"Are you ready to be charged, Mr Stavely?" His pudgy fingers played with the file in front of him.

"Charged with what?" Tom asked hoarsely.

"You know that." The big, artificial bright-eyed smile again.

"If you're going to charge me, get on with it and stop arsing around." The words were forced out by despair.

"You had a motive to kill Ernest Ashton if this story about your father is true."

"Ernest is alive isn't he?"

"He says you tried to kill him."

He had guessed that he might have to face this one. "Tried - and failed? He's as weak as water. How could I fail to kill that old man if I wanted to?"

"You thought you had killed him. You threw his pill on the floor and choked him on his water. He passed out."

"That's not a very compelling story, Inspector. You don't kill somebody by dropping pills on the floor." Just the right implication of ridicule, and there was another lull. He could hear Stelios's slightly asthmatic breathing. He also noticed that Stelios's hands had a slight tremor.

"You did drop the pill, though?"

"No. I don't know anything about it."

"He alleges that you killed Stuart."

The old man was a viper. He had wondered whether Ernest would go this far, and in a way wasn't sorry that he had; it was an allegation Tom thought could never stand, and it illuminated how cracked the old man was.

"Why would I try to kill my friend of forty years? That is really a lunatic allegation from a man who isn't in possession of his senses. A man who is a pathological liar."

"Jealousy of Stuart Ashton."

"Jealousy of Stuart won't survive as a motive. I live in another country. I have a completely separate life. I'm a visitor here for a few days for my daughter's wedding. What on earth would I gain? You won't get an ounce of support for that nutty idea from either Stuart's wife, or his sister, my ex-wife."

"But why should Sir Ernest bother to lie at all, unless to protect himself, because he tried to kill his son?"

Tom thought that Stelios had moved away from threatening that charges were imminent, to speculating about causes, but it might be a tactic of his.

"We've come full circle, haven't we?" Tom said. "Well, I doubt whether he wanted to kill Stuart, but you can hypothesize about it. I'm pretty sure they were talking about the gun. They were talking about it earlier in the evening and the account you have from Ernest is from a sick old man, who was drunk, scared and in agony over the death."

"Why?"

"Because his son was dead and he was involved in an accident that didn't need to happen. Grief. Remorse. Excuses."

"Sir Ernest didn't love his son."

"The affection between parents and children is like a seesaw."

"The forensic tests on the hands of the son, and the

clothes of he and his father, support the fact that they were grasping each other."

"That doesn't take you far, Inspector. It could have been a happy embrace. It could have been that Ernest had a seizure while they were talking, and had to be lifted on to the bed. Maybe they argued over the gun and came to grips. I don't know. Nobody will ever know."

"Isn't it the height of improbability to find a gun in the bedroom of a man like Sir Ernest Ashton?"

"Not really. Ernest used to shoot rabbits from the bedroom window with a .22, until a few years ago."

Stelios was beginning to look peeved as Tom tried to rebut his arguments; his cheeks were flushed. Tom was heartened by the thought that Stelios wasn't ready to make charges, and that could mean that last night's summons was merely gratuitous cruelty.

"Mrs Dilsey says you and Stuart weren't so friendly. You were shouting at each other in the library earlier in the evening."

"It was boisterous good humour. We spent the whole evening drinking from around 7 to 3am. Together."

"But Stuart had a poor relationship with his father. I have this from the housekeeper, and Tia Ashton. He might have attempted to kill his father. He had a motive. His father was facing disgrace."

"Ernest isn't saying that, is he? I think they were talking or even arguing over the merits of a gun."

Stelios sat back, frustrated. "Are you are covering up for the family?"

At last, Stelios had touched the core of it, but he wasn't sure. "Why should I get involved in the Ashton family affairs and chance a charge of obstruction? If Ernest murdered his son, nature is going to be his executioner. He'll die soon.

He's far too ill to face a trial. I honestly don't think there is anything in this situation for you, Inspector."

"We have to complete our investigation. We're also looking at Sir Ernest Ashton's involvement in your father's death. We've seen the material gathered by *The Mountaineer* magazine. We've compared it with his evidence in the coroner's court. There's a material difference. Sir Ernest says Stavely died at about eight thousand feet on the way up while he went on to the peak. If, however, it was Stavely who went on to the peak and was killed later, and Ashton claimed the conquest, it's a very suspicious situation."

"What does it really matter? My father was killed going up or going down."

"Don't you want to find out?"

"Not particularly. I'm afraid this is turning over cold stones. It doesn't lead anywhere, Inspector."

"Do you believe Ernest Ashton killed your father?"

"No. I think he is a monstrous liar with an ego as big as Mt Vogel, and that he's now broken down, but I don't think he is a murderer." He knew better than anybody else that Ernest Ashton could be a double murderer, but making accusations like that would only heat up the police interest in the case.

Stelios stopped to consider this.

"Look, Inspector, I want to go home. I want my passport back."

"You're a very long way from going home at the moment, Mr Stavely, and you're on the brink of facing a charge of murder of one man and attempted murder of another, and at the very least a charge of perverting the course of justice."

"You don't have a case."

"Look at the circumstantial evidence, man. You're in the house and involved with both men on the night. Your fingerprints are on the weapon and on the bedroom glass. Your shirt was bloodstained..." Stelios's steady stare was tinged with malevolence.

The words left Tom at the bottom of a deep depression and with a sense of horror that the police might just manage to stitch together a prima facie case out of the rags of suspicion. Stelios wanted a charge. He was a hunter. But the facts would have to be sieved through the Crown Law Office before that could happen. Maybe the particular Crown Prosecutor who would make the analysis in this case would be a chancer, a gung-ho operator who thought that it was better to haul a suspect into court and make him squirm, rather than wait for cut and dried certainties. It was a prospect which made Tom choke.

He sat through a performance of *Oh What a Lovely War!* in Christchurch in order to see Robyn, although he was too preoccupied to enjoy it. She had given him a ticket and he couldn't refuse, especially as he was going to beg - he'd try not to let it show - a favour. He did note that it was a convincing production, well-attended and amusing. The theatre group were talented amateurs.

He felt like a beleaguered general himself, trying to fight his campaign with the police. Since he learned from Stelios of Ernest's allegations against him personally, flimsy in fact as they were, he had toyed whether to commit the further crime of attempting to pervert the course of justice by persuading Robyn to influence the old man.

They met in the small café behind the theatre immediately after the performance. Robyn was open-eyed with success, brusque and hurried, looking forward to getting away to the post-performance party. People stopped at their table to congratulate her. The coffee was too hot to drink.

He had never shared with her his anxiety about whether he might himself be charged, and, submerged in grief herself, she had no appreciation of the possibility. Stelios had been deliberately threatening, and Tom was aware that he himself was too immersed in the nuances of his interrogation to form any balanced idea of the extent to which he was in danger. He had been more candid with Alison, about what was happening, but even with her he had been restrained about his worries, although she sensed them. The telephone conveyed emotional tones quite subtly. He had lacerated himself for his decision, if it could be called that, to try to persuade the police it was an accident – a few words uttered out of loyalty when his mind was in a fog.

"The play was great. You've built on your skills," he said, trying to claim her exclusive attention in the noisy café.

"I'm very pleased with it. You don't look well, Tom. What's the matter?"

"It's this police enquiry. I'm tied down here. It's rather depressed my days of leisure at Tamaki Downs."

"Why is it dragging on so? Every so often this Greek inspector pops up. He's not exactly sinister, but he seems confident that he knows what I'm thinking. What does he expect to find?"

"He wants to hang the death on somebody. Ernest or – or me."

She had a rueful grin. "You're not a very convincing murderer, Tom. Stuart's dead and Dad's nearly dead. What does it all matter?"

"Sure, but Ernest has gone a bit further. He's said I killed Stuart and tried to kill him."

"He doesn't love you, but that's a pretty way out thing to say. Why would he go that far?"

"Partly venom, partly self-protection, I expect. He's saying I dropped his pill on the floor when he had a seizure."

"Does what he says make any difference, Tom? After all, he's..."

"It could. We have a violent death and the police want a perpetrator. There are only two people in the game now, Ernest and me."

"Are you worried?"

"Not seriously," he said, managing the gross untruth calmly, "but I don't want to get further involved in this. Robyn, could I put it to you another way? The only story which will close the enquiry decently for Stuart and the family is that the fatality was the result of an accident between two drunks with a gun."

"It's not very palatable, but I guess that's true. So..."

"So you might point this out to Ernest."

"Uh-huh."

"His rancour against me may be less than his concern for the family reputation. He's not in danger himself; he's too ill. I don't think from what I know of the criminal law that charges of murder, attempted murder or obstruction could be sustained against me, but the problem is that a mere trial could besmirch me. It's about my reputation as a professional man. It's mud. It sticks."

"Your reputation. Yes, I see it," Robyn said. "It's ironic, isn't it, that Stuart was so concerned with his reputation, and now you."

15

He had a further peremptory call from the police three days after his meeting with Robyn. It came at ten o'clock in the evening of a day he had spent walking the Downs. He was tired and slightly drunk, trying to anaesthetise his pain and avoid calls from reporters. He was told again to be at Timaru police station at 9am. It was no use trying to ask the officer who called what it was about. He was awake the entire night, striding around the house, trying to read, drinking, drifting into violent and surreal imaginings. When he delivered himself to the police in the morning, he was a ruin.

At first, the duty officer was ignorant. "Thomas Stavely… What's it about?"

"I don't know. I was told to be here." He wasn't going to say, 'It's something about me being charged with murder.'

The officer frowned at him and disappeared from the desk. When he came back, he began to thumb through a pile of papers in a tray beside him. He produced a brown envelope, opened it and withdrew the familiar dark blue passport.

Tom Stavely was flooded with warmth and weakness.

The officer scrutinised his face, compared it with the document, and said, "Sign this."

"Is this all?"

"Was there something else, Mr Stavely?"

"No…" He turned away, swaying clumsily.

He stood in the foyer for a moment, steadying himself. It was over! As he walked toward the swing doors to go out, Stelios and three of his assistants were sweeping up the steps, dark-suited and brisk, like important politicians. Stelios saw him.

"Ah, Mr Stavely!" He grabbed Tom's arm and pulled him aside to an ante room. "I hadn't planned to see you again, but we might as well take this opportunity."

Stelios's fingers on his arm made ice in his stomach. "I can go, can't I Inspector...?"

Stelios's black eyes bulged up at him. "Uncertain, aren't you? You bloody well ought to be, mate. I believe you were in the room and tried to murder Ernest Ashton, if not the son. There's something going on in the Ashton family that we don't know anything about, and you've all clammed up."

"Why can't you rest easy with the evidence you have? It is what it is. But you want more. You don't have to *get* me, do you?"

But Stelios did have to get him. He was Stelios's target. Stelios wanted a conviction. The Crown Prosecutor had apparently reviewed the evidence and decided that it fell short of a prima facie case against him. In Stelios's mythology, *he*, Stelios, had fallen short. A violent homicide case was going to be closed without a prosecution. There would be an unpleasant inquest; an open verdict or a verdict of death by misadventure. Mysteries led to speculation, and one speculation was defective police work. He thought Stelios disliked him, not in a very personal way, but rather as the quarry who escaped, and perhaps a little because Stelios saw him, wrongly, as part of the privileged Ashton clan.

"Rest easy with the *lack* of evidence, you mean?" Stelios said, poking a soft brown forefinger into his chest. "No way. We'll be watching you. We don't close these files, you know.

If we find anything, we'll come after you. You've heard of extradition, haven't you?"

Although he thought Stelios's threat unreal, it made him shiver. Cruelty was all Stelios had left.

He left the station and paused for a moment in Evans Street, feeling his whole body re-energise itself and begin to glow. If the pubs had been open, he would have treated himself to several beers before driving back to Tamaki Downs.

He was sitting with Robyn in a café in Riccarton. He had a little time before he boarded the flight back to London, and she had asked to see him before he departed. They had taken the time together to visit Len and, as always, Tom came away with a feeling of impotence. However much he wanted to help Len, there was nothing he could do except endure the spectacle.

For a while they were silent. Stuart's funeral had taken place the previous day at the Canterbury Cathedral and it had been crowded. There was no shadow of Mt Vogel over the gathering that Tom could discern, only many people confused by the sudden departure of a local personality. Petra and Darren interrupted their cruise on the Great Barrier Reef and flew back from Cairns. He saw them at the church and afterwards at The George hotel where Robyn hosted a gathering for the family and closest friends. He had one of those awkward and inarticulate conversations with them. 'All it amounted to,' he would tell Alison, 'was Darren stepping restively from foot to foot and looking round the room like a giraffe, and Petra assuring me that she had no time because they were going back to Sydney that evening. I will say that she looked upset.'

Robyn said, "It was a terrible day yesterday, Tom, and I want to forget it. I want to thank you for dealing with the police and the media over the past few weeks. Tia and I were overwhelmed. I just couldn't handle it. You were the one person who could talk with an authentic voice, because of your father's involvement. You're right about having a private burial for Dad. He hasn't got long. He doesn't know it, but he's really under a cloud. The rest of the family are hardly touched, and it's not so bad for Tia and me. It's just embarrassing... what people must be thinking. This must have been disruptive for you – your job and everything."

He had tried to deal with the newspaper and television journalists in the furore which accompanied the police investigation, repeating the mantra that it was two drunks with a gun, and that what happened on Mt Vogel was a mystery. He went on with this as a kind of personal memorial to Stuart, despite his realisation that Alison had been right and he should have told the truth. He had suffered in proportion.

"You've got through so far, Robyn. I don't know that I've done much. I was nearly burned myself! Anyway, the media interest will continue for a while. It's a hell of a story with a lot of room for doubt and speculation. What the Swiss found or saw will be examined very closely. As I've told you, I've had a lot of approaches from reporters, which I've rejected. After the newspaper and TV hacks, there will be the adventure writers and biographers, I'm afraid, and you'll have to deal with them."

"Tia and I have just taken your advice and accepted what you said about the deaths, but I never could see Dad and Stuart chatting about guns in broad daylight, let alone at three or four in the morning. But I kept quiet, and poor Tia is absolutely crushed."

He decided to tell Robyn the truth. In so many ways, she was like her father; tough, arrogant, wilful. She could take it, and there was no reason why she shouldn't share the burden of the truth with him.

"No, it wasn't an accident with a gun, Robyn. Your father killed Stuart when he thought Stuart was coming for him. He expected Stuart to accost him, and he was prepared for it with a loaded shotgun."

"Oh, Tom, no." The lines around Robyn's mouth pulled taut, her eyes closed and she trembled.

"That's murder."

"Oh no."

"I tried to stop Stuart going to your father's room, but he was drunk and wouldn't be stopped."

"Couldn't you...?"

"I put my hands on him. He resented it. To stop him, I'd have had to knock him unconscious. My concern was that Stuart might hurt the old man. I hadn't reckoned on –"

"How can you possibly know this?" Her voice was faint.

"I was a few yards behind Stuart as he headed for your father's room. I saw everything."

"You never said that to the police."

"Of course not. Stuart, murdered by his own father. That *would* have been a story on top of the Mt Vogel vileness. I thought that there should be a better end for Stuart. When Ernest blamed me, I was alarmed, but I thought his lies would fall down."

"I don't think he was in his right mind... although he is my father, I can believe he was capable of what you say, so many years of... hatred."

"What Ernest said to the police – conceding it was two drunks with a gun – was enough to get me off the hook. Thanks to you. Just enough in lieu of other evidence."

She lowered her head. "You saved us even further ignominy, then." She reached out her hand and placed it on top of his on the table. She toyed with the spoon in her coffee, looking down. "Let's put this behind us, Tom, try to forget it as far as possible, and look forward. Len needs you."

"I don't see that my presence or absence matters that much to Len. I mean, Len can virtually only sit there. He can't talk much. I can't teach him, or show him anything. He doesn't really need a parent, and the arrangements for his care are very good." He sounded more defensive than he would have wished.

"You think that nurses and care assistants are a substitute for his father? He wants, and to some extent needs, the contact with *you*. A nurse may mean a lot, but not as much as his father. Just your company. Being there. He needs you to look into his eyes, hold his hand, put your arm round his shoulders. You and I are more meaningful than anybody. It's not a matter of bringing presents or teaching him things. He's a kid of eighteen; all alone in a chair. He's conscious. He can see things. He can't understand much. He can't do anything. He can't speak. He's just a human consciousness that we've created. He's nothing except a consciousness. But he has a quality of life. He's handled lovingly by nurses and doctors, but what *you* bring him with your company, because he does know you, is inestimable, and to him, beautiful and irreplaceable."

He was surprised at her tender understanding. For once, she wasn't simply goading him; and she was to a large extent right. He was so used to her prepared lines, her speeches; so used to looking behind the actor's script and trying to find the actor. He could remind her about Peter, and her abject failure to understand what they had consigned Peter to, but she would have her defences ready.

"I'll keep in touch with Len by letter and phone, and try to get out here more often."

"That's not communicating, Tom. Len can't read. And he can't talk on the telephone. Other people have to interpret these things to him."

"It's a sign that I'm..."

"Signs aren't enough. You should be *here*. You should have been here in the past for Petra, but that doesn't matter so much now. But you should be here now, for Len."

"I certainly think about it a lot."

When he told Alison about this exchange, it would raise an old issue. She would say something like, 'You have to think why you're here in England, Tom. Not just why you should be in New Zealand. I know you love me, and if I want to be here in London, that's a weighty argument with you for being here, but we both know it's not the whole story. There's another reason for being in London. You've exiled yourself.' 'Never,' he would reply.

He did honestly see himself as venturing out from his birthplace positively, not as escaping or trying to cut himself off from it. But Alison would roll her eyes sceptically. 'It's true. You're escaping from the image of the farm boy. It dogs you. You thought that by marrying into the Ashton clan you'd escape, but it didn't work that way. If you'd married anybody *but* an Ashton, you'd have been free, especially if they came from outside Springvale. By marrying Robyn you became part of the Ashton breeding stock and still, in their eyes, and your own, a farm boy. You had to get out.'

Getting out was the very advice that he had given to Stuart, many times. He would deny that it applied to him in his discussion with Alison as he had in the past, but he knew there was a tincture of truth in it. Breeding stock.

Robyn went on urgently, "But typically, you never do

anything, Tom. You could have not only a good life here, but
you could have a career. You could join one of the big firms
in Christchurch. They'd fall over themselves to have you.
You still have years of working life in you."

"They would like to have me, not because I'm me, but
because I'd bring in the Ashton empire."

"You're underestimating yourself, but alright. If that
offends you, you could start your own firm. Do it your way."

"I could."

"Please think about it, because I want to say something
else. It's a bit crass talking about it here, but..." She glanced
around at the diners chatting excitedly over their wine. They
leaned toward each other to hear more clearly. "Dad's will
leaves everything to me – now Stuart has gone, and there's a
trust for Petra and Len. Tia has Stuart's estate, and she wants
to manage Tamaki Downs. She's going to do it. And she's
going to have a baby. You should stay and take charge of
everything – all the family stuff, including the companies."

"That's more or less the offer I had from Ernest years
ago and turned down."

"I know. But he'll soon be out of the picture, and you'd
be close to Petra, and Len, and your other two kids would
have a good life. They're young enough not to have their
schooling disrupted too much. And Alison, surely, has some
feeling for this place. After all, her parents have settled here."

"She likes it here, but..."

"Or you could take the chair at the Ashton Group, and
some of our other companies, and get involved more actively
as a CEO if you wanted. What do you want? You have a
world of choices. Legal practice. The motor industry, or oil
and gas? A big shareholding would go with the job. It's a hell
of an offer, Tom, and your terms are virtually for the asking.
Mark knows everything and you could talk to him. He

knows I want you to take over."

He thought that perversely she still wanted to keep him close, or perhaps it was the mother of two children wanting their father close.

"One of Ernest's brothers or the cousins might want to do it."

"They'd defer to you. I've spoken with them. They think a lot of you - you know that. None of them is as well qualified as you."

"I doubt that."

"I was going to get Mark to write to you with a formal offer, but you're here…"

"It's a very generous offer, Robyn, and I appreciate it."

Well, that was true, even if his stuffy response made him sound like a politician, but he would say to Alison, 'I don't dislike Robyn, I just hate her on occasions, and we've always been at odds, even before we were married. I wouldn't feel easy with her as a major voice in my life, although I could handle it. And it would be a sound position for us and the kids. Better than I'll ever do in London.'

Alison would echo the peculiarity that Robyn couldn't seem to quit him, but she would be noncommittal about the proposal, because she would want *him* to take the decision about his future work. If he were to decide on legal practice or the Ashton job, he was sure she would support him in returning to New Zealand. But at the same time, he knew that she wanted to stay in London. She loved their home in Fulham.

Lurking uneasily behind such a conversation would be Alison's perception that he was in flight from the farm boy image, and that he ought never to be foolish enough to return to its roots. Although he would, if he accepted Robyn's offer, be in charge of all the family resources, Alison would contend that in the Ashtons' eyes he would still be no more than the Admirable Crighton. She would probably say, if he pressed her for a view, 'Any *other* job in New Zealand, yes, if you really want it.'

Robyn took his thoughtful reception of her proposal as encouragement and sounded enthusiastic. "I want our finances in the hands of the family. I trust you as a businessman, Tom. And you and your family will be set up for life. So it's not a big ask, is it?"

"No." It was in fact, to him, a monstrous ask.

She put her other hand on his. Both his hands were now pinned down by hers. She looked at him, unblinking. Her eyes had rich, brown irises in nets of blood. "We have had some wonderful times, Tom."

"Valuable memories... I agree." But he would say to Alison, 'She began practicing her skills on me, playing the tender, somewhat lost, ex-wife.'

"Don't give all this up, Tom - Tamaki Downs, the Ashtons," Robyn pleaded.

For him, there would always be this dichotomy: part of him here, part of him in England. It didn't make a lot of sense to yearn for *this* place, to have paintings of Ruapehu and the Clutha River on the walls of his home in London, and read W.H. Oliver and Keith Sinclair and John Mulgan from twelve thousand miles away, but that was the way it was; it was the way it would probably continue to be as his commitment in London deepened, with the roots put down by the children, and eventually their children.

"Well, what do you think, Tom? New Zealand could be a remote province of England to the south of Cornwall."

"It isn't. Not even conceptually. It's a long way away."

"People call it 'Little England'."

"Maybe it is, climatically, ethnically and politically, but it's a long way away."

"Does distance matter when you can fly it in thirty hours, and see and talk to people any day on a video link?"

"Yes. There's a sense of remoteness; four million people sailing alone in a lifeboat on the cold southern seas."

"Oh, Tom, what a disappointing and fanciful thought." She withdrew her hands from his.

"It's a very complicated situation emotionally, Robyn, but I can't settle down here."

"You could fly to London or New York whenever you like."

"I know. I'm trying to say that it doesn't quite work like that."

"What do you mean, Tom?"

"You get stuck here."

16

He returned to London and the familiar rhythm of work, and weekends with Alison and the boys. He felt he'd escaped, but the notebook and what to do with it still troubled him. It was a few months later that he broached the subject to Alison on a sunny afternoon as they sat reading the Sunday papers in the new conservatory they had added to their home.

"I don't follow you, Tom; what should you do with it? You don't *have* to do anything, but you speak as though you do."

"I mean, I just have to make a personal decision. Maybe it's to do nothing, but I haven't made that decision - yet."

"What could you do?"

"Release the notebook to the media."

"It would look vindictive to the Ashtons. How would Petra feel?"

"She should face facts," he said sharply.

"I don't think she would see it that way. I would guess her grandfather's achievements don't mean much to her, but the family name does."

"That old bastard is still on his pedestal, with a bit of mud sticking to him, Alison. He committed a monstrous fraud and it ought to be exposed."

"Vogel was climbed that day. The record books are right on that. Does it matter precisely who did it?" She managed to make this sound distant and unimportant.

"Yes, if you've sung your achievement all over the world. I think Ernest wrote *The Fatal Snows* to psyche himself into an imaginary world where he had climbed the mountain."

"Is Ernest's fading fame very important now, Tom?"

"Yes."

"So you really want to give your father his due? After all, he was a courageous mountaineer."

"A mad one, more like. No, I honestly don't want to justify him. What set him off up the mountain against Ernest's arguably correct judgment that they ought to turn back, we'll never know."

"You held off releasing the truth to protect Stuart. Doesn't that apply now that he's dead?"

"I don't think so. His view of his own celebrity was swollen, but it *was* extensive in fact in New Zealand. I could accept that and keep quiet, but now that he's dead, it will shrink to family-size. Ernest is different."

Her face had a grim seriousness which he saw only rarely. "So you're going to…"

"What do you think I should do?"

"Nothing, Tom," she replied without hesitation.

A restless month later he wrote the following letter:

Dear Robyn,

One thing that I believe only Ernest, Stuart and I knew definitely was that there was a notebook of my father's which clearly establishes that he alone climbed Mt Vogel. The Swiss claimed to have seen it; their phone video showed a document but no conclusive text. The Mountaineer Magazine *story and photos, and speculation by others, cast a lot of grave doubt, but couldn't be* definitive without the actual notebook. You may remember our conversation in the library before Petra's wedding, when you asked why Ernest couldn't sue for libel. He couldn't sue, because the rumours were true. His failure to sue in turn emboldened the media in their speculation.

I have the notebook and out of consideration for Stuart's career I would not have revealed it had he lived. Much that he had worked for was in a sense dependent upon his father's achievements and reputation - misguided as that may have been - and to that extent his own reputation would have suffered. At about the time of his death, I was thinking of handing the notebook to him, but these thoughts do not apply now.

I have considered it carefully, and I have no loyalty to Ernest. I don't see why, now that the issues around the conquest have been lulled for want of further evidence, that Ernest should remain in the record books as one of our foremost mountaineers, and why The Fatal Snows should continue to be regarded as an outstanding factual narrative when it is, in truth, fiction.

I don't have any anxious thoughts of justifying my father, but it seems right that he should have the credit for what he did.

All those things being said, and I feel them strongly, these events have blighted the Ashton family and I have no wish to add to that. I am therefore enclosing the original notebook which you may keep or destroy, pass around the family or publish as you wish.

Yours sincerely,

Tom